By

Published by DREAMSPINNER PRESS
http://www.dreamspinnerpress.com

# RACING
## FOR THE SUN
### AMY LANE

*Dreamspinner Press*

Published by
Dreamspinner Press
5032 Capital Circle SW
Ste 2, PMB# 279
Tallahassee, FL 32305-7886
USA
http://www.dreamspinnerpress.com/

Racing for the Sun
Copyright © 2013 by Amy Lane

Cover Art by Reese Dante
http://www.reesedante.com

ISBN: 978-1-62380-647-7
Digital ISBN: 978-1-62380-648-4

Printed in the United States of America
First Edition
April 2013

As always to Mate, to Mary, and to broken people who live and love and dream. And also, thanks to Will, who did scads of research on cars because I said, "Hey, does anyone know anything about street racing?"

# THE MEET

MY NAME is Jasper Anderson Atchison. People call me Ace.

I am a murderer and a thief, but if Sonny still wants me, I will call myself a good man.

Right now, I am driving a rented car through the Mojave Desert toward Bakersfield from Barstow. There's a girl next to me who I should have left in Barstow, but I may be taking her home for a spell before she moves on, because that seems to be my job. I seem to be the one who will fix what is broken. But that is not important—in fact, the girl, bless her, isn't important. What is important is that I get us back to the hospital in Bakersfield before Sonny wakes up and knows that I am gone. That's important, because if anybody asks, I don't want Sonny to lie. He's not no damned good at it. He needs to think I was right there, watching over him as he slept, like I promised. But I promised I'd keep him safe too, and he is in a hospital right now, so that's not saying much.

Then, we never *did* say much, me and Sonny. Never did say much at all.

MY FOLKS were all right people—not warm, but not rough. Fed us, clothed us, gave us stuff for Christmas. But I was the youngest of six, and that makes things crowded, and it makes you damned near invisible.

By the time I graduated, invisible was the only thing I was good at.

I decided I might as well be invisible someplace else. I got good marks, but Dad worked a factory job and Mom worked register in a gas station. Good marks, bad marks, there weren't no money for school. I signed up for the army, shipped out to the Mideast. Wasn't great, didn't suck, I signed up again. Got promoted to staff sergeant with the re-up, and there I was, in charge of new recruits, when Sonny showed up in my unit.

Now I ain't that tall and I'm not that wide—five feet ten inches when I stretch my neck, maybe 180 when I've been working out—but I still felt bigger'n Sonny. He's maybe five six, and if he's taller, it's 'cause he's lying, and 120 soaking wet.

Sonny *made* himself small. He was standing just as straight and looking just as stiff as the other recruits, but something in his stomach or his shoulders—he was *wishing* I'd just ignore him.

He looked like a dog slinking outside a gas station, hoping he gets fed more than he's fearing he'll get the fist.

Made me squirmy, that look. Like he was thinking I'd be the one to give him the fist. Now it's true I don't go around adopting orphans, but I don't go around kicking 'em either. So I gave the new guys the spiel, sun up, sun down, where the schedule was, where the rifle practice was, how soon they'd be expected to report. The other rookies I sent to their bunks, but Sonny I asked to stay behind.

"Private Daye—wait? Really? Someone named you Sonny Daye?"

Sonny has gray eyes in a poky sort of face—the kind with the cheekbones poking out and the chin poking out and the edges of the eyes sort of poking over the side of the temple—and he narrowed those gray eyes at me and scowled.

And didn't answer.

Well, hell. I had to get power-tripping on his ass, and that was not what I'd had in mind. "Private, it was a simple question—did your parents really name you Sonny Daye?"

The boy's face twisted in agony. He was eighteen—eighteen years and three months, if his reg papers were any close to right—but he looked younger 'cause of his size. His face was small and his teeth were crowded, and the looks he kept giving me... well, I backed up a step so as not to spook him into running out into the damned desert and stepping on a land mine.

"That's not your name, is it?" I asked, shooting in the dark.

He broke attention to look me full in the face. His mouth was open, moist and full, and he licked his lips with purpose.

"I'll do anything," he said, and no man in the world could misinterpret what he meant by that.

I swallowed.

There was a temptation there, a growing knowledge I wasn't ready to face.

But whether he knew it or not, he was offering me more than sex right then, he was offering me dishonor, and whether I was invisible or not, my folks had raised me right.

"You are not at ease, Private," I barked, and he went back to being at attention. I stood there for a second and watched, scowling, as a drop of sweat traveled from his temple, down his cheek, and near his ear. There was the barest amount of stubble there to get in the way of that sweat, but the skin was tanned like it had seen hard weather. Eighteen? I could see it. But it hadn't been eighteen easy.

"You had to be desperate," I said, "to risk prison time by lying to the US government."

He swallowed and kept his eyes trained forward. I was only a little smart. *Someone* who came before me had to have noticed that this boy had lied to be here. That same someone had to have helped him fake it too—Social Security number, ID, checking account, birth certificate—someone with connections.

"You're eighteen, though," I said, making sure.

"Yessir!" he snapped out, with so much force I could tell he was relieved to tell the truth.

"Boy," I said, though he was a bare three years younger than me, "have I beat you?"

His gray eyes grew large in that tanned face. "Sir-no-sir!"

"Has anyone in the service beat you?"

He jerked his head back with so much surprise that, once again, I was relieved. "Sir-no-sir!"

"Do you want to be beat?"

He cringed sideways like he knew what it was like to dodge a blow. "Sir? No, sir."

I nodded. "Then you will stand tall when you are at attention, and you will behave as though there is no beating—none—waiting around the corner, do you hear me?"

"Sir-no-sir?"

I sighed and stepped into his space, lowered my head, and spoke personally. "Sonny Daye? You want to last a *week* here in this fucking oven, where people are either bored, trigger-happy, or just fucked in the head from both? Then you need to act like you will not get beat. You have to tell people your sergeant will get them for you? You do that, but it won't make you popular. But you tell yourself what you got to so that you stand tall, or you will not last here, do you understand?"

I watched his Adam's apple bob. "Sir-yes-sir."

"Good. It says here your specialty is machinery and cars. Great. You stow your shit in your bunk and report to Master Sergeant Galway by the auto bay there with all them Hummers. He's a fucker, and he ranks me, so you walk in there like you own the fucking place, and if you've got to pick up a wrench and kneecap him, you don't let him lay a finger on you. I've got your back."

He swallowed and actually looked at me. "Thank you, Staff Sergeant," he said, nodding. "I can defend myself."

I nodded. "Good. Now you gotta act like you deserve to be defended, or that won't help you. Hear me?"

And he nodded again and set his jaw.

"Dismissed."

He marched out of there with his shoulders set and that aggressive jut to his jaw, and I breathed a little easier. Yeah, sure, he might be an asshole to his bunkmates, but they'd leave him alone. He needed to learn, I thought, irritated. He needed to not be meat.

I kept a weather eye out for him, as they say. Saw him sitting alone at mess but scowling at anyone who sat next to him. I'd walk by, bend down, say a word—who would give him hell, who was good to know. He took my advice and pretty soon, I sat with my rank, he sat with his, but he wasn't alone. I felt like I'd done my job then, and it felt good.

Master Sergeant Galway, just like I thought, had it out for him just for breathing.

Galway was an evil fucker, with red hair he kept brutally buzzed, big green freckles he protected with zinc oxide in that violent sunshine, and a scar—one he'd signed up with—ripping from the corner of his mouth to the corner of his eye. He'd told recruitment it had been a car wreck he'd survived. All that time I'd spent invisible? I wasn't always a good boy. I knew a knife wound when I saw it.

Last boy who'd been under Galway's care in the auto bay had walked in front of a bank of sandbags during a shelling.

Galway said the boy was weak. I suspected he had a way of making men weak.

Two weeks after *my* boy got there, he walked into mess with a black eye. He met my eyes as he stood in line for chow, and I nodded.

He nodded back.

That day, after mess, I paid a visit to the auto bay. Said I needed to requisition a Hummer—and I did—for Master Sergeant Kennedy, who was putting together two teams of recon to make sure no one was moving in on us. We were outside of Pakistan, and I wasn't high enough to be in the know, but I knew people were running around like headless chickens and that the privates were running message after message that they didn't know about and didn't want to.

There was going to be action, something big, and if the good master sergeant wanted to check for bogeymen, I wasn't gonna tell him no.

I got there just in time. Sonny was standing in the corner, a lug wrench in his hand, looking at the other two privates and Master Sergeant Galway like he was going to take them down. Galway was holding onto his arm, furious, while Daye's jaw was clenched like this was his last stand.

"Private Daye!" I snapped out, and without flinching, without questioning, he jerked his spine upright, dropped the wrench, and stood at attention.

"Staff Sergeant!"

"Master Sergeant Kennedy needs his Hummer ready, complete with ordinance, as well as two other vehicles. Go out and start outfitting those, and I'll come help in a moment."

"Sir-yes-sir!" His voice rang in the hot confines of the concrete-floored auto bay. Then he turned, grabbed his box of tools, and trotted out to the Hummers.

"Master Sergeant?" I inquired courteously. "Is there something I should know about?"

Now, if Daye had been insubordinate or had asked for what had just been happening, this would be the time to say something. But Galway turned his head and spat, the spittle steaming on the concrete.

"You're not in position to know shit," he snarled, and the look he cast behind him to the other privates said volumes.

They were scared of him too. I was only a little smart, but I knew that.

I shook my head and went out to Sonny.

"Private?" I said as he busied himself with loading ordinance into the Hummer.

"Sir?" he said, looking sideways.

"There a Hummer we can outfit?"

"Yessir."

"You want to see more of this godforsaken desert?"

A smile pulled at that flat, grim mouth. "Sir-yes-sir!"

I nodded. "Then set about that when you're done. I'm off duty for the day."

Suddenly the military crispness relaxed a little. "Sir?" he asked conspiratorially, and I liked that little half smile so much I leaned in for the conspiracy.

"Yeah?"

"Do I have permission to modify our vehicle?" he asked, his gray eyes growing big enough to almost glow.

"We don't have *that* much time, Private."

"Meet me back here in an hour," he said.

"Will do, Private," I said, nodding. I turned back around and saw Galway giving us the hairy eyeball, so I saluted smartly and walked back to my bunk for my flak jacket and helmet, because it was fucking Afghanistan, and even a joyride didn't come without body armor.

Two hours later, I rode a rocket through the desert.

Yeah, it had all the outward appearance of a gas-fueled Hummer, but you stepped on that gas pedal? There was nothing but wind and grit in your face and a steering wheel that read your mind.

I swear that thing was soaring, off-road—I swerved around rock outcroppings, small stands of brush, and once? A motherfucking cobra—and Sonny sat in the passenger seat, hanging on to the roadie bar for dear life, fingers turning white he was clutching it so hard. If there wasn't a look on his face like he was flying, I woulda said he was scared to death, but there *was* that look, and all I could hear in my head was my own voice going, "Faster! Faster!" when my brother took me out for a ride when I was twelve.

He wanted to go faster, and I obliged.

The cliff wall, the same color as the sand, brought us up short. I didn't see it, and the abrupt 360 I pulled to keep us from slamming face-first into a hunk of rock left us breathless and shaking with adrenaline as I pulled the thing to a stop in the shade.

I half laughed, not really afraid, and looked at Sonny. His eyes were squeezed shut with fear, and I felt bad.

"Sorry 'bout that, Private," I said, trying for courtesy.

"I'm gonna hafta change my shorts," he snapped, only half kidding, and I squashed a smile down.

"Well, I hope you did your laundry," I told him soberly.

His grin caught me by surprise. "Sir-yes-sir!"

I laughed. "Man, Sonny, I do not know what you did to this thing, but it's like magic. If anyone else drives this vehicle, they will think they stole a flying carpet instead."

Sonny ducked his head, looking bashful. "Thank you," he mumbled. "You drive like a tornado."

I laughed some more, happy like I hadn't been since I was a little kid and Jake was still my hero. "My brother taught me," I said. "He used to street race. Damn, he was good."

"Was?" he asked, and I looked away.

"Was," I told him, because Jake had driven his car up on the railroad tracks to be hit by an oncoming train when I was a senior in high school. He'd been twenty-six then, with a job at the cannery and his second baby on the way. People said he'd turned off the ignition and just sat there, head back, eyes closed, waiting. But I didn't want to talk about that, not to Sonny, not now. "But I miss racing," I said to fill the silence. "Best time ever."

"You can make money on it," Sonny said, sounding glad he had something to contribute.

"Yeah? Yeah—Jake used to make money. Said he could make more if he could forget he wanted to live." But he'd forgotten at the end, hadn't he? "Maybe when I get back, I'll do that. Just buy myself a car, soup it up."

"I'd trick it out for you," Sonny said, and I looked to my side to see him looking at me earnestly. "I'd make it fly. You'd dust everyone. We'd make a shitload."

"Enough to—"

"Start my own garage," he said, his voice dreamy, and I knew this was something he'd thought about.

I smiled a little, thought to give him his pipe dream. "Yeah, sure, Sonny. We'll do that. Take the pay we save, buy ourselves a car, a little garage. Make us some money. Get a bigger garage and live someplace nice. Why not?"

He looked fierce then, like I'd given him a dream and a backbone, a reason to sink his teeth into the world.

"That's a promise," he said, his voice guttural. "You can't go back."

I blinked. I hadn't realized I'd married the guy just by feeding his dream. But then…. "Why not?" I shrugged. "Got nothin' better to do when I get back."

He nodded and spat into the dust. "Good," he said, as if we'd sealed something. I guess maybe we had. "Now let's get back and I can fix the mods on this thing so no one knows I've been fucking with it. Galway'll fuck me sideways if he knows."

Something hot and alien stopped my breathing then. "He'd do that?"

Sonny shrugged. "Sure. Why not. Those guys, they'll do anything if it hurts you."

He sounded like he knew.

SO NO more black eyes after that. But neither of us stopped watching his back. Unfortunately we were at war, and things had a way of stabbing you, shooting you, or reaming you from behind, no matter how hard you tried to sprout eyeballs in the back of your head.

Sonny adapted to the army, though. He didn't fit in, but he adapted. There were locals that slept near the camp. The official rule was not to encourage them, not to buy from them, not to get attached to them—but they were folks, same as us. Some of the boys, the ones who grew up with those parents who watched their every move? Those guys had trouble watching the ten-year-olds with the M16s. Me? My folks didn't know what we were doing, as long as we got home in time for dinner. I watched my brother slice a piece off his best friend once just because the guy was standing too close to him. The guy ended up with a scar that looked just like Galway's, except across his chest, and he didn't stop wanting to stand too close to Jake. Jake just stopped objecting, that was all.

So I didn't mind the boys with the guns, but I did mind watching them surf through our garbage to eat, so I started sneaking food to them. Sonny saw me and started doing the same.

On the one hand, it didn't feel honest. It felt like feeding cats, and they weren't cats, they were people, starving people, children running in linen diapers and nothing else, their feet bare on the burning sands of the road.

On the other, we didn't make the world and we didn't make the war. We just pulled a trigger in it when we were asked, and that was all we had. We wanted to feed people like cats? Well, it was better'n shooting them like cats, and I knew guys back home who would do that too.

So we fed the children, and knew they brought the food to their parents in their little tents, and knew that sometimes it went to feed the babies and sometimes it went to feed the dads. All we could do was bring the scraps. It had to be enough.

You feed a cat, and it gets attached, and it was the same for Sonny. He had a little girl, thin, brown, swathed in lengths of cloth like they all were. This one, though—she had a red ribbon, soiled and limp, tied to her wrist like a bracelet. Sonny gave it to her—I think he got it from one of the girls, a copter pilot—and she wore it all the time, smiling at him with quick flashes of white teeth. She couldn't have been more than nine or ten.

She followed him around when she could, and he let her carry his tools and gave her money for the help. The money was good, and the food was probably better, but mostly? She was like me, I guess. Her mom had a thousand kids, and there were a thousand thousand people in that camp by our base, and she was lost, another set of bare feet and a high-pitched voice, unless she was with Sonny and he made her feel special.

The day we got hit, the fuckers attacking us, they didn't give a damn about all those locals hanging near the Americans. They just ripped right through like butter.

We had bunkers ready for the attack, and there I was with all the new recruits, listening to the fire and the screams and the chaos, when I looked around and realized I couldn't see Sonny.

Something horrible roiled through me. He would have been in the auto bay—that was safe, wasn't it? With his little barefoot shadow in his wake?

I looked at my guys. They were safe, they had ordnance—and there was a Marine Special Ops guy who had stopped for a shower, shit, and shave and gotten caught with us Army grunts when the firing started. They were safer with him than with ten of me.

"You got these guys?" I asked, listening to see if the shelling had started up on the other side of camp.

Lance Corporal Burton looked at me as though that were the stupidest question on the planet. He was a black guy, pleasant round face, light-brown skin, shaved smooth, which he didn't have to do as a jarhead, but he had the kind of head it looked good on, so why not?

"Good," I said, taking his silence for acquiescence, which was stupid, but I was worried. "I gotta go check on my buddy. His guys don't have his back."

Burton raised his eyebrows. "Your guys don't have his back?"

I squinted at him. "We don't all come from a fire cradle, like you all," I said, thinking about the way those Marines had each other's backs through fucking lava storms and ice bombs and shit. "Sometimes we're just grunts and bullies, same as any other schoolyard."

Burton looked at the new recruits, who were sitting, a little shell-shocked, but sound, cradling their M16s like newborn children.

"Yeah. We'll live," he said sourly, and I had a feeling they'd live because he knew how to aim, but still. It was Sonny and he was alone.

"I owe you," I said, and he shook his head.

"Man, just have your guy's back," he said in disgust, and I took that for what it was, and ducked out of the bunker and held my breath.

It was about a hundred yards from that bunker to the auto bay, and maybe the longest run of my life. There were some portable buildings in the way, the mess hall, the showers—I wasn't all that exposed, but everyone else was behind barriers, and I felt as naked as I've ever felt in my life.

Still, my breathing didn't get any better as I slid into the auto bay. In fact, if anything, it got worse.

I could hear Galway taunting Sonny, even over the retreating shellfire.

"C'mon, Daye, give her up. Your little raghead friend, she ain't got no business here. You kick her outta this here bunker or I'll shoot her myself!"

"She'll die out there!" Sonny protested. It was about the only time I ever heard him stand up for someone.

I ran full tilt into the auto bay and saw that Galway's other cronies were nowhere to be seen. It was just him, Sonny, and a terrified nine-year-old girl.

"Galway, stand down!" I snapped, and it might have worked, but he'd studied ranks same as me, and his stars and bars were more and better.

"What did you say to me, you insubordinate little shit?" he snarled, and I looked up to see Sonny, his back to the little girl as she wept in the corner. A shell went off, nearer than the last one, and she screamed a little and whimpered, and I thought about what a shitty thing war was, especially for this poor kid here.

"I said leave 'em alone! It's not like he can fire his weapon!" And it was true. There were tiny little window ports on the shelling side of the auto bay, supported by sandbags, but at the moment? There were two latrines and a shower between the auto bay and whoever was throwing shells at us. Unless someone snuck in past our outer defenses, there wasn't nobody to shoot at through that little window.

"And I said he's got a little raghead girl in here and that's against regulations—that kid needs to go!"

"She'll be killed," I said, and I knew, somewhere in the back of my mind, that it was the same thing Sonny had said. It was basic, wasn't it? Basic humanity? But then, Galway wasn't hardly human.

At that moment, the guys throwing the shells got smart and added some extra oomph to their ordinance. The two latrines went up in a spatter of sun-boiled shit and a corner of the auto bay, pulverized in an instant. I was thrown down face-first, and so was Galway, and I pulled myself up when I heard Sonny's wail from under a pile of rubble.

Oh God. He was hurt. I imagined him, bloody, ripped, dying, and for a moment my world became a telescope, me on the far, small end, all the bad things I imagined about Sonny on the big-seeing magnified end, and I thought my breath would stop.

I started digging through the rubble, ignoring Galway, and when I pulled up the sandbags under the broil of the sun, I saw he might have had some scrapes and bruises, but he wasn't hurt.

The little girl, though, the one with the red ribbon on her wrist—her skull was caved in. Her tiny little face didn't hardly look human, and the blood was seeping up through the gray dust that covered them both. Sonny was cradling her and weeping even as Galway pulled himself up off of the ground.

"*Shut up!* Stop whining, you little faggot!" He was screaming, which was stupid because our ears were all ringing and he couldn't hear his own voice. I know everything *I* heard sounded like it came from the bottom of a pool.

I looked up, and he was advancing in on us, his M16 in his hand and a look I didn't like at all in his eyes.

I don't know what I would have done then. At least that's what I tell myself. I had my own weapon, a standard-issue Beretta, in my hand, aimed straight on Galway with the safety off. I stood there, finger on the trigger, yelling although I couldn't hear my own words, and that's what we were doing when the next shell hit us.

My gun went off and Galway's face dissolved at the same time. The explosion pitched me forward and buried me under sandbags, and this time, it was Sonny digging me out of them.

"My gun," I said when I could pull myself to my knees.

Sonny said something, but I couldn't hear him. I must have asked "what" about six thousand times, because finally he turned me, and what I saw….

He'd taken the little girl's body and laid her facedown in the puddle of her blood. He'd put my gun in her hands.

The angle was right, I realized, my head ringing, a pain in my ribs and my shoulder I couldn't seem to breathe past. The angle was right. She could have shot him as he was advancing on her and Sonny. But that's not what had happened. What had happened was I had shot my own man in the face and I wasn't sure if I meant to or not, but I'd been aiming, I'd been aiming when the shell went off.

The shells weren't going off anymore.

I shook my head, dazed, short of breath, trying to figure the story, trying to figure what Sonny had planned with that little girl and my gun and a dead master sergeant. Sonny, tears tracking through the grime, was yelling at me something I couldn't hear.

I stood up and said, "I hope they go easy at the court-martial," and it was the last thing I managed before my knees gave out and my lungs were set fire and I looked down and saw I'd taken shrapnel and I might not survive to see this mess untangled.

# SHAKING HANDS

TURNED out, nobody asked me shit.

I was under, and Sonny told the story. He said I'd been taken out with the first shelling, and my gun had been knocked out of my hand. The girl had grabbed it, and Galway had come after her. She'd taken him out right before the second shell.

He told me what had "happened" when I was still groggy from the anesthesia, and I remember squinting at him.

"That's the worst story in the history of stories in the history of history." I *was* still stoned, mind you.

Sonny shrugged. "No court-martial for you" is what he said, and I was passing out again.

"That's something," I said before my vision went black.

It was.

My body mended, our base camp moved and rebuilt, and in six weeks I was doing PT and morning call, same as everyone else.

Sonny became my shadow.

We didn't talk about Galway, or the day of the shelling, or the lie, or the fact that the more I thought about it, the more I pulled that trigger before that last big shell hit. What we *did* talk about was street racing. How we were going to get home and he was going to fix up cars and I was going to drive them, how we'd go from town to town and we'd make up our money for a garage, for a little house, for a dog. Sonny wanted a dog, a midsize dog, he specified. Sort of a mix of things, something that would love him forever and not ask too many questions. He'd put a red bandana around its neck and it would be his. I hadn't had any dogs growing up and thought that sounded fine. Sonny's garage, Sonny's dream, Sonny's dog.

Beat what I had going on at home by a mile.

Or a quarter mile on a deserted track in a small-assed town.

I got my papers about a month before Sonny would get his. I didn't much like leaving him alone, although Galway was dead and the auto bay was run by a perfectly decent master sergeant now. I just didn't trust that last four weeks.

I asked Burton to keep an eye on him, since the guy was in and out of our camp more than most of our COs anyway.

Burton shrugged, said he would. I told the guy to look me up when his term was up. He smiled slightly. He was going to college after this; I knew it. I was still going nowhere.

"If you need your car fixed," I said lamely, even though all I did was drive 'em. He coulda been an asshole about that; we both knew it. He wasn't, though. Shook my hand like a friend, said, "Keep outta trouble, Ace. I'll keep your boy safe."

I felt better then, knowing Burton would come through.

The day I shipped home, I went looking for Sonny, thinking he'd want to say good-bye. He was under a car, same as any other day.

"Sonny," I called, then looked at all the other mechanics staring at me like I'd lost my mind. "Private Daye!"

"I'm busy, sir."

"I'm shipping out." It was stupid. He knew I was shipping out. He couldn't even come out and shake my hand?

"I know it." His voice was still muffled by the underside of the Jeep he was working on—but by something else too.

I swallowed hard and crouched down, looking around me. The master sergeant saw me sort of begging with my eyes. He rolled his own eyes in disgust and made himself scarce, and since the other guys in the bay were working on their own vehicles and not minding me, I figured there weren't nothing I was gonna do here that they'd need to see.

"This is stupid, Sonny," I said quietly to the pair of legs sticking out under the Jeep. "I've got your number, I know when you'll be in San Diego. I'll meet you there like I promised. I just want a handshake, that's all."

"You'll get a handshake when you meet me," he muttered, face still under the car.

"I can't get one now?" I was laughing a little, because he was being such a little kid.

Sonny was on a little wheeled dolly, the kind with the pillow for the back of the head, and he scooted that thing just far forward enough to glare at me through the grime on his face. It was oil-based grime. Water slid right off, not leaving a track or a trace.

"Right now, you are just some asshole I knew in the army," Sonny said, his eyes squinted mostly shut so I couldn't see they were red. "You meet me in San Diego, you'll be my friend."

I took a deep breath. Killing for a guy didn't buy you a handshake? Well, maybe not.

"I'll be there," I promised quietly. "You keep your nose clean and stay not shot, and I'll be there."

He grunted and squeezed his eyes shut tight. "Buy us a car while you got the time," he said. "I want to work on it as soon as I get there."

And with that, he scooted that dolly back under the car without another word. I sighed, patted his thigh perfunctorily, and grinned when I heard a thunk and a curse as he jerked and hit his head.

"Serves you right," I said, my voice all mildness. "Shake a man's hand while you got the chance." And then I left.

Unlike Sonny, I didn't have no doubts we'd be seeing each other again.

BEING in the service was decent. People tell you when to get up, tell you when to eat. People tell you what you're supposed to be doing when you're on duty—not too much thinking, that's my favorite part. Thinking gets you in trouble. Thinking gets you feeding kids behind the barracks, and thinking gets you standing with a gun on a superior officer in the middle of a firefight.

Thinking gets you working security at the coliseum in San Diego at night while you work fast food in the day. I wasn't proud. I promised Sonny a car when he got out, which meant I needed a little apartment to sleep in and cash on hand, because what we were looking for was something stock that could be taken to the next level.

I found it at last—a basic Taurus SHO in wasp yellow, running good, all legal—and I bought it with a smile, wondering what Sonny would do to it. It had been in an accident, and the front end had been crushed and then replaced with one off a pick-n-pull, and I figured Sonny would have something to do with that too, because you don't want no substandard construction when you're going 200 miles an hour. He was going to want to reinforce the frame, add NOS, take off the smog, and make it pretty.

The woman selling it was in her thirties—her daughter had wrecked it, and they'd salvaged the car after it had been declared totaled. She needed the money, but I wanted the car at $3K. We compromised when I paid the $3K but spent the night making her $2K worth of happy.

Now you'd think I'd be thrilled to get a $2,000 discount and some pussy on the side, and she wasn't bad-looking or anything, but, well, I've learned to fake it real good.

See, the trick is, you go down on girls long enough, lick them until they scream and shudder and their parts are all shiny and quivery, keep two fingers inside, pushing until you find their spot, and after that? You only have to fuck them long enough to make them come again. You can make yourself hard while you do the licking, if you close your eyes and think of something else, and they think it's them turning you on. It's a small lie, really, if it makes 'em happy, right? If you did your job right the first time, it doesn't take long, and that's a blessing. Then, as long as you got a rubber on (and I always got a rubber on), you can thrust a couple of times, and she's all tender, right? She thinks you fuck like a god, and you wait until she spasms all over, goes limp, and then go real fast and groan like it feels so good you can't stop yourself.

And there you go. She comes, she thinks you came, and you can make her feel good and walk away.

Just don't look yourself in the mirror too soon afterward, because you might not like what you see.

And really don't remember that, while you were licking her lady parts until she left scratch marks on your scalp, what you saw when you were stroking yourself off was a set of gray eyes and a mouth, slightly open, lean lips moist, while a vulnerable young man promised you anything and everything you'd never let yourself hope for, even in a dream.

But it got us the car. Odds were good Sonny wouldn't ask how I got it cheap, because the reason I needed it cheap was such a good one.

I found us a garage. Not the dream garage Sonny wanted, but I had my salary saved from four years in the service, and I put a down payment on a place in a little town called Victoriana, which sat between Santee and Lakeside. There weren't nothing there but a Carl's Junior, one of those big gas places with a Subway and a Baskin Robbins inside, as well as T-shirts, books on tape, travel blankets, and the like, and that garage, complete with a shitty little mother-in-law cottage in the dust behind it.

I spent an hour standing inside that tiny house. It had a living room, a bedroom, a swamp cooler, a kitchenette, and a tiny bathroom with a shower and a mirror cabinet and a toilet, sink, and vanity and nothing else—you could see it all in one glance, really, but I stood there, sweltering since the swamp cooler hadn't been turned on and trying to decide how I was going to outfit that place. I knew what I wanted, but I didn't know what Sonny expected. In the end, I did what I would've done if that extra $2,000 hadn't been a hardship, and I'd been able to call that woman back after I left.

I bought a queen-size for the bedroom, and a futon for the living room, and a dresser for each. The dresser in the living room could double as an end table. I put a lamp on it and my shit inside and congratulated myself on buying one of the pricier futon mattresses so my back didn't get screwed up.

I got a real good mattress for the queen-size too, and tried not to feel sorry for myself when I did.

*So what?* I told myself. So what if he didn't want me. Wouldn't even shake my hand when I left. So what. He hadn't meant that offer in the beginning. He'd been desperate. I told myself I was too good to take something someone didn't really want to give me. Then I remembered what I'd been giving to the women I'd been with and felt like shit.

That night—the night after our furniture arrived—I drove to the stadium and put on my uniform and stood watch as a bunch of pretty girls and boys ran around in their best clothes and listened to a techno band I ain't never heard of.

I kept my game face on, my staff sergeant face, and most of 'em stayed in line. No walking on the floor unless you had a pass, no sitting in a seat that wasn't yours, no filming the band (which was pretty stupid anyway, since the band was in the middle of all these special effects that boggled most cameras), and no getting so high you couldn't stand.

The first band was over and the second one came on when a little girl walked up to me—not much older than eighteen, if that's how old she was. She had dark hair, dark eyes, and pale skin much like my own, actually. She was delicate as a flute of champagne and three times as bubbly. She tripped over her own feet, fell into my arms, laughed giddily for a minute, and abruptly passed out and threw up on me.

Gross.

I carried her to first aid, where they pumped her stomach even while I walked out. The employee room had extra T-shirts and I had a pair of black sweats, and I went to the nearest men's room to try to wash the stench of vomit off my skin.

I ended up stripped to my skivvies, wiping at my underwear with the crumbly paper towels until you could see the outline of my cock through them, and trying not to drop my clean stuff in the sink.

Guys came and went, most of them not giving me a second look, and then the leader band started its opening set and, thank God, the place cleared out.

It's about then I gave it up on the tighty-whities and pulled the sweats on commando, and then looked up to see a guy watching me in the mirror.

He had tousled bleached hair and blue eyes, and his mouth was parted, moist, and his pink tongue was between his lean lips. I took a sudden gulping breath, and even as I watched in the mirror, big patches blotched deep red on my chest, and my face heated. My hair is dark and curly, and I wear thin sideburns and a ducktail, like a gang-banger in '60s Texas, and my eyes are dark brown. You wouldn't think my skin would be so fair, but it is, and as our eyes locked, that damning flush traveled from my chin to my abdomen and bloomed hectically over my cheeks.

I pulled my T-shirt over my head hastily, knowing my little pink nipples had pebbled and that under my sweats, my cock was hanging heavily against my thigh.

I felt him pressed against my back, his hand down the ass of my sweats, just as my head popped out of my T-shirt, and our eyes met in the mirror again.

He leaned forward and licked my ear, causing my cock to pump solidly with blood, making an obvious tent in my pants.

"I would get on my knees and swallow you whole," he whispered, and I must have made a sound, a whimper, a plea, because he grabbed my hips and turned me around, hands shoving at my clothes.

For a moment I closed my eyes and pictured him kneeling in front of me in his V-neck sweater and the jeans that dropped so low I knew he waxed. In my mind I saw his hand wrapped around my cock, white fingers not meeting, and that's when my eyes popped open and I put my hands on his as they rested on my hipbones, ready to drag my sweats farther.

"No," I said, but not rough. "I'm sorry. Not you."

He stood up slowly, reluctantly, and moved into my space, pressing up against my front. "You waiting for a girl to suck your balls, sugar? Because not the way that thing's poking at me."

I swallowed and, if possible, blushed even more. "No," I whispered. "Not a girl. You're nice, but I need this job."

And now he flushed, the blood moving up his face, and he took a step back, adjusting himself unnecessarily.

"I'm sorry," he said, embarrassed. "Daddy's money... you forget—"

I shook my head. I was remembering the way my brother had sliced up his best friend, the knife appearing out nowhere, sliding cleanly through Ronnie's T-shirt, his flesh, and Ronnie had stumbled back but hadn't protested, hadn't even asked Jake what the fuck he was doing.

*Don't stand so close to me!*

*Okay, Jakey. You let me know when it's okay.*

No irony either. Just acceptance.

"You wanted me," I said, my voice somebody else's. "That's okay. You're hot. But… but it's not what I'm looking for right now, and like I said—"

"You need this job." The guy nodded, and I felt better. He moved past me to wash his hands, and I grabbed my boots and my socks and leaned against the wall to put them on.

"Are you out?" he asked, looking at me with what I could tell was courage, and I couldn't shit on that.

"No," I said, and even though I'd said no, there was an acknowledgement of which box I was in. "I might never be."

Sonny had offered me the same thing this guy just had, but he'd offered it to me in desperation. I didn't want it in desperation. I wanted it to be real.

"That's too bad," the guy said, and his smile was kind. "I'd be gentle."

My own smile was hard, and it was the only smile I had. "I wouldn't be," I said, my voice gravel and grit and dust. "Gentle isn't what I've got."

The guy shuddered and held onto the sink. "Oh. My. God." He leaned his head down and made a couple of helpless, impotent thrusts with his hips. "I've got to go beat off in a corner, soldier, because you are *not* making me want you any less."

The guy left then, walking funny, and I closed my eyes and waited until my heart stopped thundering in my ears. I could see it so plainly—him pressed up against the wall, our pants around our ankles, my dick pushing hard and slick into his sphincter.

It made me ache, and I knew what I'd be doing on my new futon that night, in the sweltering darkness of the ova of our dream, but even then, when I wouldn't say the words, any words, to myself, I knew why I didn't take that guy against the wall and fuck him until he screamed, job or no job.

It wasn't because I was honorable, or smart, or straight.

It was because he wasn't the right guy.

THAT night I thought of Sonny as I laid on my little futon and tried to put that dream of him to bed. Whatever I was didn't mean Sonny was, and even if he *was* that, it didn't mean he wanted me. It just meant we were, that was all.

And I had promised him a place, and even if this wasn't the big place I wanted for the two of us eventually, I had a start to our dream, a chance to ride cars like tornadoes through the dusty streets, an excuse for working shoulder to shoulder with him in the garage.

So I lay there, naked, a fan blowing from the swamp cooler, trying to take the sweat off my body. I couldn't think of Sonny doing things to me like that guy in the restroom. I couldn't, not and not cry because it would never end happy.

I just lay there instead, gazing into the darkness and feeling my fingertips across my stomach, along the length of my cock, teasing my nipples, and stopping every so often for a pinch.

My abdomen was lean and muscled, and the skin there was tender, so I teased that for a while, then tickled the hair on my balls until they drew up tight, as hard as my cock was now on my stomach.

I drew my knees up, spreading my ass to catch the air from the fan, and knew this for a plain luxury, something I hadn't never been able to do before, because whether it was my folks' house or the military bunk, fact was being *truly* alone was not something that had happened to me often, and it figured that now that I was, I was thinking of who I wanted with me.

I wrapped my hands around my cock, my thumb not quite touching my fingertips, and squeezed hard at the base, stroking up. My precome shot, warm and slippery, and I wet my fingers in it and used them to stretch my asshole while I stroked. It was awkward, doing that, one hand reaching behind, the other hand stroking, but my body was hungry, driven. I squeezed my cock and stroked it fast, my fist making slurping noises in the wet spurting mess of precome. My fingers burned, not lubed enough but scissoring anyway, stretching as I reamed myself because that's what faggots wanted, wasn't it? Something in their ass and a hand or a mouth on their cocks? Wasn't that what I was? A faggot? A bent-over asshole that needed a dick, a pumping dick that needed a mouth, a cocksucking bitch, a comewhore with a prick, a—

Oh God! I saw Sonny on his knees, my cock stretching his mouth, his gray eyes looking at me with the same hunger that was searing my skin in my own bed, and I screamed into the silence of the little apartment, come scalding over my hand, my ass clenching on my own fingers before my spasming, coming body clenched so tight they were squeezed out. I groaned then, wanting them back, wanting something, anything, oh God, please, *anything*—

And I saw Sonny again, swallowing, bending over, letting me lick him in all the places he most wanted hid.

My cock gave one more pathetic squirt and my body shuddered out its last orgasmic spasm. I pulled my elbows in to my chest and rolled over on my side in a puddle of my own come, and tried not to let my after-sex groans turn into sobs.


A WEEK later, I picked him up at the airport, still in his fatigues, weary and grimy from the two days of travel it took to get from the Mideast to San Diego—to home.

I was waiting by the luggage turntable and had already pulled off his duffel—DAYE in big black letters on the OD green side—when he trotted over. Fatigue had aged him for the evening, sunken his eyes in his skull, drawn his mouth tight, given him scowl lines from his nose to the corner of his lips. But when he saw me, some of that fell away, and he walked up tentatively, his hand extended like he was afraid I'd refuse.

I took his hand and then pulled him in roughly so we could bump chests and I could thump him on the back twice.

"Good to see you, Private," I said as we pulled back. His eyes rabbited left and then right, and that quickly he settled down.

"Field promotion," he said, his mouth twitching up. "I'm corporal now."

"Nice," I said, seeing the change in his uniform now that he mentioned it. My stomach washed cold. "You were out in the shit?"

He shook his head. "Naw. Had a three-star there trying to get the fuck out of Pakistan before things went south. I fixed his Hummer, made it faster. He sent the promotion when we lived through the attack."

Officers. Seriously. "Was Burton there?" I asked, still grateful for his help.

"Yeah—he's the one who told three-star I could fix the Hummer."

I laughed a little. "Well, Corporal, we've got about an hour to the garage. You want to stop and eat on the way?"

More of that age fell away—the lines around his mouth, some of the wrinkles at the corners of his eyes. "A milkshake," he said eagerly. "A real one. From Sonic or Baskin Robbins. Can we do that?"

"Yeah. Yeah. No problem. If we go Sonic, will you eat a burger or something?" His wrists were still thin, and his pointed chin seemed about to split out of his skin.

His eyes lost focus, and I shouldered his duffel and started to steer him out of the terminal. "Yeah," he said, like that took a lot of thought. "It's been a while since I ate."

I didn't say anything, but I wondered if it hadn't been that whole month since I'd left.

I explained the setup as he wolfed down a burger and *two* chocolate-banana shakes at Sonic. I told him the garage had tools and such, but it hadn't really been touched in a couple of years, and that I'd put in new carpet and added another swamp cooler to the bedroom. I even started watering the dust around the cottage, but so far, all I had was mud.

"Why didn't you work on the garage?" Sonny asked, his voice losing some coherence as I pulled out of Sonic.

"That's your place, Sonny. I can help and all, but I can't do what you do."

"Why didn't you put my bunk in there?" he asked, and I swallowed, not wanting to talk about the futon and the bed and mattress.

"'Cause it's a garage, not a home," I snapped. "I'm sorry it's not in a nice place with a big house nearby instead of a shitty little one, but I kept some of my salary. We can work for that place, okay?"

"No, that's not what I—" Sonny made a sound of frustration and pulled off his hat, then smoothed his hand through the short blond hair that was just barely long enough to show he'd missed his last haircut. "I don't need a bedroom, you know, or a place. I just need the garage."

"Well, tough. You've got the bedroom, I've got the futon, and we both have a shitty swamp cooler and a big-assed fan until shit cools off in October." It was May.

"Well that's just silly. A futon'll screw up your back."

I shook my head, so pissed for a moment I couldn't talk and could barely see. "Sonny, shut up. I got you a place to sleep, we got a refrigerator that don't let the milk go sour, and you can work on the car and get us some gigs while I do my thing and keep us fed."

Sonny squinted at me. "What're you doing?"

"Frying burgers. Why's it matter?"

"Don't you have more money saved than that?" he asked, and I glared. This was not going the way I'd thought it would.

"I told you, I've got half my savings waiting to get a better spot. I figure we'll race, we'll add the winnings to the pot, and that way we'll be able to move outta the fucking desert sometime before it kills us, you think?"

"Better spot?" Sonny asked through a yawn. "I already got a bedroom. I didn't know there was a dream bigger'n that."

I'd hit my limit then and wanted to demand what sort of world he thought we lived in that this shitty garage apartment on a stretch south of nowhere was the best of his dream, but he'd closed his eyes—just shut them, there in the front seat of the Taurus—and curled into a ball on the front seat. I reached over him at the next stoplight and moved the seat back, then pushed him a little so he wasn't leaning his head against the armrest like a broke-necked puppy, and that's how he stayed for the next forty-five minutes, not even snoring he was so tired.

# LOCKBOXES AND STRAY DOGS

SONNY staggered into the apartment without even looking around, which I'd kind of expected. I saw him strip to his skivvies and a T-shirt and then fall into the new bed with the new clean sheets like he could have dropped on a sand dune and slept just as easy. I sort of expected that too—it was how I spent my first three days in a hotel room when I arrived.

I imagine he slept most of the next day while I worked both jobs. I left him with cereal and milk, some sodas in the fridge, and the key to the garage. When I got back from the coliseum around 1:00 a.m., he was in the garage, up to his elbows in a tub of water and disinfectant, scrubbing out around two years of dust, spiders, and grime.

I stepped out of the car and yawned, about done with my day. He looked up from his scrubbing, though, and said, "You wanna help? I'm almost done with it."

Well, okay. It was about the only time he'd ever asked for my company. I took a scrub brush and went.

I checked him out as we worked, watched his face move like he was talking to people but not enough to actually open his mouth, and wondered what sort of conversations he was having. He was in the middle of a doozy when I leaned my head against the recently cleaned wall and dozed off.

He shook me awake before my face hit the concrete, and then offered me a hand up. I took it because my body hurt after a long fucking day, and I felt my knees protest.

"I gotta get you some pillows," I mumbled.

He stepped into my body and draped my arm over his shoulders.

"This shit's no good for your knees. And a dolly too, like they had in the desert. And more disinfectant, something good, 'cause this shit don't work. And some gloves for your hands, 'cause—"

"And some fucking sleep, brother." His voice was low, and he stopped and pressed the button that closed the bay door before turning off the light in the garage and turning on the one that lit up the muddy yard between the garage and the house.

"Yeah. Sleep's good."

"You got both jobs tomorrow?" he asked, and I had to think about that one.

"No. Wait. Yeah. I don't know. Schedule's on the fridge."

"Yeah, well, which one pays more?"

"Security," I told him. I'd woken up a little, and I was hot and sweaty. I'd taken off my jacket and left it in the car, but I'd been on my hands and knees in my boots and polyester pants and black SECURITY T-shirt—complete with a stun-gun holster and my Taser tucked inside. "But it's only four nights a week."

"Yeah, well, we put my money out to keep us alive some while we build up the car, and you can quit the one at McDonald's. Do you really fucking work at McDonald's?"

"Yup," I said, hating the fact that I could still smell the grill on my skin on top of everything else.

"Why'd you sign up to work there? Pussy?"

I grimaced. "Is all underage. Or even if it's exactly aged, it's all too damned young."

"Yeah," he said, sighing. "Just as well. You can't bring anyone back here, you understand?"

I blinked hard, because I wouldn't have in the first place, but I still didn't understand. "Deal," I said, wishing for some brain cells and a way to read his mind.

We got to the front door, and he swung it open for me. I pulled away, feeling like I stank to high heaven. "I'll take the shower first, 'kay? God, three days in the desert was honest sweat, at least. Working in that kitchen is all food grease."

"Yeah, you do that. You eat?"

I nodded. "Yeah. Sandwich before work."

"Oh." He looked crestfallen. Had he wanted to cook for me? That would have been nice.

"I'll be out," I told him, and then, just like we were in the military, I locked the Taser in my top drawer with my Berretta and the belt, then stripped to the skin, threw my clothes in the basket next to the end table, and sorted through my drawers for clean boxer shorts.

There were a couple of towels hanging on the shower, and I didn't feel like breaking out a new one, so I was naked and dangling when I turned back around to walk the five steps across the living room to the tiny bathroom in the corner.

And that's when I saw Sonny's eyes on my body. I swallowed, not sure why he'd be looking there with such amazement.

"That's fuckin' huge," he said almost accusingly, and I knew my skin was blotching from embarrassment under his eyes.

"It's what God gave me," I said, knowing from all that time in the military and in locker rooms as a kid that it wasn't quite what the big guy had handed out to everyone else.

"Yeah, well." He said it like it was a whole sentence by itself, and then turned away toward the kitchen. "I'll make you a snack."

"That's appreciated, but 'yeah, well' what?" Perversely, I didn't hide myself, just stood there, arms crossed, equipment hanging against my thigh. Maybe he could be embarrassed into finishing his sentence.

"Yeah, well." He looked up at me from under lowered eyebrows. "I'll bet the girls like that thing plenty."

I grimaced, hating this conversation. "That's not the part they like the most," I muttered and headed for the shower before I had to clarify that. God. God, I hated hiding. I hadn't been fond of it before the army, and the army had made me forget for a while. But now, I had the memory of the woman who sold us her Ford burning behind my eyeballs, and not a single memory of a touch I really wanted to make it feel better.

And Sonny looking at me shyly, but at the same time like I somehow let him down.

Sonny had rooted around the kitchen and cooked me a late dinner, which was nice. I got out of the shower and into a pair of briefs, and there was a gi-fucking-gantic plate of eggs, sort of fluffy, and he'd put garlic salt and cheese on them too, so they tasted real good.

I sat at the little counter dividing the kitchen from, well, my bedroom, actually, and ate the food automatically, trying to focus on the refrigerator.

"Yup," I mumbled through a mouthful of eggs. "Six-hour shift tomorrow, but nothing at the coliseum. I'll be home around five."

"I've got saved pay too," Sonny said abruptly. Without asking, he pulled a stool up next to me and hopped on, leaning into my space with a fork to eat off my plate. The closeness was nice, I thought, bemused. I don't know if anyone had eaten off my plate since I was six and could stab my sister's hand with a fork.

"Yeah, well, you said you didn't do much on leave."

Sonny let out a grunt. "What was I going to do, someplace I didn't know, no one to tell me what to do? Anyway, I got money. Racing season gets big in a month, and I can't do this shit alone. Especially if we open the garage for actual business. You quit your

McDonald's job with all the underage poontang, and I'll pitch in my share."

I should have jumped at it—God, I was tired. But I'd had this… this stupid vision. I'd wanted to take care of him. I hesitated just long enough, because he stabbed at a bite of eggs viciously.

"Don't worry 'bout getting girls. They'll be lining up to jump on that thing when you start winning races."

I flicked him on the temple. "Could give a crap about girls on my pole," I snapped, enjoying his surprise. "Just…." I shoved the rest of the eggs at him, and he ate without reservation. "Never mind."

"No, not never mind. Why you wanna keep that job?"

"Hate that job. I'll quit, okay?"

"Yeah, why's it so hard to give up?"

I shook my head and stood up, away from the warmth of his body and the smell of cooking and garage grease and antiseptic. "It's not. I get plans in my head is all. I'm obliged to you."

He cocked his head. "You don't *like* owing me?" Oh fuck. He was getting hurt.

"I wanted to give you something," I said, not sure how this could sound anything less than what it was. "But you're right. You can't do this alone, and I can't work three jobs."

Sonny looked at me blankly. "You wanted to give me something?" he mumbled. "You gave me… Staff Sergeant, you gave me lots."

I sank down on the futon, feeling foolish. "Call me Ace," I snapped.

"'Kay, Ace. I'm going to shower." And just like that, he walked into the bathroom and turned on the water.

He left the eggs on the counter, and I got up, still in my briefs, and washed the dishes while he was in there. Then, knowing I was dying with tired and no kind of rational, I opened the futon and slid under the sheets.

The swamp cooler worked better now, especially since it had help, so it was comfortable, and the rumble-whine of it working actually soothed me. My eyes were mostly closed when Sonny came out of the bathroom, a towel wrapped tightly around his hips. He walked by the bed and looked down at me for a moment.

"You asleep, Staff Sergeant?"

"'Lmost."

"I'll turn out the light, then."

"Yeah. Night, Sonny."

"You quitting tomorrow?"

"Yeah."

"Good."

And with that, he leaned forward and turned off the light. As he did, the towel parted a little, and I saw a dark-brown mark, like a scar, that disappeared in the shadow of the towel. I filed it away for later, because there was so much that towel obscured that I wanted to see anyway, it was just one more mystery for me to fill my dreams with.

"Staff Sergeant?" Sonny's voice sounded smaller in the dark.

"Yeah?"

"I'm... I don't sleep well in new places. I'm putting my gun under my pillow."

"That's hella fucking stupid," I told him, waking up a little. "Lock your gun in your drawer. Put your *knife* under your pillow."

I saw Sonny's lean face in the darkness and could tell he was fitting that together like a new bolt in an engine.

"That's a real good idea," he said, and I nodded. I kept mine in the same place.

"Just make sure you stack a couple of pillows on top of it—them bowie knives, they're lumpy."

"Thanks, Serge—"

"Night, Sonny."

"Night."

Okay. Small dreams on top of large ones. We wanted a bigger garage in a suburb without dust. We wanted a dog. We wanted to race like the fucking wind. *I* wanted to see more of that scar. And *I* wanted him to call me Ace.

SO I quit frying burgers the next day, not bothering about a two weeks' notice and feeling a little guilty over that. I'd always been taught to respect a job, but Sonny hadn't been shitting around. There were already races every weekend with small pots and big ones and some just to be seen, and if you wanted to race for the big pots, you had to race in the ones to be seen. If we were going to compete, we needed to trick out the Taurus, and in order to do that, we needed to fix up the garage and pretend it was a business.

It might not have set well with my dumbass plans, but Sonny had a point—I did him more good in the garage than at a grill, and that was the truth.

We cleaned the place out first and then assessed our tool situation. We were lucky there—an air compressor, the basic gauges you needed for modern computer-driven engines—all that shit was still there in the shop. I said, "Shouldn't we stock up on stuff?" and Sonny looked at me blankly.

"Why?"

"Well, tires and stuff. There's some things—water pumps, hoses, belts, tires—that shit goes out, and it's real simple to replace. Right here, across from the gas station—we're gonna want to be able to sell that, you know?"

Sonny's blank look still didn't focus. "We don't even have a cash register."

"Well, we'll have to get one too. You *did* expect this to be a business, right?"

There was a moment, then, of total confusion. "But… but that's a legit thing, right there."

Now I was the one feeling blank. "Well, we're not running a chop shop!"

And suddenly, there was focus. "Oh! Okay, then. Well, yeah. I guess you're right. I'll… well, shit. We're gonna need some sort of computer and—"

"We can get a tablet today," I said, thinking about my stash of money and how much I had to spare. "And a cash box and receipts and stuff. And a printer."

Hell. This was an entire shitload of crap I hadn't thought of yet. Well, a dream, right?

"I got money," Sonny said like he was reading my mind. "I got more'n you think. Not enough for that house somewhere green, but I got it. You're right." He swallowed. "Yeah. You're right. It should be legit."

I didn't even know what to say to that. "I had no idea you thought it wouldn't be." My heart was pounding like I'd had a near miss of some sort, and my hands had gone cold and clammy. "What… where… how were you brought up that you'd think it wouldn't be?"

"Let's go get that tablet after lunch," he said. "Peanut butter and jelly or mac'n'cheese?" He'd been fascinated by our capacity to choose and make the food we wanted, even if we were constrained by budget. He'd been going to the dollar food store to see what canned goods from Serbia or Taiwan he could find, just to make the recipes he found on the backs of old magazines. Exotic things like Beanee Weenees and Hamburger Helper. I'd grown up on PB&J and mac'n'cheese—I didn't never see these things as luxuries, but Sonny did.

I looked at him, hoping for something more, and he looked back, the sweat seeping down his neck and soaking the collar of his OD-green T-shirt.

"Mac'n'cheese," I said after a minute. "With hot dogs."

Sonny brightened and ran through the back door of the garage to the house, away from my questions, to make gourmet kid food on the stove.

So after about a week, we started getting deliveries. We set up a joint bank account, and that's when I found out it was Sonny's *only* bank account: he'd cashed out his bank account at the military commissary because he didn't trust that walking away from the army didn't mean walking away from his pay. We had to count it out in front of the bank clerk, like drug dealers, and I wasn't sure my eyes were ever going to shrink back down to normal size, just thinking about it.

I should have known, I guess, from that first moment, when I knew whoever he had been before the army, it *wasn't* Sonny Daye. But something about the way he kept fingering his bankbook suspiciously, looking at the total like it was going to change, deplete in front of his eyes like a computer total in a spy movie, made my heart trip-hammer hard in my stomach. Near misses. Every quiet moment with him was a near miss.

"You want to keep that in your drawer?" I asked him courteously, and his fingers tightened on it. I swallowed. "Or under your pillow."

I watched him take a deep breath, like he was reminding himself of something. "It's your money too," he said. "Where do you keep yours?"

"Recently? It's been on the coffee table with the computer tablet," I said, trying to remember. "Other'n that, I keep it with my passport and my social security card, in a little file box—you've got one too, right?"

Sonny shook his head. "I've got a pocket in my duffle," he said seriously, and I swallowed. I had questions burning so bad in my throat they gave me heartburn, and no way to ask.

"Well, we'll get you a file box when we go get receipts," I said. "We'll keep it separate from the cash box and the envelope and all."

Sonny nodded, and for a moment he looked a little overwhelmed.

"Want to get a shake on the way?" I asked, and he smiled. The bank was thirty minutes out of our little town/pit-stop, and we were going grocery shopping too, since we were there and I didn't work that night.

"Yeah. Can we get a *blender* at the Walmart? I bet I can make shakes too, if I have ice cream and ice and some strawberries and—"

I shrugged. "Yeah, sure. Your money, Cochise—you go ahead and spend some."

Once again I felt the sudden shift of Sonny's focus to my face. "Thanks," he said briefly, and I didn't know what for. "For helping me be a grown-up. I don't got no one else to ask."

I shifted as we got into the Ford and turned on the air conditioner. "My brother," I said out of nowhere. "My oldest one. He was a good grown-up for a while."

"Was?"

"Drove his car on the railroad tracks and parked," I said shortly. "I guess there's some parts of being grown-up that hurt too much to do."

Sonny grunted, and I didn't know what else to say. "Did you...." He stopped. "Did you love him?" he asked after a minute, and I looked at him, because it was a curious question. Most people just said they were sorry, or that was too bad. People just assumed you loved your family, right? Even distant family was loved in a distant way.

"Yeah," I said, thinking it to be true. "I did. He was good to me, tried to be a role model, that sort of thing. Took me driving. Let me hang around and annoy the shit out of him and his friends. He knocked up a girl right out of high school, though." I shook my head. "Changed."

"Why? Was she a bitch?"

That jerked my head back sure enough. "She was a nice girl," I said, because Juanita was a nice girl—or had been, until seven years with Jake had made her bitter. "Wasn't the right person, I don't think," I said thoughtfully.

"Who was the right person?" Sonny asked, and for a moment I was tired of the two of us keeping our secrets in our own separate lockboxes.

"Same guy who went to prison for knocking over a 7-Eleven right before Jake stopped his car on the tracks. I hear he's out now, but he's missing most of his teeth."

Sonny sucked in a breath, a hard one. "I don't know what to say to that," he said after a moment, sounding as lost as I felt when I thought about it.

"I think it would have sucked," I said, "if Jake and Ronnie had run away together. For a year or two, it would have sucked for them. But this? It's sucked worse, longer. That's what I think."

"That's a fair thing to think," he said after a moment. "I'm sorry it sucks."

I shrugged. I wanted to tell him everything then, about tagging along after Jake from the time I was a kid, about thinking he walked on water. I wanted to tell him about seeing him cut a slice out of Ronnie, about seeing them kissing in a darkened corner of an alleyway before the stitches healed. I wanted to tell him about the fight he'd had with Ronnie, about how Jake had wanted to come out and Ronnie had said no, and how Jake had run off to sleep with his best friend after that, and Ronnie's life had gotten worse and harder and worse.

I wanted to tell Sonny everything, including the way his eyes had followed me for much of the last two years, whether he'd been in the same room or even the same country as me or not.

But he'd just gotten a checking account of his very own, one not in the military, from a bank he picked out. His dream was so secret, he'd planned to hide it from the law like his knife under his pillow and the scar he was so very careful not to let me see.

He was just becoming himself, a mouse out of his cage. He changed his name and was reborn, spending his cradle days in the army and learning to walk now.

Sonny Daye did not need me spilling my slippery heart under his shoes.

SO WE worked side by side, and it was all right—better than the army, that was for sure. We bought a television, new, and satellite channels, and the nights I had off, we watched movies and miniseries and ball games and concerts and… well, *everything*. Sonny watched it eagerly, with the same enthusiasm he'd shown mac'n'cheese and Beanee Weenees. Like it was the height of luxury.

I started wondering what he'd do if I gave him some slacks and one of those nice button-up shirts and took him to a place with a tablecloth. I'd never been myself, but there was something frustrating about him and that television and that kid's food. I liked that shit—I liked sharing it with him—but I knew there was something more. Did he?

THE day we got the tires—five sets in three different sizes—I ran across the street for some giant sodas on ice, which was one of the few luxuries we allowed ourselves to buy from the service station store, 'cause that shit was expensive. I'd just run around the side of the store to drop off a napkin in the trash when I saw some kids cornering a girl.

I'd seen them around: somewhere in a five-mile radius there had to be a high school, a tiny one, the kind with a graduating class of a hundred or so and a population that was 95 percent Hispanic.

The girl was crying, and the head boy in the pack was jeering at her and pointing to his crotch. Wonderful. I heard the word *puta* and saw them advancing and swore. I set my sodas down and took a couple of steps in, wondering what I thought made me look like a hero.

"So," I asked, stepping between the girl and the four cats moving in on the little mouse, "what are you all, ten?"

"Thirteen," the lead boy said. He was pretty—had the big sloe eyes, the long face, and the delicate nose and chin that some of the Mex kids did. Ronnie had been that pretty before his life turned to shit.

"So, is that old enough now? Did we get old enough to call girls whores when we're thirteen? Last I heard, you had to be a man to use that word."

The boy laughed and spat. "She is a whore—ask her. I paid her twenty dollars and she sucked my thing."

I turned around and looked at the girl, standing in her neon knit shirt and hip-dropped jeans, both of them ripped. She was trying so hard to look twenty. She was crying and she wouldn't meet my eyes. Poor baby. Twenty dollars must have sounded like a good deal at the time.

"You know where Afghanistan is?" I asked, reaching into the sheath at the waist of my cargo shorts and pulling out my bowie knife. Carefully, I started to scrape the grease out from under my fingernails.

"Yeah," the kid said, backing up at the sight of the knife. "It's a long fucking way away."

"Sure is," I said. "You know, in some places in the Middle East, they stone a whore to death for putting out. You know what 'stoning' is, don't you?"

The kid grinned at his buddies. "Smoking shitloads of weed?"

I flipped the knife over my hand and caught the handle again. "Not even close. It's when two hundred or so people throw rocks at the girl in the middle of the road until they cave in her skull and she dies."

There were shocked gasps, and some unease. Good, you little shits, choke on *that.*

"Now that's a pretty serious thing to do to a fourteen, fifteen-year-old girl. Who'd want to risk that for what you kids got? So you know what that tells me?"

"I don't know," said the kid, looking stunned. "What?"

"That girl wouldn't be putting out if she had any other way to eat, or buy clothes, or medicine. You know what else it tells me?"

The kid shook his head. His eyes were big and fixed on the knife, and I was glad I had his attention at least.

"That the guy sticking his dick where it don't belong should get at least that much grief, you think?"

The kid paled. "Man, she's the *puta.*"

"Yeah, but you're the dick who made her one. It's a two-way street, little man, and right now, you've reached the end of it."

You get bored in the desert. You stand and twirl your knife and teach each other dumb tricks and practice throwing. There are these big fucking scorpion spiders out there, and you get good chucking your bowie knife at them to see if you can cut off a head. So what I was doing with that thing, setting it in motion in my right hand like it was a cheerleader's baton, that wasn't no hairy deal—but to a kid trying to be hard?

I looked like a badass, and I knew it. Jake used to play with his switchblade in front of me and the other middle schoolers for the same reason.

The kid spat on the ground and his cronies followed, and then the four of them slunk off like beat dogs, growling and snapping behind them.

I stood there, cleaning the nails on my other hand and then working to trim my cuticles, until they were all gone, and then, without looking at the girl, I went to get mine and Sonny's sodas.

Well, some helpful soul had thrown them away and ignored the potential for gang rape going on in their backyard. Fucking awesome.

I heard a noise behind me and I turned. The girl was a mess, mascara running into her brown eyes and down her heart-shaped face, her hands and knees scraped, bits of the star thistles and the weeds that surrounded the back of the gas station caught in her hair and her clothes.

Oh hell. Sonny said he wanted a dog. I didn't think this was what he had in mind. But I couldn't just leave her like that. The memory of that girl, her head caved in, as Sonny wept over her body, was right there, pulsing at my eyes. And that kid—let him put his thing in her mouth? Boy, that must have been a real treat for her, right? Because it's not like a thirteen-year-old boy knows how to keep that thing clean, or what to do with a blow job other than just jerk himself off in someone else's cave.

"Kid," I asked, and she looked up at me, pathetic and demoralized. "Here, let's go get some napkins. I need to get more sodas. What's your poison? Dr Pepper? Sprite?"

She looked hopeful. "Root beer," she said quickly, and I shrugged.

"Why not. I think they got some. Grab some candy while you're at it. Let's bring Sonny some sugar."

She had a whole little sack of crap in one hand and her giant sixty-four-ounce root beer in the other, and the two of us stood at the edge of the pavement for a moment and watched on either side of the road. Cars could see the big red light flashing for about a mile in either direction, and there was about twenty feet in the middle of the street that was supposed to let pedestrians pass. But there were semis going eighty miles an hour and family minivans going a hundred, and the odds of those things slowing down, red light or no red light, was something I didn't know enough decimal numbers to calculate. We stood there for a moment and determined that any approaching vehicle was at least a mile away, and then hurried anyway, because if they were going a hundred miles an hour, that distance could be deceiving.

We walked into the shade of the garage and set the sodas and the M&M's and Jolly Ranchers on the workbench.

Sonny looked up from pricing spark plugs with a scanner and blinked. "Who's that?"

"A kid."

"What's she doing here?"

"Regretting her shitty life choices and looking for a bathroom." We had cleaned out the employee bathroom three days ago, when I got tired of going across the mud, looking for a place to leak. I'd even put in an air freshener and one of those magic toilet cleaners that all you had to do was squirt it and it cleaned away the ring.

"She got a name?"

I looked at the girl, who had picked out a root beer and her candy without saying much. She'd moved quickly, though, like she was doubting her good fortune, and that had been enough.

"You got a name?"

"Alba," she said shortly, and I looked at Sonny.

"Alba."

"Aces. What's she doing here?"

"Helping out," I said, and she shot me a look of disbelief. "Twenty bucks a day. Stocking, pricing, cleaning the bathroom. Talking to people if we get any. Doing her homework after school. If she wants to."

She looked at the two of us, me slouching by the door to the little office, Sonny standing there, the new scanner forgotten in his hand. "The office is for pigs," she said. "You got a bucket and soap?"

We both pointed to the broom closet.

"Clean up first," I said. "I'll get you a T-shirt."

Her eyes darted to me, and then to Sonny, and then back to me again. I guess she decided he didn't count, because she looked me in the eyes and said, "I am, you know. I am a *puta* like the boys say."

Sonny jerked his head up like something hit him hard in the nads.

I shrugged. "You're a girl. You got time to be something different."

"My mommy, she say I'm a *puta* for life."

"She's full of shit," I told her. I heard Ronnie in my head, loud and echoing like he was in the garage with us. *Once we're fags, Jake, we're fags for life. You want that? You want your folks looking at you like that? Your little brother? Forever?* "You stop putting out for cash, you stop being a whore. That easy."

The girl looked stricken for a moment, like I'd rearranged her worldview, and then grunted. "Go get that T-shirt. I'll clean that pig place."

"See?" I said, not even raising my eyebrows at her giving orders like that. "You're a nagging bitch already."

She smiled then like I'd paid her a compliment, and disappeared into the bathroom. I went to run to the house when Sonny grunted and I turned around.

"*Puta?*"

"She fucked up," I said evenly.

"Girls are trouble."

I swallowed. "We can keep this one safe."

Sonny looked down at the pricer in his hands. "Don't expect me to talk to her."

He hadn't talked to the last one, just let her follow him around, showed her how to hand him tools and hold shit when he needed it.

"You don't talk to anybody," I said and hoped I didn't sound bitter. I didn't wait to see what he'd say to that; I ran and got the shirt instead.


SHE came by after school every day, dressed in a T-shirt and shorts that didn't show too much of her ass. Once, she walked in wearing a T-shirt was so tight I could tell her nipples were crooked, and had a neck that plunged down to her skinny little bra clasp. Sonny took one look at her, turned around, walked out of the garage, and came back in a minute with one of *his* T-shirts, the old army ones, and she looked at it distrustfully.

"Ace's shirts are white," she said, and Sonny curled up a lean upper lip.

"My shirts are smaller," he said. "You can show your tits without selling 'em. It's an art. Learn it."

She glared at him, and for a moment I thought she was going to throw the shirt back at him.

I met her eyes then and shook my head.

"I may be a *puta*, but he's a dick!" she snapped, and I laughed.

"You're not a whore—but he *is* a dick. We're getting the sign today, so we're opening tomorrow. It's Saturday. Can you be here?"

She nodded. "I'll be here. We're gonna have real people here? Not just broke-down hard-lucks?"

I grimaced. "God, let's hope so. After all this hoopla, customers would be nice."

We'd already had a couple of nibbles from people with flats and broken radiators and such, and we'd helped them out and patched their tires and their radiators and all, but we'd explained we weren't really ready for them. They'd been nice, most of 'em, and given us cash for our trouble. The first time, Sonny had just looked at that cash sitting in the bottom of the box and then looked at me, puzzled.

"Whaddawedo with that?"

I looked back. "Put it in the joint bank account. Put it back in the business."

"What if we get more?"

"Then we add it to the savings for the better garage in the better place."

Sonny looked around our little garage in the middle of the fucking desert. "This is, like, a business."

I blinked at him. "Yes, Sonny. It is a business. And it's going to keep us in racing cars, right?"

Sonny looked mournfully at the Taurus then. He'd wanted to work on it for the past three weeks, but we'd been using it as a workhorse to start the business and as my commuter car.

"I'd like to race just one car," he muttered, and I agreed. We were almost set up, and more and more I'd been working on the shop and he'd been working on the car—but even that was driving him crazy because I'd had to take it to work four nights a week.

"Five days," he snapped at one point. "I need your car spread out and nekkid on my bay for five days, and it'll be balls-to-the-walls, hot-lubed-piston action for fuckin' ever! Is there any fuckin' way you can give me five fuckin' days?"

It had been the first thing he'd asked for since he'd arrived.

"I'll ask Getch," I said reluctantly. George Getchell, my supervisor—an okay guy. Homophobic as hell, but good to his kids, nice to his wife, went to church every Sunday. My folks would love him. I didn't talk about him too much to Sonny, but every time he talked about the "faggoty little rich boys" who bought tickets to the events at the coliseum, I remembered my knife and one of those scorpion-spider things in Afghanistan. Sometimes I wonder how much of me was forged in that desert, and what kind of materials I brought there in the first place.

Sonny looked at me shrewdly. "Why don't you like him?"

"He hates faggots," I said and blessed that he knew about Jake. That would make it personal, and he didn't have to know the truth.

"That word should mean something else," Sonny said ruminatively. "It sounds uglier than what it really is."

All pretense dropped away, and I suddenly put my heart in my smile. "It used to mean wood sticks," I said, remembering my old high school English. "And there's a kind of... of lace stitch thing that's called faggoting."

"That shit's not bad." He settled his arms across his chest. "Maybe it's not the word. Maybe it's people like Getch." His eyes darted to my face then. "You got a good smile," he said abruptly. "You don't smile enough."

"You smile less," I told him. "I'll ask Getch for the time off, maybe swap some shifts. I'll get you your five days."

And *then* Sonny smiled. "Good. If we could have them during opening weekend, you can cover the small shit, I'll work on the car. Weekend after that, we'll race."

I grimaced, mostly to hide the fact that five billion different things were happening in my body from that smile. "Hell—I'll need to get that off too!"

Sonny shook his head. "Naw—them's just basketball games. They end by ten. Racing don't get good until after that."

I did some of the math in my head. "Yeah, but where's the race, Sonny?"

He smiled a little, and it was almost as good as the big one, which sucked, because I was still all red and flushed and swollen in places from the first time. "There's one not far from here. Don't worry. We'll make it."

"Yeah, well, I'd like to take the car out before then."

Again, that slight smile. "It's gonna be great, Ace. Trust me on this. I'll make that thing fly for you."

I nodded, and he reached over and clapped my shoulder. "You look hella nervous. Don't worry. You're a better driver'n all those other guys. You don't fear nothin'."

"That's bullshit," I said, but I turned away before he could ask me what I feared.

That night, I kept far to my side of the futon as we watched television before bed. He sat at the opposite end, quiet as he always was, eyes wide and glued to the television. We were watching *Person of Interest* that night, and he had a faint brow furrow as he watched.

"That little guy's real smart," he said during the commercial.

"Yeah."

"Lots of school."

"Yeah."

"I don't got no school."

I wasn't surprised. The army said you were supposed to at least graduate high school, but however he faked his name, he must have faked a diploma too and the entrance exams as well. There was bucketloads of shit Sonny didn't know. I mean, I had a basic high school education and the shit I learned in the army, so I knew a little. But Sonny didn't know basic shit. He didn't know that England had its own literature. He told me once that he'd been surprised there weren't more black people in Afghanistan, and then he realized he'd been thinking about Africa, and that had been the first time in his life he'd looked at a globe and really thought shit out. He could make change and deal with cash, but I was pricing the spark plugs with a 10 percent markup from the dealer, and he was lost. I explained fractions and percentage to him, and he caught on real quick, but I wondered. Entrance exams—we'd all had to take 'em. How *had* Sonny got into the army?

Who'd cleared him? Who'd let him go like that? How'd he get ID in a fake name? How'd he get a plane ticket to Fort Benning for boot camp? Who had helped him out, and why?

"I figured," I told him mildly.

He looked down. "I'm stupid."

"No! You just ain't been told lots of stuff. You pick it up quick, though. I don't know how you got into the army without no high school education, but you're getting it a little at a time."

He looked up, a quick smile on his face for a moment—probably from the compliment—before something wiped it off. "You know how I got into the army," he said, his voice deadly quiet. "I offered it to you that first day, but you didn't want it."

And heaven help me, I was going to be honest with him, and tell him that I *had* wanted it, so bad I still burned with that moment, but before I could, his voice grew deeper and harsher. "See. I'm just like Alba. I'm a *puta* too."

I gave a sharp bark of a laugh. "Hell, Sonny—how do you think I got the damned car so cheap?"

He looked up, shocked, and the shame washed me to my toes.

"Everyone's soul is for sale," I said after a moment, hating myself for making it true. "What you got to determine is what sort of price is on it. What'd you get for what you were offering? Is it something you can live with?" I was asking the question in general, like rhetorically, but Sonny sucked in a breath and seemed to take it serious.

"What'd I get?" he muttered. "Freedom—*that's* what I got. Hells yeah, it was worth it!"

I shook my head. "Good. Wherever you came from, if you're glad you're here, it was worth it."

Suddenly he reached over and touched my knee, and I jerked my gaze toward his. "What'd you get?" he asked. "Besides one of the top-ten street racers in history."

I loved how he said that with no irony whatsoever.

But even more, I loved how gray his eyes were, how they seemed to be focused on me for once, how he knew one of the worst things about me, and he still leaned forward and touched my knee, wanted to know my opinion, believed what I said.

"I wanted your dream," I said, aching to put my hand on top of his. "I was trying to get you everything—the car, the garage, the home—but I knew I couldn't make it perfect. Not at the first go. I got a chance to keep reaching for you—it, for you—that's all."

For a moment we were connected, and his gray eyes searched me to my soul. I must not have been pure enough, though, because eventually he looked away. The television show was back on; maybe he was watching it.

"I woulda paid the two grand," he said after a moment. "Save your pecker for the girls on the track. They *want* to be used."

Well, that was fair, I thought, feeling like shit. Of course, it wasn't the noblest thing I'd ever done, and he had a point.

"I don't want no track girl," I told him patiently, and he flicked a glance at me, seeming to be bored.

"You will," he said. "Everyone wants 'em. They're faster'n the cars."

He went to bed after the show was over, but he must have sensed something of my misery, because he stopped for a minute after clicking off the set.

"Ace, I don't know what you're so upset about," he muttered. "I'm a whore too—what's my opinion matter?"

The past month of working elbow to elbow with him trammeled up in my chest, my throat, behind my eyes, and it felt like bloody sand. "You missed the point. You're not a whore, and Alba isn't a *puta*, and apparently the only one who's covered in come is me."

Sonny recoiled from me like I slapped him. "You're not a whore," he whispered. "I'm sorry. I'm stupid. You know that."

"You're not stupid," I said, feeling stubborn. "You're not stupid, you're not a whore, and I'm just tired. Go to sleep, Sonny. I've got my last shift at the coliseum tomorrow, and it's gonna be a fucking long day."

Sonny made a little whine then, but I couldn't look at him. I sat there on my corner of the futon, my knees drawn up to my chest, just wishing he would go the fuck away.

"Ace, you know you're the best… friend?"—like he didn't know the word—"you're the best friend I've ever had. Don't take anything I say to hurt you. I'm not worth all that."

"Sonny…." God, I didn't have any fucking words. "Did I say something about going to bed? I'm not a little kid. I'll live."

He reached out awkwardly and grabbed my shoulder to squeeze it, and then made his way to bed. It wasn't much of a touch, but long after his "lying down" noises had stopped, I sat there, not bothering to make up the futon to sleep, shaking from the force of desire that swamped me, suffocated me, made my flesh ache and burn until I couldn't breathe.

# SHUT 'EM UP, SHUT 'EM DOWN

THE next night I staggered in after the coliseum job, tired to my toes. I'd been chugging caffeine and no-doze and Red Bull to get me home, and that shit had worn off as I'd pulled into the driveway in front of the little cottage. The only reason I hadn't fallen asleep in the car to get enough energy to get me through my own damned front door was that it was still ninety degrees outside, even at one in the morning.

I was not quiet as I thumped through the front door into the kitchen, and the sound of the screen door slamming was like a gunshot. I had just cleared the kitchen, and the door to Sonny's room was on my right, when a heavy arm wrapped around my chest and a knife pressed against my throat.

"Who are you?" asked a disoriented Sonny, and God bless the military.

"Staff Sergeant Jasper Anderson Atchison, Ace to my friends, *stand down*, Corporal, *stand down*!"

The knife disappeared, and for a few delirious moments, he just stood there, his front mashed to my back, his arm around my chest, his breathing harsh against my neck. A trickle of blood oozed from my neck down my collarbone, where the knife had slipped. The adrenaline eased and our breathing stilled, and he dropped his arm.

I turned around slowly, and he blinked at me like he was waking up.

"Sorry, Ace," he muttered, sounding lost. "Didn't mean to… aw, hell." He brushed my neck with his thumb and it came away red. I pulled in a breath hard through my nose and had a hell of a time letting it out.

"Kleenex," I muttered. "I'll get…."

He cupped my neck then, and his thumb brushed the line of my jaw, smearing the blood.

"I'm sorry," he said again, and I covered his hand with my own.

"It's okay. I probably scared the hell out of you, coming in the way I did."

He gave me a hunted look, eyes searching mine. "I don't sleep well with you not here," he confessed, and I nodded like I'd known that. He'd told me, it was true, but his definition of "not sleeping well" and mine were obviously worlds apart. "I'm sorry 'bout the knife."

I nodded again, needing him, needing him badly, even if it was just the closeness. I wrapped my free arm around his shoulders and brought him in for a one-armed hug.

"It's okay," I said briefly, wanting to just hold him and hold him. I shuddered once, because I was tired and weak, and then I took a step away. "Go back to sleep, Sonny. I'm real glad you took my advice about the knife instead of the gun."

He sagged then, and if I hadn't still been holding his arm, he would have fallen.

"Whoop—gotcha, don't worry, Sonny, I gotcha." I half carried, half walked him to the futon and sat, pulling him against me while he shuddered. "Sorry about that. That was stupid, sayin' that. You wouldn't have—"

"Just shut up," he muttered, cold and shaking against my side. "Just shut up. Let's just stay here a minute, and you don't talk and you don't say anything that makes me think that, okay? I don't want to hear it."

I remembered Galway's face dissolving, blood, bone, gray matter—no small, neat hole for a Beretta with hollow points, no. He was imagining that happening to me, and I tightened my arm around his shoulder and tucked his face against my neck.

I fell asleep there, which was horrible of me, I know. I hadn't taken off my gun belt or locked my Taser in the drawer or even taken off my boots. I just sat there, Sonny huddling against my side, until my body shut down, and that was it. Sometime in there, I remember *Sonny* wrestling with the harness, and the belt to my slacks, and my boots, and when I woke up the next morning, I was on the futon as a couch and not as a bed, in my T-shirt and boxers. One of our spare sheets was on top of me, and one of the pillows from Sonny's bed was under my head.

I tend to wake up and move all in one go, and I was out of bed and on my feet before I realized Sonny was up, cooking french toast.

"'S'up?" I stretched up and twisted, trying to work out the kinks from the futon.

"Breakfast," he said, looking up at me from the pan. "You woke up earlier than I expected. You were out."

I grunted and stretched again, and saw Sonny smirking at me. I looked down, and hello there, little Ace was happy to be up too.

"Damn," Sonny said, his voice pure admiration. "Damn. I thought that thing was big sleeping."

Oh, I couldn't do this with no food and no coffee, and him looking at the tent in my shorts like he wanted to go camping made it worse.

"It's only at half-mast now," I mumbled, heading for the bathroom door. "You should see it when I fuck." I ran into the door and woke up and realized what I'd said, and then dodged inside the stupid bathroom and slammed the door. Fortunately my mortification was enough to shrivel my stiffy, because otherwise I would have been in there forever.

God, he'd felt good in my arms the night before. He'd been compact and hard and limp against my side. I remembered that. All that controlled tenseness, the things he didn't say, the history he never hinted at—it had flooded out of him, and all that was left was relief and me.

And me.

I knew where my family was. My mother sent me Christmas cards every year I was deployed. I'd called to let her know I was in San Diego, and had given her the address and the phone number. She'd written me letters—three or so a year—about my three sisters and their children, and Jake's two kids and how they were doing, and my other brother, Duane, who had actually graduated from dentistry school and had a family in a suburb up in Bakersfield.

I didn't call enough, I only wrote sometimes, and they didn't know a whole lot about me, but I did have family.

Sonny Daye wasn't even his real name. As far as I knew, in two years of deployment, he hadn't gotten one damned letter. And I knew for a fact he didn't keep contact with anybody from his life before he'd enlisted, because I'd helped him program his cell phone. I'd entered the number for the parts place, the tire place, the computer place, the coliseum if he needed me, the landline to the house, the business line to the shop, and the number to my own cell phone.

I'd *made* him enter Alba's number—because I figured if anything happened to me, she could help him run the business, because she wasn't stupid—and Burton's number, because he just seemed a handy person to know.

And that was it. The end. The extent of the people in his life.

And I knew without conceit or hope that I was the one person in there he truly knew and cared anything about.

I could not, *could not* make myself the one person he couldn't depend on. But as I braced myself against the back wall and pointed my peter down, I wondered how long I could do this. Months? Years?

Until Sonny found someone and I was free?

Yeah. That one. I could do this *that* long.

Well, it was good to have a limit, I thought practically as I washed my hands and splashed water on my face. I looked critically at the little wound at my neck crease and tried to clean off the blood. It gives you strength to keep on keeping on.

And as Sonny started to talk over french toast, I thought it wouldn't be that hard. If you didn't know him, you'd think he was being low-key and laconic, but I knew him, and to me, he was damned near manic.

"'Kay, Ace, so I'm gonna replace the intake manifold so it can take the NOS, and I'm gonna put those racing tires and rims on—gonna need your help for that, 'cause we got a lift in the garage, but I ain't used it before and I don't trust it. Didn't get the shiny ones, got the good ones, so don't expect it to look like the shit, 'cause it's not. Gonna get rid of the backseat and strip the paneling down to the cage and reinforce the cage with steel—"

"Won't that slow us down?" I asked through a mouthful of french toast. It wasn't bad—he'd been watching cooking shows, and he used real french bread and added cinnamon.

Sonny glared at me. "I'm protecting your stupid melon head with your stupid ducktail and your stupid sideburns, so shut your stupid mouth."

"You don't like my sideburns?" I asked, stung, and he scowled.

"I love them. Did you see your neck in the mirror, jackass? Did you see it?"

I'd needed to scrape some of the blood off with my thumbnail and had to be very careful about the little horizontal scab. "Yeah."

"Yeah. Fuck your sideburns, save your fucking skull, okay? Can I continue?"

"By all means."

"Yeah, 'by all means' my scrawny white ass. Anyways, got a line on a better front end, and want to replace the rods, the pistons, the cams with the forged parts so the engine doesn't explode, Mr. My Sideburns Are More Important Than Brains, and we'll add fins to the back—"

"I thought that was a myth that those helped—"

"Yeah, well, I'm gonna be doing the paint job and I suck at it, and it's gonna have shitty-lookin' rims, give me some fucking vanity and hope, won't ya, Ace? Anyways, I got a full racing harness, the kind they use in stock car races—"

"The passenger seat too?"

"Why would I need that? I'm not racing—"

"You're going to be there when I test-drive, right?"

Sonny blinked. "Well, fuck a jackrabbit and make stew—you're right. Fuck. Fuck, fuck, fuck, fuck, fuck, fuck, fuck...." And with that he pulled out his phone—I already knew he had the parts people pinned to the front. "Jason? Daye. Racing harness. Passenger's side. Three days. Got it? Fucking *air mail*, where the fuck—oh. Houston. Gotcha. Yeah, everything's in Houston. Go figure." He looked at me, doing the pee-pee dance, probably because of the expense, and I nodded unequivocally. He scowled and covered the phone. "You're gonna make me wear a helmet too, aren't ya?"

"You got one for me?"

"Yeah."

"That or your flak helmet."

"Fuck a coyote—"

"And you make a roadrunner happy," I supplied, grinning when his jaw dropped open and he laughed soundlessly before speaking back into the phone.

"Yeah, and a fucking helmet too. Yeah, I don't wanna know how much it'll cost. Surprise me. Maybe I'll have heart failure, and *then* who's gonna pay the bill?"

"*I will!*" I snapped, loud enough for Jason whoever he was to hear me. I could hear laughter coming from the phone, and Sonny scowled at me.

"Yeah, fine, make it so." There was a pause. "Who in the fuck is Number One? What? You can't just go—" Sonny glared at the phone, probably because Jason just hung up on him laughing. "What in the hell?" Sonny grumbled, mostly to himself.

"Number One," I said, hiding a smile. "He's a character in *Star Trek*—like, from, I dunno, back when I was born or something. My dad watched it when my older brother was a kid, he loved it."

"*Star Trek*," Sonny muttered. "Yeah. I've heard of it. What in the fuck. What in the fuckin' hell. It's bad enough I don't know about fuckin' countries or the fuckin' constitution or any of that school shit, now people think I gotta know television shows from back in prehistoric times. Fuckin' hate that shit. How much shit I gotta know before don't nobody have to tell me nothin' and I can stop feeling like a retard." He stopped then, like he expected an answer to that.

"I think 'retard' is an ugly word too, Sonny. It's like 'faggot' and the N-word—it's sort of an insult to people who have brain problems."

Sonny's jaw dropped. "Seriously? Fuckin' *seriously*? So people can go and tell me all about some fuckin' television show, but now I'm like insulting brain-damaged people and little kids and...." He trailed off, his good mood shifted to funk—a whining car from first to second in one *wheeeeaw* of the engine. "Been called that word my whole fuckin' life. I thought it was for dumbasses, not for people born hurt."

Red filled my vision, and my stomach clenched cold. "Who in the fuck called you a retard?"

Sonny stopped like he'd been caught doing something bad. "No one I'm ever gonna see again," he said, dropping his fork.

"Eat your food," I snapped. "Eat it. It's good. It's good and you made it and if you won't tell me anything, you won't. But we're not using that word, and we're not using 'faggot' and we're not using 'whore' and we're just not. You are 'Sonny' and 'Corporal Daye' and 'Mr. Daye', and you're not even close to being a retard and...." My hand was shaking. I put my fork down and wiped my mouth. My head hurt—probably from being tired and not having coffee or soda yet— and I got up to go pour coffee, then fished the painkillers out of the cupboard by the sink. I washed one down with the other and then looked up to see Sonny shoving french toast in his mouth by the forkful.

Good. I didn't want to talk anyway.


TWO days later, there I was, asking Alba if she could work the shop.

I was excited as hell, actually. As much as we'd started it to support the racing, the fact is, it was our shop, our business, and we had built it and stocked it from the ground up. Suddenly, all the times we'd skimped on buying parts because we figured we wouldn't need 'em came to haunt me.

God, we were a business—we *promised* something, and I wanted very much to deliver.

The night before we opened, Alba showed up in the passenger seat of a giant Cadillac Seville. It was gorgeous, maroon, original white-leather interior—it was somebody's baby. A stout, plain middle-aged Hispanic woman in bicycle shorts and a gigantic T-shirt, her long, graying hair pulled into a frowzy ponytail, heaved herself to her feet on the driver's side of the car.

"Hey," Alba said, reaching into the back of the car. She came out with a big casserole dish covered in foil and a big bag of something. "This is from my mom."

I took the casserole and handed it to Sonny, who went, "Oolf," and then, "Is this the kind with the potato chips and cheese on top? I love this shit!"

"Uhm, thanks, Alba," I said, looking into the bag. I looked up. "Uhm, Mrs. Alba."

"Rodriguez, you retard!" Alba laughed, and Sonny said seriously, "We can't use that word. That's a bad word—did you know that?"

We all stopped and looked at him, and then Alba nodded her head like it made perfect sense. "Yeah, I hear you. See, that's why Mommy made the casserole and sent the stuff—"

"What's in here?" I asked, pulling out streamers and balloons and, at the bottom, cookies and a big thing of Kool-Aid with a plastic pitcher.

"It's for opening day," Alba said like I hadn't even interrupted her. "Mommy wants to say thank you for making me not a whore and all, so here you go. The cookies are for opening day. You should have snacks. So's the Kool-Aid. I'll buy ice in the morning. You should get an ice machine, you know? All the other garages have them. And a soda machine. But you just starting. I told Mommy that."

I felt a burning behind my eyes. "This is real nice," I said, smiling hesitantly. A part of me wondered if she'd be this warm if she knew the things I wanted from my partner at the garage—Latin culture ain't big on faggots, I knew that. But that's not what I said. "Uhm, Alba, your mommy knows we're gonna be street racing, right? I mean, we're not totally legit."

Alba laughed again and scattered some Spanish over at her mom, who shot it right back like little language BBs. "Yeah, she knows. She said it's how my uncle Manny sent his kids to college."

I perked up and looked at Sonny. "You think she could give us Manny's number? We need some more gigs to race!"

Sonny was still smelling the casserole, his eyes closed. "You... you all don't want any of this, right?" he asked, and I expected him to wrap his arms around the glass dish greedily. "I mean, this is all for us, right?"

Alba laughed again. She was a pretty girl, was gonna have a big rack like her mom when she got older, even though she was slim with youth and determined diet, and she looked better laughing than she had with all the crap on her face, that was for sure. "Yeah. You're funny. You act like no mommy ever cooked for you before."

Sonny's face went very, very still, and for a moment, I expected him to throw the casserole down on the ground.

"It's always a treat when one does," I said seriously. Alba looked at me, her face flushed, unhappy, and I felt bad for her. She was a kid. She had no way of knowing that when we're kids and we think all the adults around us are fucked in the head, very often they are just doing their best. She had no way of knowing that her stocky mother, who didn't want her to be a whore, was a real good mother, and that some people, like Sonny, apparently, hadn't known one that good.

"Tell your mom thank you," Sonny said, his voice as formal as he could make it. He looked at the foil-wrapped casserole dish forlornly like it had held such promise, and now it was tainted.

"Yeah, seriously." I looked over at Mrs. Rodriguez and said, "Gracias," hesitantly, smiling and hoping she'd see that was the only Spanish I knew.

She spoke to Alba then, her words hissing like cold rain on hot tin, and Alba looked up and smiled, her discomfort falling away. "She says you two need mommies. And she says she'll give your number to Manny, and he'll be in touch."

I smiled and Sonny nodded soberly. "Tell her thank you again," I said, and then, remembering my mom and all the times she'd tried to tell us about manners, I lowered my voice and spoke to Alba. "Thank-you card, right? Maybe some flowers?"

Alba nodded seriously and then sent a shy look at her mother, who was regarding us with impassive patience. "You can't tell, but Mommy likes flowers."

With that, they got back into the car and left. I put the bag of decorations and stuff in the office, and grabbed the food to keep in the house, leaving Sonny to close the garage bay door. We were going to work on the Ford some more that night, but the rest of the garage was good to go in the morning.

I washed up and dished up the casserole as soon as I got into the house and turned on the swamp coolers and fans, and Sonny came in, washed up, and sat at the counter next to me.

He fretted for a minute with his food before taking a bite and closing his eyes to savor. He'd looked this one up—potato chips, cheese, pimentos, mayonnaise, chicken, and sour cream—it seemed so easy, but every bite was a little taste of fat-laden heaven.

When he'd swallowed, he said, "I'm glad you said that, about the racing. I woulda felt like a cheat if I'd ate her food and she hadn't known that."

"Yeah," I said, taking my own bite. "We need to order more stock for the garage."

"We'll see how much business we get," he said. "After we win our first pot, I'll order again."

I looked at him, smiling a little. Sonny didn't seem to know much about his place in the world, but this, this he knew. "You are awfully damned confident about winning that pot."

He shrugged. "When we get her back together, she'll fuck the road like a pro."

I choked on my chicken casserole. "God, Sonny, the things you say. Cars fucking roads, you fucking jackrabbits—I'm serious. The shit that gets action when you open your mouth—"

It was his turn to choke on his chicken, and this time he started giggling and couldn't stop. I realized what I'd said and was suddenly torn between the swelling in my groin and my fantasy of getting some action with my dick in his open mouth, and laughing with him like a twelve-year-old because I so seldom heard him laugh.

I opted for the laughter in the end, chuckling, and before we were done, we'd managed to talk about choking on chicken and making it dirty, as well as jackrabbits fucking roads.

It was good to let loose like that. When we finished (and managed to eat the rest of our dinner too), we were too relaxed and sleepy to work on the car, and we had time. So we decided to shower and go to sleep after a little bit of television, which was good, because we had a big day in the morning.

After we turned off the TV, as I stood up and started making up the futon, Sonny stopped on his way to his room.

"Thanks," he said, his eyes darting nervously toward his room.

"For what?"

"I asked for you to get time off, and you did. And I like having you home at night. Thanks for doing this for me, Ace. For making the garage to race, and then making sure it's a good garage and doing what we need to race. I don't... I couldna done another two years in the army, and I don't think I woulda done half so good when I got back if you hadn't... I dunno. Taken my stupid dream and run with it."

I blushed—I knew he could see it—and was suddenly glad I'd gone for laughter over lust. "I'd do about anything for you, Sonny. I hope you know that."

He looked at me and moistened his lips, parting his mouth a little, his gray eyes big and limpid in the light from the lamp. Right then I was back to that day at report, and the way he'd looked at me, all suggestion, and said, "I'll do anything."

The words hung between us, and for a minute my heart beat hard, like an eagle's wings at hummingbird speed, and my flush grew worse, popped into sweat on my forehead, and I suddenly knew, in a way I'd never had before, what *want* meant, and why it was dangerous and greedy and huge.

Sonny swallowed, for a moment looking twenty instead of forty like he usually did, and gazed at me helplessly.

"I don't know if you'd do what I need," he said at last and disappeared into his room.

I made up the futon and lay down, pulling the sheet up so I could close my eyes and think of those eyes and that mouth, and stroke my cock until I came, muffling my noise behind my hand.

*Any time, Sonny. I'd do anything.*

WE WERE actually busy that first day. Not swamped, but enough people ate the cookies that there were only a few left over, and we had to make Kool-Aid twice, going into the house for the bag of ice Alba brought. It was small stuff, like Sonny predicted—tune-ups, flat tires, check the oil, plug the radiator so the car could make it to where the thing could be replaced. Alba rang up the services on the pad, put the cash in the box, printed receipts on the carbon paper in her schoolgirl handwriting, and offered folks Kool-Aid and cookies while they waited.

She was right. If we put in a soda machine and took a percentage, we'd make some money, because people sure didn't want to walk across the highway if they didn't have to.

We closed up at eight o'clock and gave Alba an extra twenty for the day. She grinned, and I told her she did a good job.

"Thank you," she said, happy. "Maybe tomorrow, I wear jeans. I can help you with the cars. It can't be that hard. You two do it, and you're not that smart." With that, she turned and ran to where her mother was waiting for her, and I thought that maybe us having the same business as her uncle had given her some cred in her mom's eyes, and that was okay.

And I guess to her, we wouldn't seem all that smart, would we? Seeing as we'd been making a business the whole time we'd thought we were running a front for our street racer.

Sonny had spent most of the day working on the racer, and he was ebullient as I locked the money box under the register.

"Two more days!" he crowed. "We can have that thing working in two more days! It'll be awesome! She'll fly! She'll—what're you lookin' so nervous for?"

I looked at the money hidden away under a basic Formica bookkeeping cabinet, and then at our stock in the office, which had been depleted. "Sonny, you'd better hope that thing is working in two days. We're gonna have over three grand here, business keeps up like it's been, and I'd like to take that shit to the bank."

Sonny's jaw dropped, and then he got a rather sly gleam in his eyes. "How much of that is real money? You know, money that's not taken by rent and supplies and food and—"

"You mean like net?"

"Okay. If we make three grand, how much of that is net?"

I shrugged. "I dunno. 'Bout seven, eight hundred dollars."

Sonny smiled big, and he started to nod. "Uh-huh. Uh-huh! Yup. That is some good news right there."

"Why? What're you thinking?"

That grin got wider, stretching his cheeks almost to his ears. I noticed that he had a space between his back teeth, like he'd had one pulled and not replaced, and wondered at that, but mostly I wanted to know why he was so damned excited. I was *worried*—that was a whole lot of money to have lying around.

"I'm thinking," he said, still bouncing on his toes, "that if we keep making that, you'll be able to quit your job, that's what I'm thinking."

I shook my head, realizing that this last month must have made him accustomed to me like he hadn't ever been accustomed to the army.

"You miss me at night, don't you?" I asked.

He looked me dead in the eye, curled up his lip thoughtfully, and nodded. "Yup. Now let's go shower. I feel like dust and armpit, and I want a big glass of ice water and a sandwich. You up for that?"

"Yes on the ice water and the sandwich," I said, smiling at the thought. "No at the dust and armpit."

Sonny laughed and slung a casual arm around my shoulders, even though I was about half a foot taller. "I knew there was a reason we got along," he said grandly, and together we shut the garage bay and headed for the little house that was coming to be our home.

THE flat stretch of desert opened up before us, and I revved the motor, my eyes narrowed.

It was my last night off before I went back to work, and four days before our first race, and Sonny said the car was ready.

He was sitting to my right, giving me a running commentary on how his baby ran, both of us sweating up a storm without AC.

"So it's a straightaway, but you're not gonna wanna jump on it at first, you're gonna wanna break the wheels loose, canya do that? Yeah, no, you can't, 'cause you're a crazy motherfucker, but you're gonna hafta do that, 'kay, Ace? And you can't turn, 'kay, so I don't care if no possum bear runs out in front of us, you're gonna go straight through it, unless it really is a bear, 'cause we'd probably survive a roll rather than a smash, but possums, you can squish 'em—"

"Gross—"

"Yeah, it's gross, don't do it on purpose, but I'm sayin'. If it's them or us, pick us, canya do that?"

"Why would you even say that?" I snapped, that turbocharge of fear and exhilaration lodging itself in my ribcage, filling my brain with fumes.

"'Cause you feed strays, Ace. You do. Girls, that cat behind the garage—"

"You fed it first—"

"So you wouldn't have to. Now shut up and listen. No sudden turns—that thing you did with the jeep that one time, that'll get us killed. Go straight, 'kay? I marked quarter mile and half mile out here—big red poles, you can't miss 'em."

I could see them from where we sat, on a starter's line, on this big flat spot. It used to be an old road, I think, but it stopped being maintained, and water washed dirt over it, and sun baked it flat, again and again for the past ten years or so.

"This ain't gonna be like real blacktop," Sonny said, like I coulda stopped him from talking. "It's gonna have a little more give, which is good, 'cause you can't come down on that gas pedal like a hammer, 'kay? A little ease at the beginning, that's all I'm askin', and no sharp turns, 'cause it'd be like bein' in a cement mixer, right? And we better hope all them forged parts hold, 'cause we need to blow 'er out and see her go, and if we break her, we're gonna be out all night waitin' for some sucker to charge us a fortune and a blow job to pick us up."

I looked at him indignantly and he waved me off.

"Don't worry, I'd give the blow job, there's some shit you don't forget—now are you ready or not?"

"Uhm, yeah, sure"—and my brain scrambled to file what he'd just said away, a fragment of the past he never mentioned and pretended he didn't have.

"'Kay." He pulled out his phone and set the app on stopwatch. "You ready, cowboy? 'Cause it's time to pony up."

"Ready," I said, and only the lure of that wide-open space in front of me could quash that image of Sonny on his knees before me.

"'Kay. Ready, steady, *go!*"

And I hit the gas pedal and launched us into space.

The steering wheel fought me at first, but Sonny had slicked that suspension up just right. I gave it a few good hard yanks and it knew I was boss, and the rest was the thrill of the desert flying by.

"Quarter!" Sonny screamed, and my heart punched through my chest like the pedal through the floor. The world blurred, a mauve-and-tan rainbow, and I saw the red post in the darkening twilight just in time.

And then I downshifted, which would turn off the turbocharging, and slowed down, shifting at the deceleration, whooping with the charge of the race. The car skidded to a halt when I spun the wheel, confident we were going slow enough to turn a doughnut and not a gyroscope, and I threw back my head and laughed, breathing so hard it was like I'd run that half mile instead of driven it.

"Boooooyaaa!" I whooped, turning my laughing face to Sonny. "How'd we do?"

He shook himself for a moment, jerking his eyes from my face like I had something in my teeth. "Good," he muttered. "Great!" he said, checking his phone, sounding surprised. "We did great! Three-point-nine to sixty, eight seconds at the quarter, thirteen at the half—man, we're good. We get 'er on some asphalt, she'll fuckin' blow 'em away!" His moment of distraction was over, and he started quivering in his seat like a dog, waiting for another go. I turned the car around and idled it up to the mile pole, guesstimating a starting line.

"We got enough NOS for one more shot?" I asked, eager to feel that engine scream at me again.

"Oh hell yes!"

The last lonely ray of sunshine slept as I pulled up to the line, and we went flying through the darkness as the evening folded the desert in hush.

# TEARING PRETTY DREAMS

SONNY dressed me the night of the race, which was probably a good thing, because I would have gone in cargo shorts and tennis shoes.

Sonny said no, that wasn't tough enough. He said I'd been a staff sergeant and that I had rank and that I needed to show some authority, which I thought sounded spiffy until he bought me brand-new jeans and a white T-shirt, which he ironed, and made me stuff the jeans into my combat boots.

I said I didn't think that looked as good as he thought it did, and he rolled his eyes.

"It doesn't have to look like everybody else, Ace. You've got that... crap. What was that show we just watched, the sad one, where everyone was singing—"

I blinked. "*West Side Story?*" That had been a wild hair and a cable special.

"Yeah. You look like one of them Jets from *West Side Story*. You got the hair, you got that... I dunno, the face—you carry the big ol' bowie knife instead of a switchblade, but I'm telling ya, this works."

He was standing in front of me, adjusting the knife-edge creases of my cotton T-shirt as he said this and looking at my fresh shave critically, probably to see if I'd missed a spot.

"They're not going to be looking at me, anyway," I said, trying to keep my voice crisp. Right in front of me. I could just frame his face with my hands and—"They're going to be looking at the car."

He shook his head and stepped closer, staring into my eyes like he could forcibly replace my brain with his own. "They will after the car wins," he said, nodding. He'd replaced the hood and the doors with carbon fiber siding and painted the thing after dropping me off at work the past four nights. It was bright yellow again, and I sort of loved it.

"So," I said, shrugging. "Let 'em look. We win, we take the pot, we blow town."

Sonny shook his head. "You don't get it, Ace. We win, you're gonna be a superstar. There's gonna be girls there—wait. That reminds me." We were standing in the living room, and he disappeared into the bathroom and came back with aftershave, which he splashed on my cheeks.

"You're priming me up for girls?" I asked, a little horrified. "What in the hell—I'm not looking to get laid tonight!"

"Well, you should be," Sonny said, nodding at me with his brow furrowed. "Winners, they got a rep to maintain. You wanna be seen with the prettiest girl. You pick 'er, you nail her, you tell her you don't do commitments, they'll think you're a god."

"Oh Jesus," I muttered, running to the bathroom to try and wipe off some of the aftershave. Between the smell and the thought of the girls, I was going to puke. "I don't want a fuckin' girl, Sonny. I don't. That's not what I'm looking for tonight—"

"Well, I don't see why not! You slept with that one girl 'cause you wanted to make a dream for *me*. This'll make the whole racing thing perfect. The girls, the car. You need something for you, Ace. Man, you been getting more and more tightly wound here—go get yourself some pussy!"

"Well, a girl's not the answer!" I snapped, knowing he probably thought that proved his point. "And don't say 'pussy'!"

Sonny scowled. "Look, them other words, I get, but I was *in* the army. That really *was* the word people used!"

"Yeah, and I used it too, but think about it. Do we want Alba to hear us usin' that word? What if we heard someone usin' that word to mean *her*. No. We're getting rid of that right now!"

Sonny gaped at me and then scowled back. "Okay, Ace, whatever the fuck you say. Wait, can I say 'fuck' now? How about 'laid' now? Can I say 'fuckin' laid'? Tell me, I need to know, because *you need to get fuckin' laid*!"

"Nice," I growled. "Are we ready to go now? Because it's almost eleven o'clock, and Temecula is over an hour away."

"Yeah—like I said, the illegal shit don't start until after midnight. And maybe, since we're doin' somethin' illegal and all, you maybe let us swear some while we're there!"

"I didn't say don't swear!" I walked to the counter, shoved my wallet in my back pocket, picked up the keys, and got two bottles of water from the fridge, bitching back the whole way. "I didn't say don't swear, I just said don't use words that make people feel like shit. A girl wants you to dirty talk them, you go ahead and say 'pussy'—she don't like that, you don't. Just don't say it in general and expect every member of the female population not to take offense, you got it?"

"Girls!" Sonny snorted. "That's funny. That's real fuckin' funny, Ace! Didn't know you were a fuckin' comedian!" He followed me out the door, and together we walked to the garage bay to get the Ford. We slid in, and I started the car, wincing at the noise.

"Why's that so fuckin' funny, asshole!" I shouted, and he glared at me and shook his head.

"I tell you I give blow jobs, and you think that means I'm gonna be screamin' at some girl during sex!" he yelled back, and before I could point out that lots of guys who didn't like sex with guys ended up giving blow jobs, I stepped on the gas. God, I wanted to continue this conversation, but I wanted to have it hushed and private and not screaming at each other with half a ton of nitro loaded into a car with an exhaust system modified to sound like the goddamned trumpet of the juggernaut.

I wanted to tell him I wanted him. I wanted to tell him I didn't want no fuckin' girls. But NOS or no, the damned car went too damned fast for any of that shit. By the time I realized I had my courage and the words would come, we were down the road.

WE PULLED up to the intersection, and I thought that this, this was perfect. It was a desert highway, off the main drag. Above the starting line there was a hanging red light that marked the intersection, and those big spotlights, running off a generator, just poured electric sunshine onto the starting line from the side of the road. There were enough people on either side of the road to clue someone in to something goin' down if they wandered into our midst, so maybe that would keep people from getting hurt.

And lined up on either side of the freeway, the coming and the going, were cars, big muscled Mustangs, classic Volvos, snotty-looking Mercs, waiting to bust off the mark against whoever they lined up with.

"How many times am I gonna have to race?" I asked, and Sonny eyeballed the crowd.

"Twice, maybe three times," he said, thinking hard. "They go off times too, and some of these may win their heat, but they're not gonna come close to you—they won't even try. I'll say three, and you can stop fussing. Here, let me off—"

"Wait! How'm I gonna find you later!" I asked, suddenly nervous.

"You won't," he muttered. "I'm finding my own way home. You're stayin' here and looking like big man race car hero so you can get your peter waxed—"

"Hey! Hey, Sonny—"

But by then he'd hopped out of the car and slammed the door, leaving me to line up and prepare to bust some balls.

And there I was at my first heat, revving the car, getting ready to back off on the gas as soon as I shifted into first. There was a girl there—big rack, tiny shorts, just like all the calendars say a racing girl should look, with tumbled brown hair and enough eye makeup to outfit a circus. She stood between the cars, a red bandana in each hand, and after she'd made eye contact with the other driver and then with me, she raised the bandanas above her head.

And then dropped them.

*VVVVRRRRRR....*

*Rooooooooooooommm....*

And I was flying in Sonny's machine, and for a quarter mile, Sonny's obsession with getting me laid, and all the things I didn't know about Sonny and blow jobs and whether they were freely given or constrained—that shit *did not exist.* I was riding in Sonny's soul, and we were fucking free!

I came back to earth at the finish line, but not for long. As soon as I slowed down, a dozen people mobbed the car, holding up their stopwatches, showing me that I'd pretty much beat all comers. I rolled down my window and said, "Don't I have to run another race?"

Another pretty girl, this one blonde, said, "Only so we can see you do that again!" So I took a mile-long square loop around and back to the freeway. We had to stop and wait for one person to turn left and then drift away at sixty miles an hour until they passed the marker, and then wait for another person to come up the same way (I had to go off road to let 'em pass), and then, finally, I was up next to a Mercedes Benz 300 SL. It was old, but the silver paint and bright chrome made it seem slick and slippery and old school, and the engine in that thing— well, Sonny had told me about Nissans and GTs and all sorts of amazing cars out there, and this engine—it was something fearsome.

My skin and blood were all het up from the thrill of going up against something that cherry, and I looked out at the crowd and saw Sonny, gnawing his lower lip as he concentrated on me. I grinned at him and gave him the thumbs-up, and he startled out of himself and waved like a little kid.

Oh God. How could he be looking at me like a little kid when he was the one who got me here?

There was no time to be thinking about that again, because suddenly there we were, and there was the girl, licking her lips at me, and the bandanas dropped.

And Sonny and I went flying again.


WE WON. There was a guy up at the start of the race, and when I got back, a crowd gathered around a fire, all of the cars of both racers and watchers were parked on the side of the road, and in general, it was like a big parking lot party.

I parked somewheres I could get out easy and went looking for Sonny. I got stopped by a big Hispanic guy, probably the size of two of me and one of Sonny, his bald head covered with tattoos.

He stuck out a meaty brown hand and shook my smaller white one. "Nice driving," he grunted. I couldn't tell how much of an accent he had, but maybe part of that was pure freaking terror.

"Thanks," I said. "The car's what did it!"

"Naw, a car like that? Needs a strong hand at the wheel or it'll get away from you. Here—here's the pot."

And that simple, he thrust a wad of bills in my hands. I put it in my pocket without counting it, and then I felt a hand fishing around there, pulling out the bills. I looked up, and there was Sonny counting.

"We're short a hundred," he said, and then, before Mr. Terrifying Bald Man With Tattoos could say anything, he wrinkled his nose. "Shit, that's the fuckin' entrance fee. My bad. I was tryin' to get to you before Ace ran."

Bald Man With Tattoos looked down at Sonny in mild surprise and then looked back at me. "You know this rat terrier?" he asked, with the implication that he could easily flick Sonny across the desert with one jerk of his gigantic fingers.

"My racing partner," I said. "He built the car."

"You helped," Sonny said without looking at me. He nodded at Bald Man. "Thanks, Ortiz. You run a right race."

Ortiz nodded. "Thanks, little man. You bring your boy back here again—everyone's gonna wanna beat you."

"First weekend of the month?" Sonny said, all business, and the guy nodded again.

"You know it. Now there's cold beers at the cooler and women who want to suck your balls. Enjoy the party!"

And with that, Ortiz made his way through the crowd, leaving me with the uncomfortable notion that he was imagining me getting my balls sucked, when the only one I wanted to have any interest in my balls at all was Sonny.

"Oh my God!" I crowed as he left. I turned to Sonny, all excitement. "Oh my God—did you see that Mercedes? Holy fuck, Sonny—what could you do with one of those? Could we get you one of those? Those are so classy! I wanna see you behind the wheel like you own the fucking world—"

Sonny squinted at me in the bright electric light. "What in the hell are you babbling about?" He looked around the pit with all the people, and we both spotted the brunette girl who'd dropped the flags at the same time. She looked at me, predatory-like, and licked her lips, and I was surprised she didn't spread her legs and show me her coochie. "See? Her. She's the one. She probably does all the winners." There was another shove in my pockets, and I heard the crinkle of foil and felt the little bulge of an ampoule.

"Jesus, Sonny," I snapped, suddenly out of patience for this game. I was high, I was happy—I didn't care if all he wanted was to get ice cream on the way home, I wanted to spend this with *Sonny*. "Even if you don't want me yourself, would you stop shoving me at—"

A guy had come up behind Sonny and put a proprietary hand on Sonny's shoulder. Sonny shrugged him off, but he nodded at the guy, cordially.

My body got so cold I thought I might piss ice.

"You ready for that ride home," the guy asked, and Sonny scowled at him.

"I told you I'd pay you," he said. "Don't be making no assumptions how. I got cash and a knife."

The guy held up his hands in front of him like he was facing a Chihuahua that was going all pit bull on his ass. "Hey, no assumptions here, Sonny. Just thought you'd want to know it was on the table."

Sonny relaxed. "I'll let you know if I want to take it off," he grumbled, and then he looked at me square in the eyes. "Go find a girl, Ace. I'll see you back at the house."

And then he disappeared into the crowd with a guy with tousled dark hair and artful stubble, who had no problems putting his hands on Sonny's shoulder and telling him what was what.

My shame ate at my stomach, and I'd taken the first step to go chase them down when suddenly the girl popped up right there at my shoulder.

"Hey, soldier," she purred, and I looked at her helplessly, hurt and lost and pissed. Her lips were warm and full, and her painted face was exquisite, with eyes so big they were trying to swallow my soul.

They might have succeeded too, if Sonny hadn't just walked off with the damned thing in his pocket, crinkling like condom foil and just as fucking used.


AT FOUR in the morning, I was parked in front of the garage, drinking a six-pack one beer at a time.

I'd brought the beer with me because the car was Sonny's soul and I wasn't going to drive it drunk, no matter how hopeless I felt.

Couldn't crash Sonny's soul. It was fragile. I tilted the bottle up and I could smell it on my hand, stronger than the NOS fumes, stronger than gas, stronger than sweat or beer.

That word I told Sonny not to use, and it was all over my hand.

I gulped the beer hurriedly so I wouldn't throw up.

*"Whatsamatter, soldier, you blow your wad on the road?"*

*I pulled my hand from her pants and tried to wipe it off on the inside of my shirt.*

*"Did you enjoy yourself?" I asked, buttoning her teeny-tiny cutoffs. She was leaning against the car, her legs spread, on the far side of the all the lights. She looked wanton and sexy and beautiful, and I wished I could wipe my face and drink some acid so I wouldn't even taste her kisses in my mouth.*

*"Yeah, but I usually get more 'n a finger bang," she said, but it had to have been a helluva bang, because she'd been screaming the whole time and she was having trouble getting her voice to go all snotty like she wanted it to.*

*"Well, I don't know you well enough for anything more," I apologized. I pushed my hands through her hair, pulled her close, and kissed with just a little tongue. "But I sure do appreciate the offer."*

*I'd grabbed the six-pack on the way to the car, and now I offered her one. She took it, and I kissed her forehead.*

*"That's all?" she asked, clearly puzzled, and I nodded.*

*"Maybe I'll see you next month."*

*She looked at me, jaw dropped, as I got in the car and pulled away. The other five beers seemed to be screaming my name the whole way back.*

And now I was in front of the garage, and I couldn't make myself drive the car inside and I couldn't make myself go in the house. God. What if that guy was there? I didn't see his car, but what if he was? What if I could smell them, smell their sex, in my house, the house I'd picked for Sonny that wasn't good enough. What if Sonny had the guy's marks on his body and I had to look at him in the morning and know I'd wanted him, wanted him for more than two years, and couldn't have him, because I'd been too careful, too scared, and someone else had marked him, marked him forever, and he'd never be mine.

I dropped my head back and downed the rest of the beer and suddenly thought if I had to smell my hand one more time, I'd throw up.

I needed to clean it.

I opened the garage bay and started rooting around at the sink. We had borax there, the kind that would kill the grease on the hands, and we had wire brushes and shit, and yeah. It'd be like getting engine grease from my skin. That's it. I could do it. It'd be okay. Engine grease. I could do it. Okay.

I wasn't all that drunk, but I was pissed and sad and desperate, and I was knocking shit over—the generator got knocked on its side, and I hit a Peg-Board with all sorts of tools hanging from it. They fell down with a clatter, but I didn't care. I got to the sink and pulled out the borax and the brush and started scrubbing, muttering to myself about getting it off, getting it off, I didn't fucking want it on me any fucking more.

"Ace? What in the hell?"

I whirled and there was Sonny, looking sleep-tousled but wearing sleep shorts and a T-shirt.

"Had to get it clean," I muttered, and his eyes got big.

"Did you drive that car *drunk*?"

"No!" I shouted, scrubbing hard enough to draw blood. *Clean enough, I guess. Clean as I'll ever be.* "No, I did *not* drive your car drunk. I drove it here, and then I sat here and *got* drunk, are you happy now? Have I lived my life like you wanted? Are you fucking satisfied?"

My hand was bleeding and it was stinging and it still wasn't clean.

Sonny grunted. "Well are you just going to leave it out there?" he asked, hurt.

"Yeah, Sonny. Because now I'm too drunk to park the fucking car!" It was mostly a lie. The beer was burning off in my shame and my humiliation and my horrible, corrosive jealousy.

Sonny grunted and went to get the car into the garage bay, and I sat there, watching the hot water rinse the blood and pussy off my hand. The car stopped bram-bam-bamming in the garage, and the bay door shut, and still I sat there, feeling the sting of the hot water and the borax and the scratches from the steel brush.

Sonny was behind me suddenly, and I watched as he reached around and shut off the water. "Here," he said gently, patting my hand with a paper towel. "Damn, Ace—I didn't know getting laid would fuck you up this bad."

I shoved him square in the middle of the chest, and he stumbled back.

"I did *not* get laid!" I shouted. "I did *not* get laid! I got enough trouble with pussy on my hand! Do you think I want it anywhere else!"

"You said not to use that word!" he said, genuinely shocked, and I turned around and slugged the paper towel dispenser, screaming because it hurt.

"Did getting laid help *you*, Sonny?" I snarled. "Did it help *you*? Are *you* all relaxed now? Are his marks on your skin now? Do you smell like his come? I smell like some girl's pussy, do you smell like his ass?"

"Ain't nobody claimed me!" Sonny snapped, throwing himself forward, all chest, to stand toe to toe with me. "You just sit there and look at me with big eyes like you want me, but you ain't done nothin' 'bout it. I figure it's 'cause that's what friends do when they don't fuck each other. How the fuck should I know?"

"I'd do *anything* for you! *Anything*—I said it, and I said it, and you shove me at a girl and just fuckin' ditch me, and it should be *my* mark on your body, and *my* cock in your ass and *my* come on your skin!"

"Ain't nobody marked me!" Sonny yelled. "I jack off every night wishing it was you, and yeah, I was tempted, I wanted *somebody* touching me, but you're right next door, Ace! How'm I gonna want someone else!"

I was breathing hard, like a racer, and I needed to touch him, *needed* it, so I put my left hand, the clean one, up at the base of his throat, where I could feel his breathing and his pulse pounding and the rasp of his words.

"*I* want you!" I said hoarsely. "*I* want you."

Sonny tried to knock my hand away. "Don't touch me with no girl on your cock," he whispered.

"I ain't got no girl on my cock," I whispered back.

"*Don't touch me with no girl on your cock!*" Sonny hollered, and I pushed him back, back against the wall where the Peg-Board had been before I'd knocked it down.

"I ain't got no girl on my cock," I said, keeping my voice even, and then it couldn't be even, it had to be loud, and it had to be mad. "*I ain't got no girl on my cock!* I got girl on my *hand,* but I scrubbed it as much as I can, and you're gonna have to be happy with that, Sonny, you're gonna have to be happy with me just this clean, 'cause I want you, I want you, and I'm gonna mark you and I'm gonna—"

"You'd better fuck me," Sonny demanded, fierce and unrepentant, and for a moment I quailed.

"I'm so—"

"I don't care if there's pain," he snarled. "I don't care if there's pain, I don't care if it hurts. You'd better take me and fuck me and mark me... all of it, Ace. I need it all. I ain't goin' round in this world unclaimed, you hear me? You can kiss me and I can suck you off and you can say it warn't nothin', but not if you fuck me. You fuck me and—"

I kissed him, a hard, angry kiss, all teeth and tongue and clash. He kissed me back, and my lip hurt and I tasted blood, but it might've been his. I wanted to eat him alive, but I thrust my tongue in his mouth instead, tasting, devouring, needing, needing, *needing, fucking needing!*

He unbuckled my jeans and shoved them down at my hips, grabbed my cock in both hands and squeezed. I groaned and kissed him some more, needing so much from him I coulda killed him to get it. He broke off the kiss, fell to his knees, and took me in his mouth, clamping his lips around my crown and then thrusting his head forward on it. He gagged about halfway but kept it there anyway, swallowing, swallowing, and the feel of my cockhead against his tongue made me see stars. I grabbed at his shoulders, 'cause he said to fuck him and I wasn't going back on that, and he stayed for a moment, fumbling with the back of my jeans.

I kept pulling and he came back with the little ampoule of lube, which he cracked open and smeared all over my cock. The lube was hot from my pocket and his hand was rough and hard on my cock, and I needed it that way, needed it hot and rough and hard, but his touch was too much. I was going to shoot, and I got him by the armpits this time, hauled him up, kissed him hard, and whirled him around against the wall, shoving his shorts down with one hand while I pinned him there with the other, raw one. He thrust his ass out, and I bent my knees, found his asshole with my cock, and thrust forward, hard and without mercy.

"*Yes!*" he cried. "*Yes! All of it! All of it! Fucking all!*"

I slammed forward, all violence and hurt, and then pulled back and slammed again. He pushed against the wall and wiggled his tight ass back at me, and I kept thrusting, hard, fast, angry, and he kept driving me on.

"Yes, yes, God yes, fucking God, Ace, fuck me. Fuck me. Fuck me. *Fuck me!*" He screamed that last one loud and dropped his left hand from the wall, and I knew he was working himself because I could hear the slurping sounds of his hand on his cock.

Sweat poured down me, down my chest, dripping off my balls, down my sides, but I kept going. All of my body was in this, every muscle clenched and locked, the nerves in my cock shrieking as I tried to claw my way inside Sonny's body, and it was too soon, too soon, but my nuts were drawing up under me and my skin was washing cold and my stomach was clenching and everything behind my eyes was getting ready to blow up in a burst of red and white.

"*Come*," I gasped at Sonny. "*Come, dammit!*" And I leaned forward, dropped my head, and bit him sharp on the side of the neck.

He screamed and shuddered, his body spasming against and around mine. I grabbed him around the hips with both hands and threw my body against his fast, and that was it. The whirlpool sucked me under and spit me out and the world exploded and I poured, hot and mean, coming in his ass with so much force he yelled, "*Yes, I fucking feel it!*" while he was clenching around my cock so tight I couldn't move anymore.

I wrapped my arms around his chest and kept lurching inside him, wanting to crawl inside him for real, needing him all around me, needing to know he couldn't escape me, wouldn't go anywhere. He was Sonny and I had wanted him so long and my cock might be happy but the whole rest of me was going to need reassurance that this moment, hot and angry and whole, was the two of us and wasn't going away.

I PANTED into his neck for a few moments, our bodies plastered together by sex and sweat and come.

"We need to move," I muttered, and Sonny turned his head to the side and kissed me.

"No," he muttered. "Not yet."

"I want to shower with you," I said, and he shook his head.

"I want you on my skin and inside me some more."

I kissed the back of his neck, the curve of his ear, the line on his jaw, and he turned his head again and I got his lips one more time.

"Shower with me and I'll mark you again," I whispered.

I didn't just hear his whimper, I felt it vibrating against my tongue, along my stomach, and down where his body was still clenched around my cock.

"You gotta promise, Ace."

I nuzzled the secret place between his shoulder and his neck. "With everything in me," I mumbled, nuzzling again and then licking and then suckling hard.

He groaned, and I reached down and felt his dick for the first time. It was still sticky from come, and I reveled in it, played in it, feeling it between my fingers as I stroked him, and then massaged it into his balls.

My own dick started to harden inside him again. I thrust forward a little, and he leaned his forehead against the wall with a little "Ah-ah-ah...."

I groaned and sucked on his neck. His cock gave a little spasm in my palm, and I stroked again until it gave one last spurt and went limp. His groan shook me all the way in the groin and I pulled my hand back and licked, tasting. He turned his head the other way and opened his mouth. I popped my thumb in, still covered in his come, and he pulled on it, suckling and tickling with his tongue.

I grew a little harder and he let my thumb slip out, turned, and pulled my head down to kiss me.

This kiss was a little slower, a little less angry, but it still wasn't soft.

He pulled away, leaving my cock cooling in a gush of my own come down his cheeks and thighs, and regarded me with those gray eyes. "You promised," he said. "You promised you'd mark me again. No going back. We'll take a shower, but you got to do it again."

We dragged our pants up, shut off the light, locked up, and half walked, half carried each other across the mud of the yard, and fell past the kitchen and into the front room. I had to sit down on the futon while Sonny helped me off with my boots, and then I stood up and stripped off my shirt while Sonny did the same.

The bathroom really was tiny. There was barely room for the two of us to stand in the shower, but it was enough. I took the washcloth and washed him, and this, of all things, was the part that went gentle.

I ran the cloth along his shoulders and his lower back, thinking that he was small, from his height to his width. His body was tight and muscled but not big. All of his size was in his attitude, his fierceness, his determination to make a place in the world. I'd spent my childhood being invisible. I don't know how Sonny spent his childhood—he never mentioned it—but I know he spent his adulthood insisting on his place.

I was gentle with his privates, with his asshole, which was stretched wide. I sluiced lots of warm water there and was gentle with the washcloth, and he leaned back in my arms and, for the only time since I'd known him, allowed someone to do for him.

I held him up when his knees got wobbly. He leaned his head against my shoulder and trusted.

By the time I put the washcloth down, it was all I could do to wrap my arms around him and hold tight, so tight, until the water turned cold and we had to get out.

We dried off and he kissed my collarbone as we stood in the tiny bathroom, dripping on one of two rugs I'd bought. We were naked except for the dog tags we never took off, and that felt right. I looked down into his face and framed it with my hands.

"You're mine," I said gruffly. "I'll take you again if you want, but if I never fucked you even one more time, you'd still be mine." The washcloth had come away pinkish, and the thought of doing that to him again so soon made my stomach clench.

He nodded and kissed my chin, my jaw, and I tipped my head back and let him kiss my throat. One kiss at a time, one touch of his lips sliding on my skin, he worked his way down, down, down, until he sank on his knees in front of me and took my cock in his mouth.

Warm. That was my first thought. Warm. He sucked and there was pressure, and then he swirled his tongue around the head, and there was pleasure. He brought one hand up to cup my balls and wrapped the other around my backside so his fingertips could probe my crease.

I was hard in a minute.

He was going too fast, though—too fast, too hard—and I needed him to slow down. I put my hands on his head and said, "Easy," my voice deep and harsh because it felt so good it hurt.

Like that, he slowed down, backed off, and stopped squeezing my nuts so hard. I shuddered, though, when the hand at my backside got adventurous. I couldn't complain, I thought dimly. I'd shoved my cock in his ass without a hello or how-are-you. When he spat on his fingers and then spread the wet around my entrance, I forced myself to relax.

He pulled back then and looked up at me, his fingers dirty dancing around my asshole and his eyes serious.

"You ever done that before?" he asked, and I shook my head, then lowered one hand to cup his cheek.

"You're my first," I said, swallowing. All the things I didn't know about Sonny, and I knew I wasn't the first man inside his body, the first man he'd ever touched with his mouth.

His face twisted for a moment. "I wish you were my first," he said, his voice cracking. "I wish I only ever belonged to you."

"Shh...." I would have pulled him up then, but Sonny doesn't take time out for sentiment. He opened his mouth and sucked me in again, playing with my ass and massaging my balls. Without even meaning to, I thrust forward and groaned. He pulled back and licked my head, probing my slit, playing with that tight little tendon on the underside, and I leaned my head back, cracking it on the medicine cabinet and not caring. "I'm the only one who matters," I told him, before my brain blew up again and my body erupted. "I'm the only one you'll ever belong to again."

It could have been a gasp, as he lunged forward and tried to swallow me, cock first. It could have been harsh breathing and arousal, and I would have bought it, but I came, my vision burning white and red, and then I hauled him up to kiss him. He tasted salty and bitter from my come, and salty and sweet from that thing neither of us would talk about, and I wiped his cheeks with my thumbs and again and again until I gave up and pushed his head to my chest, and the two of us stood naked and shaking in the eighty degrees of the steamed bathroom.

Finally, my back started killing me from being bent backward over the sink and I gave a shaky little sigh. "Sonny?"

"Yeah?"

"I'll mark you some more in the morning. Right now, I'd really like to go to bed with you."

Sonny nodded against me. "Yeah, Ace. No problem. We'll sleep in my bed. I don't like you on the futon, it's hell on the back."

I wanted to laugh, but I couldn't. Not yet. We put on our boxers and slid into his sheets, and I looked around his room in the dark. "Sonny?"

"Yeah?"

"Let's get some pictures or something. You need something in this room."

He was lying with his face against my chest again. "Yeah," he mumbled, almost asleep. "I was waiting for you to move in here and tell me we could do that."

"It's your room, idiot," I told him, but I think he was asleep and didn't hear me.

# ADJUSTING THE TIMING

I WASN'T used to sleeping with another body. I'd never spent the night with someone, not another girl, not anyone, and Sonny did not do things in half measures. He was there, up against my chest, all night, shivering in the heat sometimes in an attempt to get closer.

As tired as I was, it woke me up a couple of times, until about dawn, *nothing* could keep me up, and I crashed hard.

I woke to a pounding on the door and Sonny pulling himself out of bed, muttering, "Fuck, we slept in. Fuck, fuck, fuck, god*dammit*, we slept in, and now someone needs the fucking garage and we got the sign up and...." The rest of his bitching was lost as he trotted to the front door in his boxers, swearing up a storm.

Sure enough, as I rolled out of bed, there was a deep voice—sort of an arrogant know-it-all voice—saying, "The sign *does* say the garage is open, am I right?"

"Yeah, it's fuckin' open," Sonny snapped back, and I winced. Customer service was *not* his middle name. "It's fuckin' open and we slept in and forgive the hell out of *us*. Whatdija need that was so goddamned important?"

"My car's making a knocking sound," the man said, and as I pulled into the living room, I got an impression of pricey suit slacks, shirtsleeves, and expensively gelled blond hair, somewhat askew. This guy had been to Vegas and was coming back the hard way, and whatever he was driving, he did *not* want to hear it making bad noises.

"Yeah, uh," I said, trying to remember that *I* was the people person of our little duo. "Let us get dressed, get our coveralls on, have some coffee, we'll be out to look at it."

The guy looked down his aquiline nose at the both of us. "Please hurry—I'm due back in Long Beach in two hours."

Sonny made one of those faces where you wrinkle your nose and your upper lip at the same time. "Sucks to be you," he said, meaning it. "Knocking in the engine means you let it get too hot, and whether that's oil or coolant, it's gonna need some doin'. We coulda met you fully dressed like a pit crew at NASCAR and I don't think we coulda fixed that in time, you think that, Ace?"

I couldn't help it. I was gazing down at him with my jaw all soft and all of last night in my eyes. "Yeah, Sonny," I said after a pause. "Anything you say."

"Well why don't you get your queer asses out there and *see* if perhaps your long-distance diagnosis is not as accurate as you think it is."

My temper flashed. "Sonny, go get dressed," I said, the habit of command apparently as ingrained in me as the habit of obeying orders was in him. He turned and left without a word, and I looked at the man who had invaded our peace. I'd had *plans* for this morning, dammit!

"You're not 'coming out', I take it?" the man sneered, and I didn't miss his snide bitchery, but I didn't respond neither.

"Sir, do you know how far we are from the nearest towing service?" I asked, folding my arms over my bare chest and stepping out to lean against the doorframe. The guy took a step back, out to our porch, so he wasn't in our kitchen anymore, and I was relieved.

"I have no idea," he said, stopped up short. "Thirty minutes? Forty-five?"

"Two hours," I said bluntly. "Do you have any idea how much that costs?"

The guy visibly swallowed, but I was too pissed to enjoy myself.

"Yeah," I said, taking his silence for acknowledgment. "And if you get Joe Thatcher, well, he's a sonovabitch, and if he's doing something interesting, he'll double whatever you're thinking 'cause he fuckin' hates Victoriana, and who the fuck can blame him. So you got two choices. You got us, and you got two hours at the Chevron, waiting for someone *not* us. Now, with us, there's a chance your car'll get fixed before you leave. Which one of these options do you hate least."

He swallowed. "I would prefer the latter," he said, and I had to remember what I said for a moment, and that must have put some fear into him, because he started babbling. "I'm sorry. I didn't mean to imply—"

"That we're fags? You don't have to imply it, we know it. But you being a fucker about it isn't gonna get your car fixed, do you hear me?"

"Yes, sir."

Well, apparently Sonny wasn't the only one who recognized orders.

"Then give me the keys, go across to the Chevron, and get yourself a nice cool drink. Come back in an hour, and I guarantee you we'll know if you're gonna need us or Joe Thatcher."

"Yes, sir," the guy said, and he reached into his pocket and handed me a set of keys on a Jaguar key ring. Oh, awesome. Something exotic and hot. Sonny would be thrilled.

"I'll see you in an hour," I told him and then slammed the door in his face.

I turned around, and there was Sonny, in his jeans and a T-shirt, and pulling on a clean pair of coveralls. He looked up from the zipper and grinned at me.

"I like how you did that," he said up front. "You didn't hem and haw, you just said it straight out."

I couldn't smile about this. "Well, like I said. My brother and Ronnie? Their lives woulda sucked for a while if they'd come out. But it sure as shit beats what I've had in my gut for the past five years."

Sonny nodded, and I realized I wanted to say better things to him, but I couldn't, because we had to fix some asshole's car.

"C'mere," I told him, even though I was the one moving. I got close up to him so I could smell the grease that didn't ever wash out of the blue coveralls, and underneath I could smell Sonny, and our soap, and me. I palmed the back of his head with one hand, and reached down and grabbed his ass with the other, and kissed him soundly, shoving my tongue in his mouth so he'd know he was conquered, know he was mine.

He capitulated that easy—because he really *was* mine, I guess— and I pulled back for air. "You're mine," I said softly when I pulled back. It wasn't good enough, but my heart was still smarting from the way he'd pushed me on some girl and left me, like he thought I'd ever get over him. "No one treats you bad, you hear me?"

He smiled then, this sunshiney, worshipful thing that made me want to look behind me to see what god walked in.

"I'll fuck up," I warned him. "I'll fuck up, and I may even hurt you, but I'll always want you, okay?"

He nodded. "Yeah, Ace. It's all I ever wanted. That first day, I told you I'd do anything. Guess you didn't really believe me."

"I believed you," I said bleakly. "I just didn't know if you meant to be with me or to stay in the army."

Sonny wrinkled his nose. "You're not that bright sometimes, are ya?"

I shook my head, knowing it was true. "No. Not so much."

"Well, it's a good thing you got me to look after ya. Go on, get dressed. That jerkoff ain't gonna last an hour."

HE DID, actually, and I hoped he got him some aspirin or whatever for that hangover he was probably sporting. The guy had smelled like sex and alcohol and probably pills to boot.

But he sure did have a sweet ride. The XKR-S was everything a car should be—supercharged V-8, 5.0 liters, Vulcan alloy wheels, active exhaust, minimized suspension—damn, with a little bit of Sonny's magic, it could blow the Ford outta the fuckin' water.

Or it coulda before this douchebag drove it into the ground with no coolant or even water in the radiator.

"Fuck *me*," Sonny muttered, looking at the engine. "Fuck. I'm surprised it made it here. Whole thing was five minutes from becoming a real big fucking paperweight. What the hell was he thinking?"

I shrugged. "Maybe he was thinking $140K wasn't that big a deal!"

Sonny did that nose-wrinkling thing again, the one that showed his front teeth, which I sorta liked. "That's a big deal even to *that* asshole."

"Can we do anything with this mess?" I asked, and he grunted.

"Yeah. Won't take no two hours, though. Fuck me if it'll take less'n three days to get the fuckin' parts in. You go cross the street and tell him we can do this in a week, and he'd better not skin us, and if he wants it towed, we can give him someone besides Thatcher."

"Will do," I said. Then, thinking about it—and thinking about drumming up business too—I said, "Maybe we should offer him a drive into town."

Sonny looked at me with a raised eyebrow. "You think he'll take a ride in the Ford and hire me," he said, approving of the plan.

I shrugged. Wasn't nothin' Sonny couldn't do with an engine. I'd been a believer two years ago in another desert. Nothing had changed my mind since.

Sonny's eyes got all narrow and his lean mouth pulled in at the sides. He looked crafty all of a sudden, and I tilted my head, wondering what he had in mind. "If I take this job, you gotta quit the coliseum," he said, and I blinked.

"Because—"

"'Cause A, It'll make us a shit ton. B, I'll need the help. And three, I don't fuckin' like stayin' here alone."

I squirmed. "I didn't know this so much at the beginning."

"Well, you know it now. Besides. You keepin' the coliseum job, that's like, Plan B. I don't want no Plan B. This here, this is Plan A, and Plan B, and Plan Z. I want to be all your plans, you got that?" His voice cracked a little, and I took a few steps closer to him. We still weren't going all soft on each other in full view of the highway, but he needed me close.

"I just wanted to do for you, Sonny. That's all. You want me to quit that job, you think we can make enough money with the racing and the garage, I'm in."

Sonny's face worked, and I woulda done anything to help him get what he needed to say out. "I think you worry too much about doing for me," he said after a moment, glaring at the ground. "I've made it without much food and less money. But I ain't never had anybody keep me for good. I need to know you'll keep me for good."

I wanted to kiss him so badly—I even took another step forward to see if that's what he wanted, even though it was already a hundred degrees at ten o'clock in the morning.

He took a step back and glared at me, and I nodded.

"I'm keepin' you for good, Sonny. I'll quit my job tonight, okay?"

He glared. "It'll be okay when you do it," he said and then went back to the car.

And just like that, we were back to me leaving Pakistan and him not shaking my hand. I sighed. "Sonny?"

"Yeah?"

"You let me know when I'm enough for you, okay?"

Sonny squinted. "I do not know what in the *hell* you are talking about. Now take off your coveralls before you pass out and go offer that man a ride."

I did, and Peter Gaubert (pronounced "go*bear*," which was a real mindfuck—I had to see that one written down to know it) took one mile in that Ford, goin' Mach 6 while he held the radar blocker, and was convinced to let Sonny have a go at the XKR-S instead of having it towed back into LA. He also, he admitted sourly, needed to take a piss, which he did on the side of the road into the desert. I told him that maybe the sixty-four-ounce drink was a bad idea, and he told me that he would appreciate a little fucking warning before we went 120 next time. I told him the fucking warning was when I turned on the ignition and he shut the fuck up and hung on.

When I got back to Victoriana, it was time to get ready for the security job, and Sonny was elbows-deep in the damned Jag.

"I'll see you in eight," I called, going to the Ford, and he squinted.

"Bring home some groceries."

"Eight and a half," I added, and he sighed.

"Never mind. I'll get the groceries tomorrow."

"Sonny...." I took my hand off the door handle and moved up behind him as he leaned into the engine, undoing a bolt. Carefully— because my clothes were clean and his were not—I put my hands around his waist and bent down to kiss the back of his neck.

His whole body stopped, still and sweating in the heat of the garage. "What?"

"I'm coming back. And then I'm gonna shower, and we're gonna watch TV in our shorts like we always do. And then I'm gonna take you to your bed, and we're gonna spend some time in there naked, and I'm gonna sleep there with you all night. It's not gonna stop. It's not going away. Can you trust that?"

Sonny's breath went from stalled to fast, and he turned his head a little and accepted my kiss on the corner of his mouth. "Only 'cause it's you," he said quietly, and I deepened the kiss a little before pulling away.

"'Kay. You trust that for me, and I'll bring you groceries."

"Since you're coming home at night, could you bring me some ice cream?" he asked, and I kissed his temple.

"Favorite flavor?"

"Ice-cream flavor," he said seriously, so I figured on a couple of different ones until he could do better'n that, and kissed him again for good measure before hopping in the car and taking off.

SIX hours later (the event ended early, thank God—I wasn't really a fan of folk music, that ain't no lie), I stood in my boss's office and told him this was my last event.

"Too good for us, Atchison?" he asked, but there weren't no heat in it, really.

"Naw," I told him. "The garage is taking off, and Sonny don't like being home alone at night."

It didn't even hit me until it came out that it was going to sound like, well, like what we were, but even as George Getchell swung his chair around to look at me funny, my backbone was all ironed up.

"That sounds a little lame for a guy from the army," he said, and I let out a little sigh of relief, 'cause if he'd said "faggot," I may've had to go nuclear on him.

"He gets freaked out alone," I said truthfully. "He still sleeps with a knife under his pillow."

George's eyes got big. "That's a little fuckin' scary!"

I shrugged. "So do I. It's safer than the gun." And then I had a thought. "Except, now that we're sleeping together, we may want a knife under *each* pillow. That'll feel a little safer."

I didn't *have* to say it out loud, but I did enjoy the way Getch's eyes got big as he looked at me to see if I was joking.

"What, did one of you set your bed on fire?" he asked, and I shook my head.

"Jesus, Getch—you'd rather believe the worst in people than believe in gay, wouldn't you? You'll send me my last check?"

He nodded, his eyes still big, and I turned around to walk out while he was sputtering. "But... but... but you two are *veterans*!" 'Cause I'd told him something about Sonny without telling him everything.

"Still are," I said seriously. "We went to a war zone and served our country. The gay doesn't change that. Didn't change that we could do it, either. Just is. You take care of yourself, Getch. Maybe back off on the F-word a little with the next guy you know who's licensed to carry, okay?"

I didn't wait for his answer. I was done and looking forward to telling Sonny the story too.

SONNY cackled over his bowl of ice cream on the other end of the couch, one knee drawn up in front of him, the other leg extended. The blond hairs on his shins and thighs were almost invisible in the lamplight.

"You *told* him that?" he said before tasting the mint chip experimentally and then taking a bigger spoonful.

"Well, yeah. The guy was a jerk. I dunno, since I didn't have to work with him, I thought I'd shake him up a little."

Sonny giggled some more. "That's amazing. I can only say shit like that to *you*. Just *sayin'* that to this guy." He looked up at me, his eyes glowing, and I felt a stupid, goofy smile sitting slack on my face.

Sonny's sharp-eyed look of mischief faded, and I slid my hand down his ankle, cupping his tightly muscled calf in my palm. He looked down into his ice cream and smiled in a way that might have been shy. I watched him, fascinated, and took his clean foot in my hand and started rubbing. He let out a groan and I pressed harder, along the instep, putting counter-pressure on the ball of the foot, and he looked up at me, a little shocked, I think, but his mouth opened, and there was ice cream on his lower lip.

"What're you doing?" he asked.

"Does it feel okay?"

"Yeah… aaahhhh…."

"Then go back to your ice cream," I said mildly, "and tell me about the Jag."

"It's a mess," he said seriously. "That guy, Go-bert—"

"Go-*bear*—"

"That don't even make any sense. Anyway, it didn't have any coolant, and we really are gonna have to rebuild the fuckin' engine, and you told him we could do it in a week—"

"Do I need to call him and revise that so we can cancel the parts?"

"Fuck no, I'll get 'er done, but only because I know you'll take care of the rest of the tough shit, and if you don't, well, you'n me'll be working some late ni—*ights*? What in the *hell*—?"

I'd dropped a little bit of ice cream drippings on the top of his ankle, and while he watched me, gray eyes enormous, I stuck out my tongue and licked it off.

He held very still, and I took my spoon from the bowl and did it again, but this time, on the inside of his knee.

"Ace?" he whispered while I licked it off.

"Yeah?" I sat up and adjusted my position, kneeling on the floor next to him while I grabbed my bowl from the table.

"What're you doing?"

"Eating my ice cream," I said, knowing he could see my smirk and hoping he trusted it only meant good things right now.

"Yeah, but you're eating it off my… thi—*igh!*"

He'd showered, and his skin was soft and smelled like Irish Spring—man soap, in a bar, with-a-washcloth kind of soap. I could taste it a little on my ice cream, and I had to lick Sonny's hairy thighs to get it up, but that didn't bother me one bit.

"Yup," I said, pulling on Sonny's leg until it was on the ground. The next dollop I dropped was really close to the inside edge of his boxers, and he hissed as it drizzled down around his thigh.

"You'll get it on the couch!" he protested, and I pulled the towel I'd been using out from under my bowl and situated it under his ass instead.

"Nope," I told him when I was done. I smiled up at his face, wanting to taste more of him in the worst way but feeling like a kid too. Finally—*finally*—this is what we were. I had permission to touch him. I winked, stuck out my tongue, and started to lick the crease between his thigh and his balls. The ice cream had dripped, and I followed it with my tongue, shoving the boxers sideways so I could bury my face into the hollow between his ass and the futon and lick the last smear off his cheek. He was making an odd sound—something between a giggle and a gasp—and arching his back to keep his ass off the futon. I backed off so I could pull off his boxers, and then reached around for the bowl.

Sonny said, "Don't bother!" and when I turned back around, I watched while he drizzled melted ice cream on himself—he was aiming for his full purple cock, but when I launched to lick the inside of his other thigh, he gasped and spilled on his stomach instead.

"Goddammit, Ace—*nungh*...."

I licked it off his stomach, and his lower abdomen, out of his belly button, and down the side of his hipbone—everywhere, in fact, *but* his cock, which was now starting to pulse with his every breath.

What I wanted to do was go back to his thigh.

He had that scar there, brown and discolored and raised. It felt... deliberate, like a scar over a scar. I wanted to know about it—the thought of that scar, and the newer scar over it, gave me a nasty churning in the pit of my stomach, and God, I wanted to know.

But Sonny was laughing, and he was holding my head and trying to push me so I'd swallow his cock, and he was feeling sexy and happy and Jesus, just all of the things I'd ever dreamed of him being.

"Ace!" he whined, for once out of words with me, and I laughed, feeling like a champion when it didn't sound forced or distracted or any of the things I was trying so hard not to be.

"Here, dammit—gimme that bowl."

He thrust it into my hand, and I couldn't look at him now, because I'd laugh, and I had a boner too and I didn't want it to go away.

Very deliberately, I drizzled the rest of the ice cream from the head of his cock and down the length of him—he was pretty dead-on average as far as length goes, but he was my only guy, so I didn't give a good goddamn. I dripped the ice cream between his balls and then dropped a big dollop, 'cause his legs were spread and his ass was sort of raised and there was only one place that was going, and I wanted to lick that too.

In fact, I started there.

"Ace?" Sonny's voice was still high-pitched and breathless, and just hearing him say that as I spread his cheeks and watched the ice cream drip a trail toward his little indentation made my own boner give a big nasty throb.

God, it wouldn't take much to make me come, but I wasn't all that worried. Sonny was here, as vulnerable as he'd ever let himself be, and I was gonna lick ice cream out of his ass and off his cock until there wasn't no more to lick.

As soon as the little drip of green hit his pucker, he hissed and whimpered, and I didn't waste any time before going in.

I'd worried about this before—I'd seen it in vids and always thought, *Nope. I know what comes out.* But this was different. For one thing, there was ice cream, but it was more than that. There was Sonny talking in tongues while he tried to grab my hair, and there was the scar he'd forgotten about, and there was his body, which was mine to do with as I pleased.

I pleased to make him moan. I *really* did please to do that, I wanted him so bad. I wanted his panted breath and the taste of him on my tongue; I wanted to hear him beg and need. I licked his rim until there wasn't no more ice cream, and then put my thumb there to soften it while I licked the rest of the ice cream off his balls. Delicately, just to make sure they were clean, I sucked each one into my mouth and tugged gently, and kept my cool when his upper back came off the futon and he almost screamed.

"*God*, yes! Oh, fuck, Ace... please, dammit! Please, please, please, please...."

And everything else was clean, and that's when I opened my mouth and clamped my lips over my teeth and my mouth around his shaft, and sucked.

I was not expecting him to erupt, and he probably hadn't been either, because his hands flailed and he cried out, "No!" while I struggled to swallow.

I lost a bit, and it was bitter, but I was so hungry for him that it didn't bother me none. I just kept sucking on him, lowering my head until he was almost all the way down my throat, when he grabbed my hair and made a sound that wasn't all pleasure, so I let go.

I grinned at him from across the length of his compact body, come dripping from my chin, and he stared back at me, his eyes blinking to focus.

"Oh Jesus!" He reached out and cupped my face with his hand, wiping some of the come off my chin with his thumb. "Jeez, Ace, ain't ya... you know... wanting?"

I laughed and buried my face in his thigh. "Oh hell yeah." I straightened up and reached my hand into my shorts to pull my cock out, and he grabbed it and stroked it hard enough to make me gasp.

"Aw, fuck—"

"Here, move up a little!" And then he scootched down so he was sideways on the futon and my cock... well, it was just perfectly level with his mouth.

He closed his eyes first and licked it, squeezing and stroking, and my entire body shuddered.

"Oh hell... God, so good... Sonny, I'm gonna—"

He pulled his head back so he could talk, but kept up with the stroking. "Tough," he snapped sullenly. "Licking me 'til I'm out of my mind. You're gonna come in my mouth until you can't see, I'm gonna suck ya 'til your eyeballs pop outta your cock and you're fuckin' blind—" His lips tickled my cockhead as he yammered on.

"Not if you don't shut up and suck—*fuck!*" 'Cause he was true to his word.

He opened his mouth and pulled me in and squeezed my cock at the base, using his pinky finger to diddle my balls.

His eyes were closed, and even with my cock sliding in and out of his mouth, he looked earnest, like cocksucking was his best subject and he'd studied hard to make it that way, and it was my turn to stroke his cheek and run my fingers through his hair. My whole groin swelled and my balls bulged high and tight, and then he pulled back and stroked with his mouth open, and the thought of him doing that, my come squirting on his face, that was enough right there to send me over.

I came, white and thick, and he closed his eyes and took it, opening his mouth and engulfing my cockhead and then tightening his lips and sucking me dry.

I groaned, shivering hard, and the only thing behind my eyes was black. Finally, I was empty, limp and tender, and I tugged on his hair and sat down on my feet so we were eye to eye. I was still wearing my T-shirt, and I pulled it over my head and used it to wipe his face, and he looked up at me, his eyes so earnest, I had to bend and kiss him, just to put a seal on what we'd just done.

I pulled back from the kiss, smiling, and he still looked so lost.

"You liked?" I asked anxiously, and he nodded, all enthusiasm.

"It was fun," he said. "All the things I think I know, you keep teaching me they're wrong. That can be *fun!*"

That scar on his thigh was going to haunt my dreams, but right now, I just closed eyes and kissed him again, swallowing my fears like I'd swallowed his come—the bitter salty price for something I'd do again and again.

# GOOD CRASHING

FIXING the Jag was a pain in the ass, and I didn't even do most of it. That was Sonny's job, while I did the grunt work on the regular cars. Yeah, sure, I appealed to Sonny for help some of the time, but mostly I just used what we both knew about cars and felt my way along, asking questions when I needed, but not too often, or he'd snap at me and I'd know I was being a dumbass.

By the end of the week, we'd done it, though. The Jag was done, the rest of the work caught up on, and the Ford had been tuned twice and run through the desert once, just for practice.

Peter Go-bear came back looking for his car, and was surprised enough to find it ran better than before he tried to cook it raw that Sonny got insulted.

"What? You thought you left it here so we could scam you? You thought that? 'Cause I say I'm gonna fix a thing, I'm gonna damned well fix it! Why you gotta look like I'm too fuckin' stupid to fix a goddamned engine! *You're* the one who ran it without water! That thing's cherry now. It could win any street race in the world, so long's Ace was driving. You fuck that thing up now, it's all on you."

Go-bear backed up, hands in the air. "No, no, Mr. Daye, I didn't mean to imply anything. I'm just impressed." He looked at me, hoping to be bailed out, and I took pity on him.

"Sonny, back off. And stop talking about putting it in a street race. I don't think that's his thing."

But the man tilted his head to the side, the attitude looking off-kilter on his long-boned face. "Really? Do you think it would do well?" I guess rich men like to show off too—go figure.

Sonny did everything but hiss like a cat. "Not if you drove it, it wouldn't!"

Go-bear grimaced, because I guess even *he* couldn't argue with how badly his last road trip had gone. "Well, would Mr. Atchison be able to drive it and win?"

Sonny scowled. "You drove with Ace, right?"

That grimace deepened, and his dimples popped. "Yes."

He wasn't bad-looking, but Sonny wasn't having it. "Could you wear those shorts again?" he asked, and I hid a smile behind my hand while Go-bear shook his head no. "Well, that there's your answer. Ace never met a car he couldn't drive like fury. He'd win it for you, but—"

"I'd stake you," Go-bear said, and he was so enthusiastic that for a minute I got really excited.

Sonny? Not so much. "You didn't let me finish," Sonny snapped. "He don't drive no one's car but mine." And with that Sonny turned around and stalked off to Alba to give her the carefully totaled—and totally legit—invoice for Go-bear to pay before he got the keys. He also must have shot off his mouth, because she gave him an annoyed look and rolled her eyes—and the back of her middle finger when he turned around.

Go-bear looked at me, surprised, I think, at not being obeyed and fawned over. "It was a legitimate offer," he said, sounding a little hurt, and I grunted.

"I don't think he thought that's what was on the table," I apologized, and now he looked *really* surprised.

"No offense," he said, looking uncomfortable, "but, honestly, as, uhm"—his eyes darted toward Alba—"as debauched as I've been known to be, men have never been one of my quirks."

I narrowed my eyes. "Okay, so firstly, keep your eyes off our receptionist, she's sixteen!"

Go-bear took a panicked step back, and I was reassured.

"Secondly, I never said you were hitting on me. It's just...." I pursed my lips. "That yellow Ford has a part of Sonny's soul. If I drove another car, it'd be like being with another person. I'm sorry—I mean, it was a nice offer and all, but we could win a frickin' mint and it still wouldn't be worth it."

Go-bear started laughing, low and soft. "You know," he said, and he didn't say anything after that, just shook his head. I never did find out what it was I knew or he knew, but that was okay. He paid Alba on the way out, didn't hit on her, which was nice, and left a big tip for the three of us for getting the car in under budget and under time.

I walked to the back of the garage, where Sonny was washing his hands to finish up for the day, and stood next to him, close enough for our hips to touch.

"I wouldn't have driven his car," I said after a few moments of frigid silence.

Sonny looked at me sideways. "You say that. He was almost as pretty as the car."

"Yeah. But I wouldn't have driven the guy, either."

Sunny glared at me and I looked back, keeping my expression bland. He kept glaring, but I didn't blink.

Finally he chuffed out a breath and looked down at his hands before grabbing a paper towel and turning off the water.

"I do *not* know that," he said after a moment, looking down.

I glanced behind my shoulder at Alba, who was texting her friend now that our last client had gone, and then grasped his chin between my fingers and forced his eyes on me.

"You do, Sonny Daye!" I snapped. "This garage, the car, the racing, *hell*, the last two nights! What's it gonna take to prove it to you?"

Sonny couldn't look at me, but he couldn't back down either. "The more things you tell me you did for me, the less you're gonna think you owe me," he said at last, his voice miserable, and I consigned our receptionist to the four winds and pulled him into my arms. I lowered my mouth to his ear and gave him the only words I had.

"I love you," I said quietly, the sweat from our bodies soaking through our coveralls at the contact. "I didn't do this shit to get something from you, I did it so you'd know that one thing. I don't know what else to tell you 'bout that, but there it is."

I knew he'd have to chew that over like gum, so I backed away and let him do it.

I went up to Alba to tell her she was done for the day, and saw that she was staring at me—but that she was unsurprised.

"What?" I asked shortly, and she shrugged.

"Don't worry," she said back. "My mommy don't have to know."

I groaned. "God. That don't even feel honest."

"Yeah, but mommies don't always know best. Gay is all over now. Back in her day, I don't think it was a thing, or if it was it was a bad thing. So it'll be our secret, like her brother."

"Manny, the one who does street racing?"

Alba shook her head. "Chewie, the one who lives up in the hills, like hellsa far away."

I didn't have no idea which hills she meant—the ones out in the north of the state, the closer ones by the Grapevine before the state leveled out to more and more desert—I had no idea.

But she had a gay uncle, and she still wanted to be our receptionist, and right now I was feeling so raw inside that the approval of a sixteen-year-old girl was that damned important to me. "'Kay," I said. "I just don't want you lyin'."

Alba cocked her head and looked at me. "How do you love him like that? He's not very nice."

I pursed my lips. "His mouth says one thing that the rest of him don't always mean. Last time he got attached, the girl ended up dead. It hurt him."

She flinched back. "Dead?"

I hadn't thought of this in so long—it had been more'n a year since it happened. "It was in Afghanistan," I said, not wanting to think about it now either. "Don't worry. As far as I know, they don't drop shells on our head out here."

She had a pretty face—wide cheekbones, rounded little chin, big brown eyes when she didn't put crap on 'em. It hurt to see her look so sorry. "I'm sorry, Mr. Atchison. That's sad."

"You're a nice girl, sweetheart. Go home. See you tomorrow, if you got the time."

"Yeah. You go take care of your man. I promise my moms don't need to know."

God. If only it were that easy.

"Yeah, well, thanks. And watch out for that Go-bear guy. I think he's sort of a sleaze."

She nodded and we locked up. I closed the car bay and went out the back door, stopping to water the mud before I went inside. I thought that maybe, on my next trip to town, I'd stop and buy some grass seed and see if that was what it'd take to change that crap from mud to lawn—it would certainly be an improvement.

I got inside and Sonny was coming out of the bathroom, scowling at me. His skin was hot pink.

"I wish you wouldn't do that when I'm in the shower, dammit! All that's left is hot water, and it's a hundred degrees outside as it is!"

I grimaced. "Sorry, Sonny." I walked past him to the laundry room on the other side of the living room. I pulled my knife out of my pocket and put it on the laundry shelf before I dropped my coveralls into the washer along with Sonny's—we put on our fresh ones on

Saturday and did laundry over the weekend. Then I stripped naked and walked that way to the bathroom, only noticing when I got there that Sonny was staring at me.

"What?" I asked, suddenly wanting to cover my privates with my hand, which was stupid since even if we hadn't been doing what we'd been doing for the last two nights, we'd both been in the army, and you just didn't get that upset about being naked around other people after a while.

"You're mine," he said speculatively, like there was another way for a relationship to go.

"Yes. Of course I'm yours."

He narrowed his eyes. "I want to cut it into your skin. Brand you. You're mine. Don't no one but me touches you."

I shuddered, thinking about the mark on his thigh, and then I looked him dead in the eye. "You do what you got to. Just remember, I get to mark you too."

The look in his eyes went worshipful again. "You'd mark me?"

"Well, *yeah.* Mine. You think I don't want the world to know you're mine? It's what wedding rings are for, Sonny. It's why people say 'I'm taken!'. And honestly, it sounds a lot more comfortable than breaking the skin."

Sonny scowled. "But not as permanent."

"I've got to take a shower. You figure out what you want the tat to look like, Sonny, and maybe we can not scare any customers before we get it inked."

I was out of patience for the moment, and I hoped the shower could wash away some of the disappointment. He didn't believe in me. I wanted to claim him too—I got that. But he didn't believe in me. He wanted the brand so I couldn't get away. I wasn't going anywhere—I'd never planned to.

The unfairness hurt, and that was silly, since I'd known life could be unfair for just about ever.

I'd just rinsed the soap out of my hair when the door to the bathroom opened. I turned off the water and grabbed a towel, looking at Sonny after I wiped my eyes.

"What?" I asked, and he scowled. Then he dropped his shorts and propped his foot up on the toilet and showed me that scar I'd been dying to ask about. It looked worse in the daylight, without any shadows, bubbled and blistered and discolored.

"I didn't want that mark," he said, his eyebrows drawn over his eyes. "I burnt it off."

I sucked in an awful breath, but he ignored me.

"I want your mark," he said, putting his leg down. He turned to the medicine cabinet and pulled out a bottle of alcohol, and then he grabbed my knife. I hadn't noticed that he'd brought it in and set it on the counter, but there it was, the point discolored like it had recently been heated.

Oh fuck no.

Oh *fuck* no.

"A tattoo," I said, my bowels cold and my throat dry. "A brand, but someplace decent. Not—"

"Us, Ace," Sonny said, his voice uninflected. "Us. You mark me, I'll mark you."

"I ain't hurting you—"

"I hurt every minute you didn't claim me," Sonny snapped. "This? This is nothing. This is fuckin' skin, and I don't give a fuck. Mark me!" He turned to me with the knife in his hand. "*Mark me!*"

I grabbed the knife from him and turned sideways, looking at the pad of my outer arm and thinking wistfully that a tattoo of a sunrise would have looked really good right there.

Then I gouged my own skin with the point of the knife and ripped, slowly, carefully, a curve, a horizontal line, and then four lines coming out from the curve. By the time I got to the sun rays my hand was shaking so bad, and my skin was so slippery from blood, that the end of the last one was a little weak.

I turned to him, naked with my arm still dripping blood, and handed him the knife, hilt first.

He hadn't said a word the entire eternity I'd been scoring my own fucking flesh, but now he met my eyes and flipped the knife around before offering it to me again. "Now. Me."

I swallowed, and the pain in my arm surged, reminding me that I was tired and hungry, and I'd been planning on kissing Sonny tender tonight, and whatever else had been in my heart and my backbone, wounding my lover had not been it.

"I love you," I said, knowing my eyes burned now when they hadn't when I'd been ripping a knife through my own skin.

Sonny's eyes got shiny. "I know you do. Mark me."

"Sonny, a tattoo—"

"You can make it like a spade, like the playing card ace. Do it."

"Sonny—"

"*Mark me!*" he snarled. And then he held the knife, blade first, against his wrist. The entire world went very, very quiet. "Mark me, Ace, or I'll do it."

It couldn't be no harder than killing a man 'cause he threatened Private Sonny Daye, now could it?

I wished we kept whiskey in the house. We didn't, 'cause I liked the taste of beer better, but I wanted whiskey so bad as I stood there, naked, *still* naked, bleeding, and scored a basic shape in Sonny's skin.

He stared straight ahead the entire time, holding up his sleeve so I could cut the outside of his arm, and I scarred him, quickly and as painlessly as I knew. If it hurt him one tenth of what the flaming mess in my own arm hurt me, it was too damned much.

But finally it was done, and I stood, dripping with sweat and blood and sadness. Both of us were breathing fast and harsh, and I don't think my eyes were the only ones that burned.

I dropped the knife into the sink when I was done, and it clattered there for a minute before Sonny turned on the water to rinse it off.

"I gotta shower again," I said, my voice sounding tinny in my own ears, and he looked at me and stripped off, getting blood all over his clean shirt.

"I'll join you."

The water was cold this time, but that was okay. The cold was needed, and it washed away the blood and the sweat and that strange, acidic tint of despair that had sunk into the tiny room while I'd marked us both, forever.

After we got out and bandaged our arms up, Sonny microwaved us both burritos and said, "No TV, Ace. We'll go to bed."

It was barely eight o'clock, but I didn't argue. It was the first thing either one of us had said since the shower.

But there is a strange peace that comes from lying in bed in the half-light of a summer night. Sonny rested his head on my shoulder and started walking his fingers along my chest, finding the scars from that time in Afghanistan where the shrapnel had punched through my Kevlar and punctured my lungs.

"I was so scared," he said into that silent twilight. He moved his fingertips to the big scar, where they'd had to push a shunt in to reinflate my lungs. "That whole thing, I was scared. And the girl—he woulda killed her, but it didn't matter—"

"I'm sorry about the girl," I said softly. "I know you were attached."

"So were you," he accused. "You were the one who fed her. You were the one who smiled at her and she thought we were gods. How do you live with that?"

I grunted, my arm giving a big fucking throb. Sonny had given us both some ibuprofen to deal with it—the shit wasn't doing its job.

"I'll let you know when we're solid," I said, a part of me hurting more than my arm.

"We're not solid now?" Sonny asked, and the hurt in his voice about killed me.

"I don't know, Sonny—I wanted to come in and...." God, I couldn't say the words and not make them sound... small somehow. "I wanted to kiss you," I said with dignity. "And I ended up bleeding instead. I'm not sure what that makes us, but I've got a feeling solid isn't it."

He kissed the scar down by my ribs then, and I gasped, because I wasn't sure if it tickled me or ramped me up. Then he kissed the one over my belly button, and I squirmed some more.

He looked up then, the beginnings of a smile on his face, before he sobered. "Did you want to kiss me then," he asked, "before you got these?"

His gray eyes were mesmerizing.

"Yes," I whispered. "I wanted to kiss you from that first day. You said you'd do anything. I wanted to do everything to you. *For* you."

"I was there," Sonny said, that hurt again. "I was offering myself. Why didn't you take me?"

"I had to know." I pushed his hair back from his face, and he leaned into my hand. "I didn't want you because you thought you had to. I wanted you because you wanted me back."

"You're the only one." Sonny kissed that tender place on my belly again. "All the—" He stopped himself. "My entire life, you're the only one I ever wanted for myself. But... but somebody's got to claim me. I—" He swallowed. "I know it don't make no sense to you," he apologized. "But somebody's got to. If I'm gonna have you, you're the one who needs to do it."

I swallowed, for a minute glad he wasn't going to explain this to me. It didn't sound healthy, none of it, and I had a sudden thought of Burton coming into my room when I was laid up after surgery.

*"Heya, Lance Corporal. You missed Sonny, he just left."*

*"Yeah, Ace. 'Bout that guy...."*

*"He ain't giving you trouble?" I was surprised, because Sonny was the ideal soldier, mostly. He did what was asked and he didn't complain and he didn't ask questions. It was why that situation with Galway had*

*been so scary. Sonny wouldn't have asked for help. He just would have not shown up for mess one day.*

*Burton shook his head. "Not trouble so much—but he's been here every minute he's not on duty, did you know that?"*

*I shrugged. "I've been sleeping a lot," I told him, feeling lame, even then when my insides had just been my outsides in order to patch me up.*

*"Yeah, well... Ace, whatever reason you decided to adopt Sonny and make him your pet private, do me a favor. Just don't cut him loose without having someone else watch him. There is something very wobbly about that guy."*

My arm throbbed yet again. "Well, I claimed you," I said, thinking that was an understatement. "I'm yours. Maybe next time I'm thinking all night of coming in and kissing you, you can trust that you're the only one I want to kiss, okay?"

Sonny nodded soberly and laid his cheek against my stomach to rest, and that's how we fell asleep, exhausted by pain, both the one in our arms and the big one, the complex, debilitating one, inside Sonny's locked-down heart.

SONNY didn't get jealous again after that—not even when the openly gay couple with the convertible and the flat tire flirted with me heavily, going so far as to pat my ass when I turned my back. I told them no, thank you, and went on about my business, and Sonny walked up to them with a smile and said he'd killed people for less.

I don't know how serious he was, but the two guys in the convertible seemed to get the message all right.

I raced three more times, taking the pot each time, and that was sort of amazing to me—but not to Sonny. Each time he got out of the car, I'd look at him and ask for a kiss for luck. He'd look at me back, his face drawn and tight, and say, "If I thought we were depending on luck to do this, Ace, I wouldn't let you go."

Of course, once I'd shut 'em down and he had the cash in his pocket, he was a little less tight. That third time, I fucked him hard against the side of the car in the dark, beyond the crowd. It started with a kiss as we faded into the darkness, and then the kiss got hungry, ravenous, his mouth opening so hot and so sweet that I needed to touch his bare skin. We kissed until we found the car, far away from everyone else around the post-race party, and he pulled the lube out of his pocket and simply bent over, looking over his shoulder at me and whispering furiously, "*Fuck me,* Ace! Just fucking—"

He didn't have to tell me twice. God, I was hard and thick and hot and ready to breach him and pound him and fuck him…. He grunted into his bicep and lifted his ass into the air by standing on his tiptoes, and I cut loose on him like fury until he came, and then I came, and we stood there, shuddering in the dry heat of the desert night.

There was nothing to clean up with, and the smell of come even overrode the smell of nitro as we flew across the desert back home.

That night, after we put the car to bed and showered, he turned to me in the quiet and kissed me, tender and soft, liked I'd dreamed about that day before the scars on our arms, and I kissed him back the same. We touched skin to skin then, skating our palms down backs and ribs, our thumbs finding indentations at waists, in the tender crease of arm and core, neck and collarbone, thigh and taint. Every touch was heightened, every moment still and sweet, until we both gasped and heaved and came in each other's hands, and even our come seemed like a silvery miracle in the bright of the moon that shone through the bedroom window.

We were claimed, I thought as we fell asleep. Maybe we had found our way to being solid after all.

But that didn't mean that when Burton called me 'cause he had docked in San Diego and was off tour that I didn't ask him to come out and stay with us and see our setup, just so I could talk to him in private about watching after Sonny.

He came out and stayed on the futon and didn't say anything about us sleeping in the room. I'd gone to Walmart one day and spent money on a whim, buying pictures of muscle cars and frames, and put them up around the room when I got back. Sonny watched me critically and said, "I'd rather have a dog and some pictures of *it*," and I widened my eyes.

All righty, then. "I'll look," I promised. "We need something that's not gonna mind when we go out racing and who doesn't spook when we rev up the Ford."

His brows drew together like he was chewing on something, but I couldn't help him there. I figured when he knew what he had in mind, we'd fix it then. But we hadn't fixed it when Burton came by in July, driving a conservative-looking Buick something and looking a bit high class for our little corner of the desert, even in jeans and sneakers. They were *pricey* jeans and sneakers, not the faded blue kind of jeans and cheap Walmart sneakers Sonny and I wore. I'd seeded the mud hole and started watering it at night, so something was growing there, but it smelled swampy, and that was the only spot of green for what seemed like miles.

The house still needed paint. Sonny and I had spent a day off filling the attic with insulation, and that had helped with the heat, but the outside still needed paint and the inside still needed more than car posters to give it character—but it was clean, and the television was nice, and we didn't smoke, either of us, or have any nastier habits than ice cream on the couch, so it wasn't too embarrassing, and Burton seemed happy to drop his duffel next to the futon and accept a cold beer.

He came out and talked to us both, filling us in on the evac as we fixed our cars. Alba couldn't stop looking at him in his tight T-shirt and his easy white smile in his round, pleasant face.

Sonny glared at her from across the garage. "He's almost ten years older'n you, girl, stop humpin' him with your eyes!"

"Yeah, if I tried to hump Ace with my eyes, you'd skin me!" she snapped. "And you're too fuckin' ugly to eye-hump, so gimme somethin' or I bounce!"

Burton and I met eyes, completely friendlike and not humping at all, and he said, "Nice, Daye. You take candy from babies too?"

Sonny shot him an annoyed look. Sonny hadn't understood why I'd been so excited to have a friend stop by, and I didn't have words to explain it to him. A friend stopping by meant Sonny didn't have just me.

"She needs to keep her eyes to herself," he said firmly. "She has a mother, a home. Don't need to be humpin' nothin' for the fun of it."

Burton dropped his voice and said, "I thought humpin' *was* the fun of it!" and I snickered.

Sonny glared at me in particular, and I winked.

"Oh, come on now, Sonny—even *you* have to agree that 'humpin'' has got to be a little bit fun, right?"

A quirk on the corner of Sonny's mouth was his only concession to the fact that I might be right, and then he shoved himself underneath the car to crank some more on an engine bolt. One more idiot trying to ride between LA and Vegas without coolant in the radiator. I was starting to love those people—they were gonna make us rich.

Burton laughed softly and leaned on the hood of the Hyundai getting its belts replaced. "He's a barrelful of monkeys, isn't he?"

I winked. "We do okay. He just doesn't like people, that's all."

"Well, aren't *you* glad you got a lung full of shrapnel for him, then, right?"

I looked at him levelly. "Best thing I ever did."

We hadn't ever really talked about what had happened that day. Burton told the investigatory committee that I went to the auto bay to check on a buddy, and that I'd secured my own men first. He'd told me in private that Galway's reputation as a sadistic fuck had apparently trickled up, and that nobody wanted to look too closely into the death of someone who'd been known to bully his own men to suicide, and I was real fucking lucky that way. As sappy as it was, I'd tried to take the whole thing as a sign that me and Sonny were meant to be.

Burton raised his eyebrows. "I hear you."

"So," I said, twisting at a bolt, "you said you were at loose ends. Between what and what?"

There was a grunt, and I looked up to see that handsome face set into thoughtful lines. "Well, I was *going* to go back to school, since it's on the government's dime and all now, you know that."

"Uh-huh." I looked at him with admiration. "You got a future, Burton. I knew that." Me and Sonny, this was it. This was the top of our game, and I was okay with that. But a guy with a college degree trying to get his master's in engineering? That guy had the world at his feet.

Burton sighed. "Yeah. Well, I gotta tell you, school sounds really fucking boring after Iraq."

I blinked. "Yeah, well, I could use some fucking boring after that."

"And that's why you go racing every week?"

I thought about it. The speed was something—God. Yeah, well, that was hard to deny. "The army don't teach enlisted men how to fly," I said, trying to hold onto my dignity. "We gotta do that for ourselves."

He nodded slowly. "Or we can keep doing it for Uncle Sam."

I'm not smart, but he was being patient with me, making an implication that I wouldn't have leapt to straight off.

"You gonna be working for the government?" I asked, and Burton nodded. "But not… not strictly legit."

Burton shook his head no, but like he was agreeing with me, and I swallowed and went for a smile. "No little house and cozy bed for Corporal Burton?" I asked delicately, and I saw a sudden stark look on his face and realized this hadn't been an easy decision.

"Nope."

"What was her name?"

He didn't even ask me who "she" would be. "The girl I left behind? Ariana."

I didn't ask why he chose to leave that all behind. "Why tell me?"

He looked around our little place at the edge of the desert. "'Cause if I say yes, I'll be telling my folks, my girl, my squad—

everyone who knows me—that I might not ever see them again, and then I might not. But you guys—no one knows I'm here. As far as the world knows, we met at base camp and said three words to each other. I'm the only one in the military who even had an inkling about you and your man here, and you're the only one I could tell about this who wouldn't know who to blab to and wouldn't do it anyway. We got secrets together now, Ace. I trust you to have my back, 'cause I've seen what happens when you got someone else's. How's that?"

I nodded, feeling a surge of pride in my belly that I'm not sure if I could explain to anyone, even Sonny.

"Fair enough. So me and Sonny, we got your back."

Burton cast a doubtful look at Sonny's feet sticking out from under his car, and grimaced. A steady level of cursing was coming out from under the car, and judging from the volume, I figured I had about fifteen minutes before he'd admit he needed my help. Burton turned back to see me regarding him levelly.

"That's something else I need to talk to you about," I said quietly. "But not now, okay?"

Burton nodded, and I put my head back under my own hood.

"So," I said, feeling like a little kid, "are you really gonna be a spy?"

Burton all but spit out his beer, but when I looked up at him, he was wiping his mouth with the back of his hand and nodding.

"Awesome. Can you tell us how to work our racing money into our bank account without getting in trouble with the IRS?"

"That's easy—just declare it as gambling wins. It looks legit."

"You can *do* that?" I asked, seriously impressed. "Awesome! Good. That way we can make it all legal."

"Street racing isn't legal, Ace."

"Fucking brilliant," Sonny said, coming out from under the car. "Ace, did you bring him out here to dazzle us with his fucking amazing insights, or is he gonna get his hands dirty and help me with this goddamned Integra?"

"There's work gloves by the bench," I told Burton. "You don't gotta get your hands dirty—this shit don't come out."

Burton blinked slowly, thinking. "Easier than blood," he said softly, and my breath caught, because we both knew I had blood on my hands, and I suspected he had a little of his own.

"Yeah, but don't no one but us know that."

He raised his eyebrow, conceding the point, I guess, and went and got the gloves.

We'd brought in some of those premade pizzas the night before, since nobody delivered out here, and we had soda and beer and three different kinds of ice cream. (Turned out Sonny's favorite flavor was cherry almond fudge—it was pretty complicated and they didn't have it very often, but I liked it too.) For Sonny and me, it was like a party, and if Burton thought it was simple or small, he was nice enough not to say so.

We ate and talked and watched television—he liked crime shows too, and that was fun. Finally Sonny fell asleep against my shoulder, and I nudged him, kissed his temple, and told him to go to bed. He sleepwalked to the doorway, waking up enough to stare at me hard for a moment.

"You promise," he said, and I rolled my eyes.

"I promise I don't want Burton to chop my dick off if I lost my mind and ever made a move," I said dryly, and it was Sonny's turn to roll his eyes.

"Like he'd get a chance. I'd gut you first."

Of course he would. "Then you got nothing to worry about, Sonny, 'cause I'm not feeling stupid tonight. Now go to bed. We race tomorrow!"

He disappeared, and I heard him drop his shirt and shorts by the side of the bed so he could sleep in his boxers, and then fall face-first on the mattress. I tried to talk him into brushing his teeth before he went, and sometimes it stuck, but I wasn't going to nag him about it now.

I turned away from the doorway, and Burton was looking at me thoughtfully.

"He's possessive" is what he said, and I shoved the left sleeve of my T-shirt up to my shoulder. The scar was still raw and pink, but thank God the damned thing hadn't gotten infected. Burton looked at it, eyes wide, and said, "Sun-ny. Cute. Did he do that to you?"

I pursed my lips. "It wasn't like that," I said, not sure how to make him see. "He wanted me to do it to *him*. I did it to myself to try to avoid it. It didn't work."

Burton nodded. "I thought I saw something—let me guess—"

"Ace of spades," I told him, not wanting to play games.

"So what do you need me for? To try to get you out of—"

"No!" I said sharply. "No. Geez, I can't believe they want to make you a spy. You know so little about people if you were oil, your engine would fry!"

"Then what is it you want from me?" Burton asked, half laughing.

"Street racing's dangerous," I told him. "I need you to promise me something."

"Oh no," Burton said, suddenly seeing where this was going.

"Oh yeah. I need your help. Man, if anything goes wrong, you need to make sure he's okay."

"Man, I just told you—"

"No one will know," I said seriously. "He's got no one—"

"Don't *you* have family?"

I swallowed. "You saw me kiss him?"

"Yeah."

"You know what we are."

"Yeah."

"My family, they might deal with it eventually, but I'm racing now."

Burton sighed and rubbed his eyes.

"Look," I said, "I'm not asking you to marry him. I gave him your phone number. I'm just asking you to show up if he uses it, okay?"

He thought about it for a few moments more, and then looked at me. "Right. It's a trade, then. I give you my family, they need me, they contact you, you get hold of me. Sonny needs me, he contacts me. It'll work. Government doesn't need to know. I'll keep… it'll give me a hold," he said at last, honestly. "I want to do it—I do. I want to serve my country, and I've got to tell you, I'll be doing some cool-assed shit. But I'm scared." He shook his head like a dog shaking off a collar. "Man, my family—they're good people. I don't want to blow them off. This way, I can hold on to them, just a little. They'll tell me not to do it, but this way… this way, no one will know."

I nodded, feeling safer. "You need to take care of him," I whispered, looking down at the coffee table. "I'm not enough."

"You know"—Burton picked at the label of his beer—"I broke up with my girl. I told my family good-bye. I can put myself at risk. Has it occurred to you that maybe racing's not the best thing for the guy who's gonna take care of Sonny?"

Yes. Every damned time I got in the car. "It was his dream," I said, hoping I got it right. I tried—God knows I tried—but I didn't always seem to get it right with Sonny. "I… I don't think he's had many."

Burton stretched then, stood up, started scooting the coffee table out and away from the futon. I helped him, thinking the conversation was over, and folded the futon out. I'd put clean sheets on it for him, our spare blanket, and it looked like we had a real home. I had pride in that. It was small, but it was real.

"You ever think, Ace, that you're the only dream he's got?"

His voice took me by surprise—I guessed I was tired too. "No," I said after a moment. "He's got… he needs. He needs this. The car, the racing—it's a part of his soul."

Burton nodded, and I turned around to go slide in bed next to Sonny, the prospect suddenly so sweet, I almost couldn't stand it.

"I think you're wrong," Burton said softly, but I lifted my shoulder, because I thought I was right. Sonny was complicated, and love wasn't easy, and of all people, Lee Burton should know that.

Sonny's body was warm and a little sweaty as I slid in next to him, but I rubbed his back anyway so he'd know I was there.

"Good convo?" he asked sleepily, and I "uhm-hmmd" back the same way. "What'd you talk about?"

"You," I mumbled. "Want to make sure you're okay if somethin' happens to me."

His body stiffened under my hand. "I'll never be okay if something happens to you," he said earnestly, and I pushed him back against the bed.

"You have to be," I told him. "How'm I gonna go race tomorrow if I don't think you'll be okay?"

"But Ace—"

"Go to sleep," I said, my eyes falling closed. "It's all right. I'll take care of you, Sonny."

The swamp cooler was pumping extra hard that night, and Sonny still scrunched in next to me like a cuddling Chihuahua. I petted him just like he was one, and fell asleep with sweat trickling between us and sticking our skin together like paper.


THE next night, Burton rode with us out to Nevada—not Las Vegas, but a little town north, where apparently the illegal street races were the only entertainment the town had besides DISH TV.

The whole town was lined up on either side of the street, and my stomach knotted when I saw kids and pets and the whole fucking shebang there as I revved the Ford and kept her in place.

"Jesus," Burton breathed. "I did *not* think it was gonna be a circus and a carnival and a street fair, all rolled into one."

"It's usually not," Sonny said, and since he was the one who did the research into where we were going each night, I believed him. "This one's three weeks, Ace. You qualify for this heat, we get next week off, and then we come back for the final. You get blown off in this heat, depending on your time, you get to come back next week, and *then* we get the final."

"Aw, fuck! I'd better get my ass in gear, then, because that was one long-assed ride!"

"Yeah," Burton said from his spot on a milk crate bungee corded to the floor in the back, "and I did not suffer that totally shitty ride just to watch you lose."

I grinned and cracked my gum. "Sonny, show this man to a bookie." We were idling at a stoplight, and I spared a glance for my new best friend in the back. "You can put money down on us, Corporal. I'm gonna make you a rich man."

Well, not exactly rich. I did pull back on the throttle a little, 'cause if we were comin' back, I didn't want them to know everything we could do. But our time was third, and he'd bet on us to show, so he had a stack of cash to blow wherever the fuck he wanted as we drove back to Victoriana.

What he proposed to do with it baffled me.

"Naw," he said seriously. "You don't get it. Money, I got. This'll be my investment in a safe house."

"You want a room in the back?" I asked, plain flummoxed, but he nodded his head.

"Yup. Dig a foundation, add a porch, get me a mattress that does not kink the shit outta my back. A few weeks a year, I want to know I got a place. My name's not on the money, my name's not on the house. It'll be mine."

I thought that there might be scary people coming after Burton someday, and for a moment I almost said no. But I was already a murderer, and a veteran, and Sonny and I still slept with knives under our pillows and our symbols carved into each other's skin.

"It's done," I said, and Sonny nodded like there weren't no argument to be had. We said good-bye to him the next evening with some regret, 'cause he'd been good company, and Alba stared mournfully as he left.

"He'll be comin' back," Sonny said, and for a second, he almost sounded gentle. "You can flash your tits at him then."

Alba turned up her nose. "Yeah, by the time he notices *my* tits, he'll be too old to grab 'em."

"He's twenty-two," I said mildly. "In six years, you two might notice the crap out of each other."

Alba brightened then, and I told her to keep reading her book. It was something classy-like, for summer reading, and not trashy, and I thought she should maybe work harder at school and less hard at boys for a bit. She was real smart—kept the ledgers for us after I showed her how, right down to keeping our track winnings square under the title of "gambling earnings." For a minute, I wondered how right it was that I was teaching her to lie like that, but then, we'd already seen that there were worse things she could be doing with her time.

# BAD CRASHING

TWO weeks after Burton left, Sonny got to use his number.

That Nevada thing was even more crowded the third week, and Sonny and I spent the entire trip up wondering why they didn't just build a track and make it legal.

"Fees?" Sonny guessed. "Overhead? Taxes? I don't know, Ace. I'm thinking maybe it just takes away some of the fun of it."

I looked at the civilians lining the first part of the strip, knowing my stomach was turning into a roiling oil pit of anxiety just thinking about the potential for disaster.

"There's more now," I said, trying to keep the tightness from my voice. "God, can't parents get a handle on their kids? I wouldn't take my kid to something like this in a million years." No, by God, this was the sort of thing you had to sneak away with your big brother to see!

Fuck. Jake had been weighing heavy on my mind, both him and the mess that Ronnie had become after he'd gotten out of prison. I saw Sonny losing his way like that, and it made me sick to my stomach.

But then, so did losing control and taking out a family because I wasn't all the shit I thought I was behind the wheel.

Still, we'd put in our stake, and we'd lose it if we didn't race. We'd already started the work on Burton's bedroom, which was going to be better than a porch if Sonny and I had anything to do with it, and we also had our eye on an air compressor and some basic painting equipment we wanted. Since we'd started racing, people had already come to us after they'd seen us, asking us to trick up their rides, and Sonny had taken the jobs. Having the paint equipment just made that easier, that was all.

So we needed the money from this one, and I needed to hold true. Well, okay, holding true I could do.

I idled at the starting line and waited for the titty woman (it seemed that every track had one) to drop the bandanas and start the race. I tried not to flash on every goddamned reason this race needed to go hot, fast, and straight, just like every other race, and why nothing, not a goddamned thing, could go wrong.

There she was, laughing, cracking her gum, flashing rack, tossing her blonde-streaked hair, and…

*Go!*

I revved for a few RPMs just like I was supposed to and then hit it, cutting that road like ribbon, flying past the crowd and way ahead for the finish, when I saw it.

It was ahead of me, where the crowd thinned out, and first there was the dog and then the flash of pink where the girl was darting across the road, and I couldn't stop because I would hit civilians on the side, so I had to take my foot off the gas, but the NOS had already kicked in and the car was sailing through the air on fumes.

Oh fuck, oh fuck, oh fuck, I was on the right and there she was on my right and the fucking dog and the car coming up on my left and oh hell, the crowd had thinned and *fuck!*

I jumped on the brake, jerked the wheel to the left, and zoomed toward the side of the road, hoping to make it before the guy behind me tore through me in a classic T-bone and rendered me into meat.

I was going, I was going, nothing in front of me but cactus, when my car was hit on the back left by the car I couldn't quite cut off, and I was sent up, spinning, spinning, spinning, hitting the ground, but the spin never stopped, the spin never stopped, we were going round and round and round and round and—

Black.

I WOKE up in a hospital with the headache from hell.

Sonny was asleep with his head on my bed, and Burton was awake, thumbing through a magazine in the corner.

"Fuuuuuck."

Sonny's whole body jerked. "Ace? Jesus!" He stood and hovered over me, red-eyed, shaking, and I lifted my arm to touch his face only to be drawn back short. My chest was wrapped hard and tight, and my breath came in short pants, and oh, fuck, I remembered this from before.

"I punctured my lungs?" I asked, because it wasn't the sort of injury I'd expected.

"You cracked your ribs too," Sonny said, his face scrunched up. "And you broke your arm and your nose."

"You would have pulped your head if you hadn't been wearing a helmet," Burton said, and Sonny gave a little, "Oh!" and wiped his face against his shoulder.

"Yeah. You wore your helmet. I'm so fuckin' glad you listened to me and wore your fuckin' helmet."

"Why wouldn't I listen to you?" I asked hazily. My head really did hurt like a sonovabitch—or maybe just my face. "You mostly talk sense."

Sonny nodded and wiped his face again. "That's right. I do. You pay attention to me 'cause I talk sense."

I reached out for him again, ready for the pain and the catch in my side this time. "Sonny, c'mon, don't make me beg for your hand."

He fumbled for mine and then grasped it in both hands. "You shouldn'ta wrecked the fuckin' car, Ace," he mumbled. "You shoulda just kept going—"

"It was a kid, Sonny!"

"Yeah… yeah… and maybe you couldna lived with that, but God, I can't live without you, so you gotta take more better care, okay? You gotta…." He sat down because he had to, and buried his face in my thigh. I stroked his hair, comforted him the best I could, until his breathing evened out. After a minute I turned to Burton.

"How long's he been up?"

"You been out of it for about thirty-six hours," Burton said. "He called me when the ambulance got to the hospital, but I was out. I got here about two hours ago."

I nodded. "Thanks for coming. Didn't expect to call in that marker quite so fast. Where am I?"

"Hospital outside of Vegas. Don't worry 'bout your bills, though, or your car. I'm not your only visitor."

I grunted, because my head and my ribs and my chest were *really* starting to hurt. "What's that mean?" I gasped, and Burton stood up in alarm.

"It means we'll talk about it later and get you a nurse now," he muttered. "Dammit, Ace, you are not breathing right."

And then he went and got me a nurse and there was some more fuss over my lungs and getting them up to where they needed to be and doctors over the bed and my hand tingling, because Sonny had to get up and leave me, and I wanted to touch him again.

They got me settled again, and I remember some quiet hours, Sonny asleep again by my leg, Burton coming and going. I woke up the next morning and Sonny was gone and Burton was there, and he said,

"He's downstairs getting food. We got five minutes. You alert enough to talk?"

"Absolutely, 'cause, you know, that's my strong point."

Burton didn't laugh. "He would have fucking lost it, you know that, right? Man, he called me from the ambulance, and the last guy I ever heard sound that crazy was getting shipped to a prison nobody knows about."

I swallowed. "He just needs—"

"He needs *you*. You, Ace. He needs his one person to stay and take care of him, and you may find some other people in the meantime, but right now, before that happens, if you're the one who gets disappeared, he's the one who ends up in a padded cell for the criminally insane, do you get me?"

I swallowed, my mouth dry anyway. My mom's descriptions of what had happened to Ronnie were never going to leave me alone.

"I'll take care of him," I said, not able to think about dream money or the perfect house and perfect garage anymore. But I couldn't abandon them—I couldn't. I had a thought of Sonny there, someplace green, someplace we could keep a dog. Someplace not in the desert. I'd had this dream....

"I've got dreams for us," I croaked after what seemed like an eternity. "I'll make it come true, or I'll die trying."

Burton blew out a breath. "Sonny won't want a dream without you."

"I've seen a man without the one," I said, thinking of Jake, "and a man without the other," thinking of Ronnie. "The missing dream is sometimes worse than the missing man."

"Give your man a little credit," Burton said, his voice sad. "And make sure he calls me if you pull this shit again."

"Thanks for coming, sir," I said, and Burton flipped me off. I gave him an actual salute, since I figured they were one and the same.

Sonny came in as Burton was leaving, and he scowled something fierce. "Thanks for coming," he said, not meeting Burton's eyes. "You helped me out of a real spot."

Burton snorted. "Yeah, well, your friend who ran the race did most of it. I just got Ace's medical bennies put in place and found you a hotel."

Sonny shrugged, still not looking at him. "We'll make sure you got a real good room," he promised. "Maybe we'll even have a dog."

"A dog, huh?" Burton asked, raising his eyebrows. "I like the little ones. The Chi-who-whats or the Pomerani-poos."

My head still hurt and I ached all over, but Sonny was there and I could smile. "A small dog—hey, Sonny, them things can go in a big box and don't have to hear all the car noise. We might be able to do that!"

Sonny looked at me then, and I saw that his eyes were sunken and sad. "Any kind of dog'll do," he said. "I'm not feeling picky."

I smiled a little. "Awesome. Hey, Burton—we might get a dream... I mean dog!"

"You need to sleep," Sonny said, nodding to Burton as he left.

"I wanted to see you," I mumbled. "I worry, sometimes, that I'll wake up and you'll be gone."

"Yeah, well, you claimed me. It won't happen."

I didn't want to think about what Burton and I had been talking about. I was alive, and I was grateful, and Sonny looked like death.

"Sonny?" I asked, feeling pathetic. "Could you, I don't know, hold my hand again? Kiss me? Touch me somehow? I'm feeling low."

Sonny leaned over me, opening his eyes a little in surprise. "You need me?"

"Yeah," I mumbled against his lips. "I don't know why that would shock you."

"Because you're the leader," Sonny said, kissing my cheek. He lowered himself so he was resting his chin on his hands, and I stroked his hair.

"If we were in the army, that'd make sense," I told him. "But we're not. It's just the two of us. And I love you. Did I mention the love you part?"

"Yeah. Yeah. You're brave, Ace. Loving is scary. I can find another keeper, but I don't know if I'll ever feel the same thing for him that I feel for you."

It was stupid, but it felt like my breathing got easier right then. "I think that means you love me too," I said, and he nodded against his hands.

"That means you can't ever do that again," he said. "Ever."

"Well, the car's probably a wreck anyway," I said, trying to keep my grief about this secret, but Sonny's face lit up.

"That's the amazing thing, Ace! Those steel frame reinforcements held sound! The engine's good. And even better'n that, you'll never believe whose kid you didn't hit!"

I blinked at him slowly, feeling stupid. "Whose kid I *didn't* hit?"

"Yeah—that girl with the dog? You know Czerczenyev?"

"No."

"Yeah, you do, he's the guy we gave our stake money to—"

"That's your thing, Sonny, I just sit there and drive—"

"Well, that's okay, then, because you didn't hit his niece. And he's grateful. He paid for the ambulance and he had your car towed to our garage. Apparently his guys have been there doing the bodywork, taking up the slack—which is good, 'cause I didn't even think of putting up a sign until Alba called *your* cell phone all freaked out about the guys who'd sorta broken in and were working on our shit."

I felt a cold rush of retro fright, and I must have made a sound, because he grunted in sympathy.

"Yeah, well, I sorta think they're mob connected, but right now, they love us, so that's something good. Anyway, the car is good too, all expenses on him, and he gave us the pot because we were clearly winning before you decided to go all hero on his ass and not hit his third niece twice removed or what the hell ever."

"Awesome," I mumbled. "So, what do you want to do?"

Sonny made a needing sound. "I wanna wake up home, with you next to me. Honest, Ace, that's about as far as I've gotten on the wish list thing. We check that one off, maybe I'll think about next down the line."

"That's sounding real good, Sonny," I murmured. "Tell them maybe don't modify the exhaust on the Ford just yet. No need for all that noise if it's just taking us into town and back."

"Yeah," Sonny mumbled. "Maybe if it's not so loud and we're not breathin' nitro, we can get that little chi-who-poo Burton wanted. That'd be nice. The little ones snuggle, Ace. I've seen that myself."

"And crap," I told him. "They crap. We'll think about it, 'kay?"

Sonny smiled like my pessimism was comforting, and closed his eyes. I could smell him—not in a bad way, but he hadn't even left my side to shower. Burton was right. He needed keepers, and not just me. I had an option in the back of my mind, but I wasn't ready to think about it, not now, when I was counting myself lucky and glad he was there to touch.

THE hospital turned me loose a few days later, and I managed to make Sonny rent a car to go to our house three times in that space to shower, check on our mail, make sure the guys weren't giving Alba a hard time, and generally just watch shit. He was back in the evenings, though, and although he had a hotel room and probably showered there and watched a little TV, I don't think he slept there, because he did most of his sleeping right there in the hospital room while I read a Lee Childs paperback I'd had him buy me from the grocery store.

Getting the hell out of there was surely a relief, partly because I don't think the staff knew what to make of us. We didn't neck, we didn't hardly kiss, and everyone knew Sonny didn't leave my side. We were in the middle of nowhere, and our bills had all been paid by the military and what was left over had been paid by the Russian mob, and we'd clearly been in a street racing accident but not one cop showed his head. Yeah, we were an enigma all right.

Still, the nursing staff was nice to us when we left, making sure we had all the stuff we needed to clean my shunt and instructions for when to take it out. They assumed we'd go to our own doctor for that, but I'd done this drill before, and I figured I'd take care of that when I was ready. The rest would be healing, resting my ribs, sitting down when I needed it, and not spending too much time bent under the hood of a car. I hated to think of Sonny doing all the work by himself, but we got there and there was a guy I ain't never seen before working on a car I ain't never seen before.

"Hi, Hi," Sonny said, and I looked at him.

He shrugged. "It's spelled J-A-I," he told me, "and I'm not sure if it's a first name or a last name, but he's been sleeping on the futon, and I guess he already caught the gay thing before he met us. Go him."

Jai stood up and my eyes bulged. He was easily six foot nine, and he had a jaw and a neck like an anvil. Holy God. Holy fuckin' God.

"Uhm, hi, uhm, Jai," I said, my eyes bugging out of my head. He wiped the grease off his hand before shaking hands with me, delicately, like he was holding a demitasse teacup. Since even that much pressure hurt the hell out of my ribs after the ride home, I was grateful. "Sonny been treatin' you okay?"

Jai pulled up a corner of his mouth and said in a voice like Siberian rotgut poured over sandpaper, "He will not give me blow job."

My knife had been on me when I crashed the car, and it was back in a sheath on my belt now. My right hand was bound up to protect my ribs and my collarbone, so I fumbled at my waist for the damned thing with my left, only to be stopped by Sonny, his hand gentle on my own.

Jai watched the byplay in surprise. "He said he was claimed!" he snapped. "He had the mark to show for it. I will not take someone who is claimed."

"You'd better not take anyone here at *all*," I snarled. "No one. Not Sonny, not me, not Alba, not Burton if he visits—*no one*. This is a blow job-free zone here for you, do you understand?"

Jai held out both hands and backed away. "He explained it to me. You need not worry. I would not touch the girl anyway." For a moment he looked sad. "I had hoped… there are very few Russians who will admit they like men."

I let out a breath. "Yeah? Well, I'll keep a look out for your love match, and I appreciate your keeping your hands off what's mine while you're helping out. Go ahead and"—I gestured to the garage—"carry on. Sonny's gonna take me to the house now, 'kay?"

He nodded, and I'm not sure he heard the remaining jealousy, but that was okay. I wasn't sure I wanted him to.

Sonny and I got to the house at that point, and my body was done. I wanted bed and my book, and maybe something cold to drink, but I got a surprise instead.

Next to the futon was a recliner with one of those blue microfiber covers, the kind that doesn't sweat.

"Holy crap, Sonny! Look what you did!"

"Yeah, well, Burton thought it would be a good thing, and we got the winning pot, so I splurged a little. They delivered it the other day."

"I like it!" My whole body gave a throb. "Maybe I can sit there when we watch TV tonight."

"After your nap," Sonny said firmly. "And then I've got to go out to the shop, or Jai will fuckin' scare the piss out of the next customer who comes in."

I shuddered and then winced, 'cause my ribs were still fucked up. "Sonny?" God, I hated to ask this question, but I had to.

"Yeah?"

"That mark on your thigh, the one you burnt off—was that someone like Jai?"

"You mean Russian? No. We got our own scumbags in America, Ace. We don't need to borrow 'em from someplace else."

Sonny helped me into our room and set me on the edge of the bed. Before he could move away, I wrapped my arms around his waist and buried my head at his middle.

"I meant mob, criminal, that sort of thing," I said into the soft skin of his belly. He smelled showered now, like our soap, and I was home, and these things eased so much in me after that time in the hospital.

Sonny was quiet for a moment, and he spent the time smoothing back my hair. I hadn't had any goop to comb through it, and it hung, curly and irritating, over my brow and in my eyes. But it was also soft and silky, even I knew that, and he liked playing with it as I held him.

"Yeah," he said after a moment. "Very much like. Actually, more like Jai's boss, only small-time. Can we not talk about this?"

I nodded and held him closer. I knew more than I wanted to at the moment. Mostly I knew that I'd marked Sonny like he asked, and that it had seemed psychotic at the time, and every mark on our skin had scored my heart twice as deep, but that my Sonny, he wasn't stupid, and in his world, those scars might be one of the smartest things he ever had me do.

SONNY and I had agreed that the car needed a standard intake/exhaust setup, because it was gonna be our commuter car for a while. At least that's how I *thought* we were going to do it. We told Jai that the second day I was there, like it was a given.

The next day, Jai showed up in the white pre-Nissan Datsun that he drove, the kind that was so small he could steer with his knees if they weren't knocking his head around. Behind him was another guy in a suit, driving a silver Mercedes. Behind *that* guy was a guy wearing a suit, driving a preindustrial Volkswagen Rabbit. Without a word, the guy in the Rabbit got out, flipped the keys to Jai, and got back into the Mercedes, looking relieved.

Jai looked at me and said stoically, "Czerczenyev thinks it would be a very sad thing if that car never raced again." He flipped the keys to Sonny, whose blond eyebrows had about hit the edge of his hair. "There should be parts for the exhaust in the back of the car."

Sonny looked up at me and said, "Well, holy mother of fuck," and then stomped off to peer inside the Rabbit. "Yup. Sure enough. The shit's all here."

He looked over his shoulder and glared for a moment. "You should be thrilled," he said sourly and opened the car to start pulling parts out. "Look. There's even parts for a blower. Fucking aces." But he didn't sound grateful at all.

Jai's unibrow rose, and I grimaced. "It's a nice gift," I said. "Tell your boss we're grateful and that we'll make sure she runs right again, like she was supposed to, 'kay?"

Jai's expression evened out (which was a relief—he could lift weights with that unibrow!) and he smiled. "Good. I'll tell Czerczenyev. He will want to see her go."

I walked up next to Sonny and reached a hand into the car.

He smacked it. "You don't lift nothin', you don't bend over nothin', you don't fuckin' *do* nothin'. In fact, I don't even know why the fuck you're out here. Go the fuck away."

"Go to hell and stop trying to insult the nice Russian mob boss who sent his employee here so that we might not starve or go broke. It was a gift so your car could run and we could not go broke feeding it NOS and a fuck ton of gas. You think maybe you could be a little bit grateful?"

Sonny's scowl intensified, but he did raise his head and shout, "Tell your boss we both said thanks!" at Jai, which I guess means he hadn't lost all of his self-preservation, and that was a relief.

Jai nodded and smiled again, which was a little frightening because his teeth were the size of playing cards. He went back to what he was doing—checking the tire pressure of a car we were about to give back—and I turned to Sonny, who still looked like someone had curdled his milk with goat piss.

"That was real grown-up," I said. "Now you gonna tell me why this gift from the gods is a bad thing?"

"It's a wonderful thing," he snapped. "It's fucking awesome. I'm so fucking glad we can fix the car that almost got you killed. I think that's peachy! Maybe next time you can forget your helmet, and I'll get the satisfaction of seeing your brains scattered over the desert. And then mine could *fucking join them*, 'cause that's something I can't see again, Ace, but don't you fucking worry, *we got the parts to fix the goddamned car!*"

Oh Jesus.

"You didn't say you wanted to quit racing," I said quietly, and he grunted.

"It was a lot easier before I knew we had a choice."

Oh yeah.

"The racing was our dream factory, Sonny. You want to just give up on that money?"

"You promised you'd keep me!" he said stubbornly, and I would have thrown up my hands, but, well, one of them was still taped to my side because it was broken and to keep me from abusing my ribs.

"I ain't giving you back, dammit! And I ain't dyin'!"

He glared at me and walked up so we stood toe to toe. "Yeah, that's real fuckin' comforting, Ace, you standing there, sweating in the morning, taped and bruised and what the fuck else, and you sayin' you ain't dyin'! Like I'm supposed to believe *that*!"

I swallowed past a hard knot lodged right where my chest and neck met. "You don't believe that? Well you'd better believe this, and think on it hard. Do you *never* want me to drive fast through the desert again? Racing, no racing, do you *never* want to clock me doin' a hot quarter again? Do you *never* want to sit in the passenger's seat and watch the world fly by?" I swallowed again, but that knot wasn't going away.

He made a little sound—nothing you coulda heard if you were standing more'n a foot away. "I love doing that," he confessed. "I don't like driving that way, but God, I love watching you do it."

I nodded. "Jai?" I asked, turning my whole body since my neck was still stiff. "Your boss, he don't want nothin' back here, right? We don't have to do no racing for him or anything, right?"

Jai shook his head. "He says he still owes you. His niece—you almost died, and she is untouched. This? This is like flowers. Me? I'm like neighbors bringing dinner. You have yet to be paid back."

"All right, there, Dinner, thanks. That needed to be clear."

I turned back to Sonny. "Don't keep that car from being great 'cause you're afraid for me, 'kay, Sonny?" I wanted to call him "baby" or "sweetheart" or "darlin'"—but I couldn't. It wasn't who we were. But something. Something soft.

"You claimed me," Sonny whispered, looking down at the blower hood in his hands. "I ain't ever had anyone good 'til now."

I cupped the back of his neck and ignored the sun and Jai and Alba, whose mother was dropping her off. "You still got me. Let's pretend I'm living, okay?"

Sonny looked up at me, his lower lip threatening to tremble until he got it under control. "I hear you. Just don't wreck again, okay? I know you can't promise something like that, but just don't."

"Okay," I said, nodding. I took a step back. "I can tell you right now I'd like to avoid that at all cost."

He nodded and I got out of his way.

The rest of the day I stood between him and Jai, handing them tools when they asked, and sitting down when they were in rhythm, or drinking water from the ice chest we kept in the corner. Yeah, I coulda been more comfy inside in my bed or the new recliner, which I sort of loved, but Sonny needed me not to go nowhere, and for the moment, that was the best I could do.

That night I made sure to shower good before I slid into bed.

Sonny came after me, and I said, "Wait!" before he pulled back the covers. It took some maneuvering and some scooting, but eventually I lay on my side with my face about even with his thighs. The light from our window was a little bit of leftover from the Chevron station and a lot of the wide expanse of moonlight on the desert, but it was at his back, and his face and the front of his body were in darkness.

I couldn't see his face when he said, "Proud of yourself?" but I knew he was smiling.

I ran my good hand—the one under my body—along as much of his thighs as I could reach. "I will be," I said, trying not to let my uncertainty show. I fumbled with the waistband of his boxers, and Sonny took pity on me and shoved them down.

"You sound awfully cocky," Sonny said, and I grinned at him.

"I'm not, you know. I had girls before you. Lots of 'em. But no boys."

"You told me that."

"I don't know if it's settled in. That you're special. That I want things for you." I reached for his upper thigh, and he bent his knees a little, grabbed my hand, and helped it up to pet him. His cock was swelling—not fully erect, but long enough for me to push up a little and tease the head with my tongue.

Sonny let out a hiss of appreciation, and I pushed myself up some more and opened my mouth and pulled him in. He thrust into my mouth, and I started swirling my tongue, and putting pressure and suction on him with my palate, trying to make him crazy. He grabbed at my hair and moaned, "Too hard, Ace. Easy. God. You go that hard, I won't take it easy on you!"

I didn't want him to take it easy on me, but things were aching, and I guessed if we were going to do this, I was going to have to be gentle so he could. I eased up on the pressure and pulled back. "Stroke yourself, Sonny. I'll never make you come from my mouth alone."

He pulled back then and fell to his knees. He leaned his forehead against mine and said, "Just kiss me."

I closed my eyes and parted my lips and kissed. At first I hit his chin, and then the corner of his mouth, and then the space between his chin and his lip, and then the line of his jaw. He was moving his head then, making sure I hit the right places by now, and I went along. His breathing quickened, and his hips thrust against the bed.

"Scoot back," he muttered, and I felt awkward and lame as I did. He waited patiently, his hand stroking slowly along his cock, but as soon as I was back on my side of the bed, he slid in, put his head down around my waist and his groin up around my face, and suddenly I felt silly, because this was much better.

"Good idea," I muttered, and then I found better things to do with my mouth.

He thrust inside and I swallowed, trying hard not to gag. It was important, I thought, aching, that this be good for him, that it meant something, and I was almost resentful when he pulled my shorts down and started to lick my length, playing with the crown, lowering his head to my balls and using his hand to cup them and squeeze.

I groaned and swallowed him some more, restricted to using my mouth alone. When I wanted to lick him, I had to let his erection flop along my cheek, and his hips rutted desperately. I struggled with my sling so I could grab him, and he spoke sharply.

"The wantin's okay, Ace. Just open your mouth, dammit!"

I did, and his thrusts against my palate were all about restrained power. I pushed myself, gobbling him, sucking him, and his mouth on my cock made me crazy enough to suck harder and deeper. But he could cheat, I thought desperately. He squeezed my balls again and slid two spit-slicked fingers back to my asshole and probed, and I whimpered, because my mind was going blank and I couldn't... I couldn't... I couldn't....

"*Aughhhh!*" His cock flopped out of my mouth and I screamed and came deep in his throat, and he wrapped both arms around my thighs and dragged me deeper, deeper, until I felt his lips at my base and I must have been pumping directly down his gullet.

He pulled back in a minute, still swallowing, and I opened my mouth and tried to capture him. I managed a couple of laps with my tongue, and he muttered, "Right there. Stay right there."

His hand came down along his side and grasped his shaft, and I stuck out my tongue as he pumped savage and fast. His cockhead hit my tongue every so often, and my cheek sometimes, smacking across my face, and I moaned, wanting… wanting… wanting….

I barely heard his scream when he came. I was too busy closing my eyes and blowing out my nose as the come shot across my cheeks and my lips and into my hair. He groaned and pumped some more, and there went another shot, directly into my mouth, and the taste was comforting and bitter. I lunged forward, capturing him again as he pumped. I swallowed, craving it, the taste, the everything, because it meant I had given him something he couldn't give back.

Finally he finished, and he gave a big replete sigh and lifted to rest his head on my hip. "You got jizz in your eye?" he asked, laughing a little.

"I will if I open it," I told him with dignity, and he left and came back with a warm washcloth after a thousand years of darkness. He washed me up—my face, my chin, my bare chest, even my hair—and pulled my boxers up. But that was it. Whatever come we still had on our dicks, he left that. I think he liked that it was there. It was further proof he was mine.

He helped me scoot up to the pillow then, and he pulled the sheets up over the both of us and let me get settled with my head on my bicep and my arm cradling my ribs. He touched my face in the darkness, and I startled. I couldn't cup his hand; I was forced just to let him.

"Ace?"

"Yeah?"

"How come you don't go by Jasper?"

I laughed a little. "See, my older brother, he was Jake, right?"

"Yeah."

"And my mom kept getting confused whenever she went to yell for one of us. She'd go to yell at Jake and she'd get me, and she'd go to yell at me, and she'd get Jake. And Jake, he was like, eight or nine years older'n me—so just about the time him and his friends were all playing poker, I was hanging around him all the time."

"Don't you have another brother?"

"Yeah, but Duane the Dentist wasn't all that fun—I swear to God, he was planning his stock portfolio when he was ten. Anyway, I followed Jake around all the fuckin' time. And there he was, about to bet his shirt with his friends, and I walked behind the kid he thought was bluffing and said, 'Don't do it, Jake! Ronnie's got an ace!'."

Sonny laughed then and I did too, pleased that I could make him do that. "I bet he didn't let you play poker with him forever after that."

I shook my head. "Naw—Jake didn't mind. I had his back. He didn't let me blurt shit out anymore, but he kept me around. Called me his good luck charm, his 'ace in the hole'—and you know. Stuck."

Sonny laughed a little. "Can I ask you—?"

"Why'd he do it?"

"Yeah."

I sighed. "Because he loved Ronnie and was gonna leave his wife and their first kid for the guy, and then Ronnie knocked over a liquor store—something about having enough money so Jake didn't have to leave Juanita and Dulcie poor. He got caught and sent to prison, and Juanita was pregnant again, and…."

"And he didn't see any way out," Sonny said when I couldn't.

"Yeah."

"That sucks."

"Yeah."

"When I was a kid, my mom used to say we were waiting for a sunny day."

I literally stopped my chest from moving in and out, willing him to continue.

"I figured, if I saw a way out of... of a bad spot, I'd be that Sonny Daye."

I had to breathe. Had to. "What sort of—"

He kissed me gently, almost shyly. "Good night, Jasper Atchison. I know you can't hold me, 'cause of your ribs and your arm. It's okay. I'll be here in the morning."

He turned his back to me then, scooting into my body and curling up tight. I nuzzled the nape of his neck and closed my eyes tight. It was hope, that's what it was. He'd given me some hope. I needed it, I thought mournfully. There was so much that was bleak and dry, no rain anywhere. He'd picked a real good name. Didn't it seem like we were all waiting for a Sonny Daye?

"WHAT is it?" Alba asked dubiously. The thing was pink with silk flowers glued to it. Lots of them, trailing from the back like a little miniature wedding posy.

"It is a clip," Jai said, his deep voice thick and full of discomfort. "My sister makes them. I tell her I worked with young woman, she wanted you to have one."

Alba fumbled with it, worked the clasp, and said, "Oh!" And then she lied her ass off. "It's gorgeous, Jai! Thank you." With a few of those quick girl movements that never ceased to amaze me, she fashioned that thing so it was pulling some hair on the side back and holding it behind her ear. "I'll wear it all the time!"

Alba could not possibly have liked that clip. Sonny and I exchanged glances that said this. Alba wore black, white, tan, gray, and gold. She wore tight shirts, yes, and tight shorts too, but not frilly, not loud, and for fuck's sake, not *pink*.

But Jai brought her a cold soda from across the street every day. He jimmy-rigged the little fan we had in her office so it blew over ice, and helped Sonny with the swamp cooler, so that made it even nicer in there. He brought her stuffed kitten tchotchkes with giant eyes that quite frankly creeped me and Sonny the fuck out, so she could stack them around her ancient computer and it looked like a girl place.

Jai may have been looking for a guy to suck his dick, but someone out there had taught him how to treat a girl like a princess, and he was spending all his unused skill on Alba.

And Alba? Well, at first she'd been cold, and when the first stuffed kitten had arrived, she'd looked distrustfully at Jai.

"I don't put out anymore," she said flatly, and I wanted to both cheer for her and cringe for Jai.

Jai didn't bat an eyelash, though. "Good. You are a good Catholic girl. Good for you."

I was across the garage, but I didn't miss the covert look Alba shot me and Sonny as we were bent over the hood of a Dodge minivan.

"I'm a good girl now," she said. "Are you a good Catholic boy?"

Jai shook his head no. "I like dick," he said, and for a moment I thought Alba was going to ask "Dick who?" and then she shook herself all over, shot us another glance, and said, "They're taken."

Jai actually looked put out. "I know. And the little one is cute too."

I was in the middle of bristling when Alba said, "He's not the one I'd go after, but yeah. It's a shame. You know, you don't have to bring me presents. It's nice and all, but I'm really just sorta hanging out here to keep outta trouble."

And that big smile, the one with the big blocky teeth and the lifting of the barbell brow, showed up, and Alba didn't look terrified at all.

"You are good girl, like my sister. I'll bring you stuffed dog next time." He walked away and the cavalcade of creepiness continued.

Alba brought him tamale casserole that Friday, and he looked like she'd laid sunshine at his feet.

"That was real nice of you," I said quietly after he'd left for the day. "Thank you. I couldn't think of anything to give him—he's been a big help."

"I think he's just happy you talk to him," she said thoughtfully. Jai had moved out after my first couple of days back home, and we didn't know where he was living. Czerczenyev's men had been by a couple of times to check on us, wearing slick linen suits and curled lips. They'd made sure Jai was enough help, but they hadn't said hi to him once. He had ignored them like a schoolkid ignored bullies. At one point, one of them had shot a disdainful spate of Russian his way, and he'd returned with a shrugged shoulder. The rejoinder had made him draw up to his full height and snarl, and I stepped casually in front of Sonny, in case fists or car parts started to get thrown around. I needn't have worried—the two men in suits backed down, holding their hands out in front of them.

I turned to Jai when they left, and he grimaced.

"Ignore them," he said sullenly. "They think we have sex all the time. I tell them...." His eyes narrowed and a truly fearsome scowl graced his blocky features. "It is no matter. You are good men."

He turned away then, and we spent the rest of the day like we'd spent it for the past three weeks. He and Sonny worked on cars, I fetched them tools and parts, water, and ice, and held lights and helped diagnose problems, and generally did everything I could without stretching my healing body too far. It was getting better—I could lift more, wrench on more, *do* more, but every now and then I'd feel the end of something grind, and know I had to be careful if I wanted to keep breathing.

At five o'clock we'd finished all the work and cleaned the shop, and I sent him home early. "Enjoy your time off!" I said brightly.

He did not look bright in return. "I have nothing to do," he said, his tone glum. "I have no friends here. I had no friends in my old town, but at least I had sex."

I opened and closed my mouth, and Sonny said, "We can't help you with the sex. But we got a TV. You got any good movies?"

I looked at him like he'd lost his mind, but Jai brightened up. "I'll bring you a good one," he said, smiling, and I was glad we had two different kinds of ice cream, because we could offer him some when he came back.

It wasn't a bad evening—for one thing, the movie was *Drive*, and I loved it, and for another, Jai sat quiet, ate his ice cream, and mouthed all the dialogue (there wasn't much) but otherwise didn't try to talk. We put in one of our own movies—something old, 'cause Sonny liked going through the bargain bin at Walmart, and Jai smiled shyly when it was over, and left.

The next day, he brought Alba the clip.

It was a slow day—in fact, the past two had been slow—and I looked around the empty shop and sighed. We'd done plenty of work lately—enough to keep the shop in the black—but right now, there was no reason for all of us to be there.

I was going to tell Jai he could go home, but he interrupted me instead.

"You two," he said abruptly. "You should take day off. Alba takes days off. You give me days off. You two—you never leave this place."

I blinked some of the sweat out of my eyes. Desert in July—if we hadn't been drinking water by the gallon, the sweat wouldn't have lasted that long. "Leave?"

"Yes. When was last time you left?"

"I do believe that was when Sparky here tried to kill himself in the goddamned car," Sonny said sourly, and I wrinkled my nose.

"That wasn't what he was talking about," I said, liking the idea. "You mean like… like a vacation. But for two days, not ten."

"Da," Jai said, nodding.

Before Sonny could say anything else, I said, "We'll do it! We'll open up the shop tomorrow and then let you two close up. We'll be home by the next night!"

"*Ace!*" Sonny sounded outraged, and I shook him off.

"You could do that, right?"

Jai and Alba nodded.

"You need to bring us somethin'," she said. "Like if you go to Disneyland or somewhere."

I shook my head. "I can't go on no rides," I said.

"Then where in the hell—"

"You'll see," I told him, excited suddenly when I hadn't been excited about a whole lot since the car had gone spinning like a top. "Trust me, Sonny. It'll be good."

And it was.

I TOOK him to the sea.

It wasn't that far away, and once you got on Highway 1, there were lots of little towns just riding the edge of the big blue, but out in Victoriana, it wasn't something we thought about.

We should have.

As soon as I pulled into the little hotel in Carlsbad, Sonny lit up like an all-night diner. "Do you see that, Ace? There's a beach access right down the street!"

"You ever been swimming?" I asked him, and he shook his head.

"Not in the ocean," he told me, excited. "They made us learn in the army, but that was a pool. This is the *ocean.*"

It was.

Now, when I was a kid, my family had taken us here a time or two. I remember Jake trying a surfboard and my mother telling me it was too dangerous. My older sisters and I had gone bodysurfing, though, and that had been something all on its own. Walking out to where the surf churned, hopping up to let a wave take you in—it was something I hadn't never forgotten.

Me and Sonny didn't have board shorts, though—we'd packed cargo shorts and T-shirts and spare sets of skivvies—so I took us to the nearest Walgreens and grabbed the first two pair they had in our sizes. We also grabbed sunblock, since our pale white bodies would be out in the sun and not just our faces. (We normally wore baseball hats anyways—we had tans, but they weren't deep.)

I made Sonny stand still in the hotel while I put the sunblock on. I'd taken out the shunt two weeks ago and had started going without the sling the night before, and there was a simple magic in putting two hands on his body and just rubbing his skin with flat palms and cupped fingers. He went curiously still underneath my touch—he'd been itching to get outside, but suddenly his breathing went shallow, like he had to think about keeping it even, and his marvel of a little body melted into me, like Sonny was mine to take through my skin.

I dropped my head and kissed the side of his neck, and he tilted his head, letting me. I hadn't gotten his ears yet, so I licked the back of his ear, and he made a trilling sound like a happy hamster, and my hard-on was almost immediate. I ground up against him without thinking, and he thrust back, and I wrapped my good arm around his waist and tried to get ahold of the sudden hot want that shafted through me.

"Later," I whispered into his ear. My bare chest mashed against his bare back, and it was hard to remember why I was making us wait. "We can't swim at night or eat dinner after ten—*later*."

He nodded and swallowed, and stepping apart was a mutual decision. He took the sunblock from me with nervous little movements and squirted some on his fingers. "I'd best get my ears, then," he said, not meeting my eyes. "You touch my ears again, I'll spread my ass and jump up and down on your cock without lube."

"Good to know," I said through a dry throat, and then I sank to my knees, skinned his shorts down, and took him into my mouth.

He groaned, and I watched him wipe his fingers frantically on his chest because of the sunblock, and then start rubbing his own nipples because apparently that felt good. It made me hungrier, and I took him deeper in my throat, giving up breathing for a second because I wanted all of him. He rolled on my palate, filled me, stretched my jaw, and I needed him, all of him, in my throat, my mouth, my stomach. God... just....

I wrapped one arm around the back of his thighs and cupped his balls with the other and swallowed, and he grunted, grabbed my hair with his oily hands, and thrust hard. There was no finesse and no savoring, just plain hunger, and my groin ached with the need to eat him, to devour him, to have him all inside me where I could keep him safe. He thrust once, twice, and I pulled back enough to spit on my fingers and thrust them past his rim while I was pulling him in my mouth again.

That must have been what he needed, because he clutched my hair again and grunted, rabbit-fucking my mouth for a giddy second before groaning from his toes, thrusting hard, and spilling bitter and hot down my throat.

I swallowed and swallowed, my own climax exploding white behind my eyes but still leaving me wanting, wanting it all, wanting more, and I sucked him hard until he was done spurting, shaky and limp. When he slid from my lips, I leaned my head on his thigh and tried to get my breathing under control while he stroked my hair.

He laughed a little, and I looked up and saw his gaze was darting wildly, like he was disoriented, and he said, "Jesus, Ace. I gotta put sunblock on you now."

I laughed some more, shaking my head. "Naw," I panted. "Naw. Just gimme my shirt, Sonny. It's big enough, it'll cover the wet spot where I creamed in my shorts."

His laughter was disbelieving, but when I pulled back enough for him to look down and see the dark spot on my blue board shorts, he made a little moan, and it was like his knees gave out, and he sank to the carpet in front of me, pulled my head to his, and kissed me, long, slow, thorough, tasting his come in my mouth, holding my head with his sticky hands.

The kiss started out hard but slowed down, became easy, and when we pulled apart, it was like the sex had been coffee or cold soda, and I was all refreshed and ready to go see if bodysurfing was all I remembered. Sonny leaned against me, though, wrapping his arms around my waist and putting his head on my shoulder.

I kissed the top of his head and he sighed.

"Ace?"

"Yeah?"

"You said you loved me a coupla times. You mean it?"

I took a deep breath on my automatic mad. "Yeah, I mean it. You think a man just lays his balls out there on the block when they don't mean it?"

"No," he whispered against my chest. "I mean it. I think it every day. I think it every minute. But... there's... there's something about saying it that scares me. Like those are the words that'll make you disappear."

Eventually we made it to the water.

Remember when you were a kid, and you played all day, but when your parents asked you, you couldn't put a name to what you were doing? Cutting off star thistles with a stick, running up and down a curb and pretending it was a land bridge, zooming your trucks on the concrete slab of driveway, lost in what the people in them were supposedly doing?

That's magic time, that lost time. You know whatever was going on in your head, it was the biggest, most important thing in the world, but it's like someone stole it away, and all that was left was the feeling of magic.

That was the day with Sonny. We slid down every breaker we could make, we swam out until we were just bobbing heads in the current, we coasted in and fought against the tumble of the surf.

I'm sure there was a reason for which wave we hit, or why I'd pick one over the other, but neither of us could remember. The sea wrapped itself around me, put delicate pressure around all of my damaged, healing bones, and set them free from gravity for a bit. It wasn't until the last tumble into shore, when I went to push myself up and my shoulder and ribs failed me, that I even associated that low, dull ache in my side and shoulder with something I should have noticed all along.

Sonny saw it, though, and fought through the waves to help me up, looped my arm around his shoulders, and wrapped his surprisingly strong arm around my waist. He hauled me across the sand to our towels, but he didn't let me stop there. Instead, he picked up the towels and the car keys and kept us going. My side and shoulder ached, and every step was a misery of sucking need until we were at the shower.

"*Damn*," I panted. "God, I hadn't counted on that. Suddenly just got...."

"Weak. Yeah. That's what happens after a car wreck, asshole. Your whole body is presently kicking you in the ass, telling you it wasn't that fuckin' fit to begin with."

His words rang in the little concrete platform, and I looked around at the half dozen kids and the dozen or so surfers and parents who were all there doing what we were, and who were all now looking at me curiously.

I gazed blankly back and realized you could still see the bruises from where the restraining harness had held me close, right through my T-shirt. They were turning yellow but still there.

Sonny saw where I was looking and rolled his eyes. "Awesome. Here," he said, still breathless. "Let's wash the sand off, and then I'll go get the car."

I glared at him. "It's across the street, Sonny. Don't nobody need to—"

He glared back. "Please, Jasper. It's stupid, but it's something I want to do. The parking lot's almost empty, I'll bring us a change of clothes—we can go straight to go eat, and you can stop looking so chalk white under your burn."

I grimaced. You'd think with my dark hair I woulda tanned better'n Sonny, but not so much. Maybe 'cause there was red in that hair.

"Yeah," I said after a moment. "You go ahead."

He nodded shortly and went trotting off for the car, and I turned on the nearest shower. It was freezing cold, but I wasn't out of the army *that* long, and I could deal. I rinsed my face and my hair, slicking it back, and then took my shirt off and used it to rub the salt off my shoulders, stomach, and back. I finished and realized that most of the parents and children had toddled off, and it was me and two other guys, both of them with brown hair streaked blond by the sun, perfect bodies, and board shorts that didn't come from Walgreens.

They were looking at me with interest, and one of them—the one nearest my bad arm—reached out and brushed my dog tags aside to touch my scars.

I flinched back, knocking my head on the shower pole and bonking my spine painfully against the spigot.

"Not your property, pal," I snapped, and to his credit, he backed up.

"Sorry. Man, those are some wicked scars. Where'd you get them?"

I looked at the guy—he was my age, maybe, but it was getting hard to tell. I felt older than every twenty-three-year-old I'd met since I'd gotten back.

"Shrapnel," I said, looking at the seven or eight half-inch- to inch-long scars peppered over my chest. There was a fresher scar from the shunt, and tape on my ribs, so I decided to cover all my bases. "And a car wreck."

The guy went to feel me up again and I smacked his hand. "Not. Yours." I looked out for Sonny, but he was taking his time getting our stuff.

The kid looked out where Sonny had disappeared to and said, "Sorry, man. I ain't never seen scars like that. No wonder your boyfriend is all freaked out." Suddenly his hand was back, and he was tracing the scars on my arm with a tentative finger. "This wasn't shrapnel," he said, looking at me from hooded eyes.

"I did that so people would know I had a boyfriend and would *not touch me when I didn't ask,*" I snarled. "Now go away, or he will *eat your liver.*"

I don't know why they thought Sonny would be interested in their livers, or why "Go the fuck away!" wasn't enough for them, but they shook their heads and looked at me like I was tough to leave.

By the time Sonny drove up, they had backed up and were talking to me about tattoos and brands and what kind of car I had. I told them we had a Rabbit to drive and a SHO to race, and we talked about that for a bit. I was standing in the sun, pulling my fingers through my hair and wishing I'd brought a little goop to put in it, and Sonny strode up from the parking lot with a gym bag over his shoulder. With an unfriendly scowl, he eyed the two guys talking to me.

I didn't even give him a chance to be a smartass. I took two steps in, wrapped my arm around his waist, and kissed him. He opened his mouth for form, but the whole time he was glaring at me like he knew what was up.

I backed up and the two guys waved and went back out to surf, and I let out a sigh of relief.

"Are we safe now?" he snapped, and I glared back.

"They were hitting on me," I said with dignity, and he glared at them, starting off like he really *was* going to eat their livers.

"You couldn't kill them for that?" he growled, and I took a deep breath.

"I thought it would be better to just show them I meant business. Can we get changed now?"

He shook his head and glowered, grabbing my hand and hauling me to the changing rooms. There were showers in there too, and he bitched at me the whole time he was under the water. "I can't leave you, can I?"

"Now, Sonny—"

"You were just *there*. It's like when you came back with Alba, or those two guys with the car, or when I leave to get soda and when I come back suddenly Jai is all smiling. I can't just *leave* you. You pick people up!"

"I told him you were going to *eat* him!" I protested. "And it's not like I ain't taken more drastic measures!"

"I was gonna eat him?" Sonny stuck his head out of the shower at me. "I brought shampoo, if you wanted to go under again."

"I noticed, and I do. And I don't know. *I* was not scaring him off, so I made *you* sound scary."

Sonny scowled. "I *am* scary. I ain't never fought for another human being in my life, Ace, but I would kill for you, so you break their wrists if you have to, but nobody touches you but me."

I kept my smile back by a bare twist of lips. "Understood, Chief. Are you done with the shower yet? My hair's all stiff, and it looks—"

"Fuckin' hilarious, so if you don't back off and let me soap my balls, I'm gonna hide the shampoo and let you go out like that. I'll take a picture even. Gimme a second."

"I love you too, Sonny."

"Shut up, and don't go getting groped by any more rich kids in designer swimsuits. Fuckin' students. Oughtta be chained to their desks."

I grinned. I couldn't help it. God, but it was good to be wanted.

WE WENT out to dinner. Sonny drove, which was good because I could look out at the ocean under the black sky and think on something so damned vast. I could see why the sea was a magic thing then—it sure did fill my heart with wonder.

We came back and got out of the car, and I still couldn't keep my eyes off it. Sonny asked if I wanted to go for a walk, and for a moment I was going to say no, 'cause I thought he was being sarcastic. Then it hit me. It was dark out. No one was there.

"Yeah," I said quietly. "Yeah. That'd be nice."

I grabbed his hand after we'd run across the street, and no one was more surprised than me when he let us keep our hands there, clutching each other, a little uncomfortable, but twined.

We had to let go as we clambered through the dunes, but once we got to where the sand was packed tightly, *he* grabbed *my* hand, and we just walked. The waves came up and got us, but we were wearing flip-flops, so it was not a problem, and we just… walked. Quietly. I could feel the heat of his body through the chill of the night, and it was like the touch of fingertips on my skin.

I was so immersed in the smell of the ocean, the violent hush of the breakers, the feel of Sonny's rough, hard hand in mine, that Sonny's voice actually startled me.

"Why's it gotta be more?"

My shoulders twitched, and I looked directly at him. I must have smiled, because his habitual scowl eased up and he looked almost boyish.

"More what?" I asked, wanting to kiss him badly.

"More'n what we've got? I mean…." He turned away, his eyes searching the big dark for something he was trying to put words to. "I like our garage. I never thought you'd make it happen. I thought it was all… just dreaming. But you did it—you bought the garage and, well, you fucked around for the car, but you did that for me too, and you got us set up in a real business. And you rode my car and you did it all proud, and—and isn't that enough? You're right. I don't want you to stop drivin'. You love it. I love seein' you do it. But *racing?*" He shook his head. "That's the dangerous thing, Ace. I thought it would be okay. I saw you get shrapnel, I lived." He shivered then, hard, and I heard Burton's voice in my head. *He fell apart, Ace. I was worried about Section 8.* "I saw that wreck, and I...."

I pulled him into my arms then, maybe about the most tender thing we'd ever done, and he couldn't stop talking.

"Why's it gotta be more?" he demanded, his teeth chattering. God. "Why more? You keep watering the mud and it's starting to grow green, and we've got the damned Rabbit, and I've got a mark on me that I want. I want to be yours, and you're letting me. What's more to a dream than that, Ace? Tell me. Tell me what's more to a dream than that?"

I just held him, held him, looked at the stars on the horizon, the matte darkness of the clouds overhead.

"See," I said after a minute, "it's like this. I was there, the first time. I was looking for them, and they were in the alley behind the mom-and-pop store where they worked. Ronnie—he and Jake were getting all smartassed, and then Ronnie—he just... just *kissed* him. And for a minute, my world was like... perfect. 'Cause my brother could be like me, which meant I wasn't a freak, and I almost cried. And then Jake ran off. Next time Ronnie got anywhere near him, Jake pulled a knife on him—drew blood."

Sonny gasped, but I was talking and I couldn't stop.

"And Ronnie came back—just kept coming back, see? Until Jake said, 'Okay! This is us! I want this!'. And I saw their first kiss after that, and it was beautiful. And I saw this picture in my head. The two of them. Little house, green lawn, and them. And they were happy, right? Except when it came time to tell, Ronnie couldn't. Said it was gonna end bad. People would hate them. You couldn't have a happy ever after when people hate your guts. And Jake... God, he ran off and came in the next morning, covered in lipstick and smelling like sex, and he snuck into our room and took a shower... and then he just... the bus was coming and Mom was screaming for us to come downstairs and he was under the covers and he just *cried*. When Juanita came up pregnant... the look on his face, it was like he was dead already."

"Ace, but, but we've *got* each other—"

He was probably making sense, but I wasn't done. This thing, *this* story, had been inside me for years. I'd seen it. I'd seen each piece lurking in my brother's shadow, and the entire time, I'd been thinking about the end of the story.

"But I could keep seeing them," I said, "in my head! They had a little house, and we could visit. *I* could visit, and I wouldn't be invisible anymore, and they'd see me and they wouldn't care and... and I *knew*. It was that dream they wanted. And then Ronnie started using, and there was rehab, and Jake's kid was born—and I got hope. Jake woke up with his kid. He was happy. And Ronnie got out of rehab, and I heard 'em talking under my window one night. Ronnie had come over for dinner, and my folks didn't know, and Juanita didn't know, and they talked and laughed, and it was like he was family. And Ronnie told Jake under my window, the night before... you know." My voice dropped. "Before he was arrested. Said he wanted a good future for Jake's kid. Said it was his fault, they'd made a mess, and they could give Juanita and Dulcie some money, and Jake...."

I couldn't even describe the look on Jake's face that night. Jake, so much taller than Ronnie, just looking at him like the world rose and fell with Ronnie's every breath. "He didn't ask," I whispered. "He didn't ask, and the next day Ronnie got arrested. That night, Juanita told Jake she was pregnant again. The next day, I was at school and—"

I'd seen the wreck, after they'd pulled what was left of Jake out of it. He drove a Ford pickup, but even that was no match for a cargo train that couldn't stop.

I clutched Sonny so tight it made my ribs ache. "Don't you see?" I said, my voice cracking. "That dream—they needed that dream. If I want you, I need to make that dream come true."

Sonny made a noise then, like he would have said no, or told me that wasn't true, but when I looked down at him, his face was wet and shiny.

I closed my eyes, because they were burning and it hadn't spilled over.

"I'm sorry," I said thickly. "I'm sorry. I didn't mean to spill that—I'm sorry. I sound like a pussy. I'll—" I went to take a step back, but he stopped me. "What?"

"You're not invisible," he whispered. "You're the only person I ever saw. And you said I was your dream."

"Oh God, you are," I muttered and lowered my head to kiss him. He tasted hot—hot, wet, and salty—and I trapped his face between my hands. "You're my dream. I've got to do right by you." I said that last against his lips and then took them again, kissed him again, and again, and again.

He broke off, panting, and leaned his forehead against my chest. "Ace?"

"Yeah?"

"Think you'll still be hard when we get back to the hotel?"

"If not, I don't think it'll take much."

"Good. That's real good. I brought lube. I want shit done right."

We started back, both of us breathing too hard, too shaky for physical activity, torn between want and that scary shit going on in our heads.

We got back to the hotel room and kissed, slid our skin against skin. The touch of his thumb against my jaw made my breath come in shuddery. The feel of his ribs under my palms made me shake. I slid my cock inside his body while he faced me on the bed, his eyes big and luminous, his body arching in need, his cock hard and vibrating against his lower abdomen. He came in a spray of white across his chest, his stomach, his shoulders, and I came inside him, so deep I hope it disappeared, became a part of him, ingrained itself in his DNA. His blood, his bones, his heartbeat—all of it would swim with my come, and he'd feel it wrapped around him with every breath.

Me. He'd have me under his skin.

We didn't clean up afterward, just fell back on the sheets that smelled like us, and caught our breath. He put his head on my shoulder and I stroked his hair.

"Sonny?"

"Yeah?"

"Is the grass really growing?"

"I'm sorry, Ace. I think it's mostly algae."

I sighed. "Well, it's green. That's a start. How's the shop doing?"

"You know the answer to that," he said, which was true, because I did the books with Alba.

"Yeah, but I need to hear you say it."

"Fine. We're close, but not there. Right now, after this dry spell, we're not breaking even."

Fuck. Just fuck. "We start breaking even, I'll stop racing."

Sonny nodded. "I hear you. That's fair."

"We don't need to move to the suburbs if you're happy in the desert."

"I'm happy with you."

"Maybe we start advertising—put the name of the shop on the side of the Ford, we'll get more of those people who want cars like yours."

Sonny blinked. "What *is* the name of the shop?"

I laughed softly. I'd had to put down a name when I applied for the business license. "Sonny's," I said.

He turned on his stomach and looked at me. "Can we put 'Sonny and Ace' on the car?"

I kissed his forehead, then licked the salt of his sweat from my lips. "Yeah."

"We can do that. But no racing until you're healed." He palmed the tape still on my ribs, and I pressed his hand with my own.

"That's a deal," I said. "You know what else?"

"What?"

"I think we need to make this day off thing sort of regular. Like, hours and shit."

Sonny looked at me with parted lips. "Oh my God!" he said, like this had just occurred to him. "We can *do* that, can't we?"

"Yes."

"This isn't the fuckin' military, is it?"

"Not the last time I checked." I was smiling so wide, I could even feel my dimples.

Sonny nodded, and the embarrassment of all that strong emotion, that just seemed to fall away. "Good," he said, settling down on my shoulder again. Without seeming to think about it, he kissed my chest, fiddled my nipple with his tongue, and came back up, still talking. "We'll have days off. It'll be great. When you're healed, maybe we can even go to Disneyland!"

I brightened. "I haven't been there since I was a kid!"

And he sobered. "I haven't been there ever."

In the darkness, the intensity in his eyes seemed to glow. "We'll make sure we go two days, then," I said. "And we'll buy souvenirs and everything."

His smile was the kid I'd never seen him be. "Yeah?"

"Yeah."

And suddenly, he was all business again. "That reminds me—what're we gonna get Alba?"

I smiled a little and smoothed his hair back from his forehead. Neither of us had gotten our hair cut this month, and it was falling across his brow and almost in his eyes.

"We'll see," I said. "There's shops up and down Highway 1. We'll go swimming in the morning and come back shopping."

I don't know if I'd ever seen his face that sweet. "We can get something for Jai too," he said with decision. He looked at me quickly. "As a friend, right, and not 'cause he wants in my pants."

I nodded. "Would it be awful if I never thought about that?"

Sonny looked surprised but not affronted. "Why not?"

There was nothing but starlight between us. "Because you're mine. If you're anybody's, you're mine."

He smiled and rested his head on my shoulder again. "Nice," he purred. "That's nice."

And on that note, we fell asleep.

WE BROUGHT Alba a tiny carved mermaid from a store that specialized in driftwood. We got Jai a perfectly round and sanded ball. It was flat on one end so you could set it down, but the rest of it was just round, smooth like satin, marled with the wood. We even got Burton something—a thing like Jai's that didn't have no practical purpose but was just made to be set down. It was wood, warped, weathered through by water, twisted in growth, but it was sanded smooth, oiled silky, every part of it. I couldn't stop touching it, looking at it, wondering at the things the wood might possibly have done, but twisted in another way to do instead.

So that was what we got for other people. For ourselves, we got one of those blankets that had the pictures woven into it. This one had a whale, because even if we hadn't seen any, we'd like to someday, and it was pretty, and it would look good on our futon.

"Are you sure you don't want one of those driftwood things for you?" Sonny asked as we were coming out of the place that sold the wood, and I shrugged.

"It's going to live in our house. That's fair enough."

Sonny nodded. "It's nice," he decided as we came out of the store. "Buying things for people. Ain't never done that before."

I stopped for a moment, watching him as he walked away. He walked on his toes, never completely bringing his heels down, like he always had somewhere to go. When I was a kid, my folks expected us to spend our allowance on each other for Christmas. I remember the humiliation of buying dolls for my sisters—even when they were too big for them—and cars for my brothers. I saved once and bought Jake a pocketknife. It was small—especially because he was big enough and old enough to carry a switchblade—but I thought it was a good thing, 'cause it had one of those smooth wood handles and a decent blade. He'd had it in his pocket when he died. I know because they gave my mom a box of effects.

And that hurt, but I put it aside for now, because I was wondering again how Sonny grew up, to not ever buy something for somebody else. I was starting to get crazy with the wondering, because it was so much shit that added up to nowhere I wanted him to be.

I caught up with him at the Rabbit and didn't say anything about what I was thinking. I was quiet for most of the trip back.

He didn't notice. I was driving and driving fast, and he had his window down and was letting the wind hit his face, almost like a big dog in a truck. I liked watching him enjoy that—it was such a simple thing.

We stopped for gas about forty-five minutes from home, and as I came back to the car with sodas, he said, "You want me to drive? You seem tired."

I shook my head. "Nope. I'm fine."

He frowned. "You ain't said nothin'. We even passed that sign that had the letter wrong, and you didn't do more than smile."

I smiled again at the thought. It was supposed to advertise jalapeños poppers, but someone had put an *i* where the *o* was supposed to be. Sonny asked me if *my* penis popped, and, well, yeah. It was funny, not gonna lie.

"No," I said, not able to shake my thoughtfulness but not wanting to talk about it either. "Nothing wrong." I swallowed and handed him his soda—he liked the suicide kind, where there's a little of everything, which I have to confess made me want to vomit. I was *very* careful I kept my Mountain Dew separate, believe you me. Anyway, there we were, in front of the car and everything, and while he was reaching for the soda, I grabbed his wrist and pulled him into my arms. It was hot and sticky, but suddenly I was cold inside.

"Ace?"

I just shook my head and kissed him. "Nothing's wrong," I said through a rough throat. "I can't remember the last time I had so much fun, that's all."

He grinned at me, young, so young, but I wasn't going to tell him so. "You think that was good? Wait 'til we go to *Disneyland.*"

I laughed. "Let's wait," I said, deciding. "It gets cooler in October and not quite so crowded. I want to ride *everything.*"

He nodded, and I threw myself into conversation for the rest of the ride home. But that night, holding him as our sex was swamp cooled to our bodies, I thought about it again. *Where'd you come from, Sonny Daye? How do I keep you from ever going back?*

AFTER that, it took a couple of weeks to get our rhythm. We couldn't always take two days off, but we *always* took Monday off, and Jai was more than comfortable taking off Wednesday and Thursday.

And that was surprising—Jai stayed the whole time. He even stayed after I was back to full speed. After that happened, I asked him if his boss was still paying him, and he said, "Nyet."

"Well, what are *we* paying you?" I asked, horrified.

"Less than minimum wage," he said.

"Well, is your boss even making up the difference?"

"Nyet."

"Where are you staying?"

"Little house down the frontage road—there is a complex there."

Now my next question was tricky. "Uhm, I don't mind you helping, and I'm sorry the pay sucks. How long did you want to be here?"

His eyebrow rose in surprise. "Would like to keep staying. That is okay?"

"Yeah," I said, surprised. "Sure. I can't complain."

I couldn't. The guy came in early, stayed as long as we needed him, didn't mind when we brought sandwiches for lunch instead of going to Carl's Jr. *again*, and brought his fair share of ice for the ice chest and bottles of water. He continued to be civil to me and kind to Alba and helplessly, respectfully in love with Sonny.

I wasn't exactly thrilled with that last part, but I thought it did Sonny good. I had the feeling he hadn't had a lot of people in love with him. Jai's unrequited longing may not have been really good for Jai, but I thought maybe loving someone who wouldn't scorn him for it wasn't bad either.

And I thought it was good for Sonny to see there were options. I may have been the first person to love him, but I wasn't the only one who *could.*

"I'd like to keep you," I said, meaning it. "Movie night is getting to be a lot of fun!" The week before, Alba's mother had let Alba come. She'd brought tamales. I asked Alba if her mother minded her staying with three grown men, and Alba rolled her eyes.

"She saw you guys kissing that one day. She says I'm safer here than I am at school, and she lights a candle for you at every service."

She'd brought girl movies—*One for the Money* and *Mona Lisa Smile*—but that was okay. We sat through them patiently, and let her cry at the end of *Mona Lisa Smile*, and told her that she *could* go to Europe if she really wanted to. She hugged us when Jai left to give her a ride home, and Sonny looked at me a little funny.

"Was it like this?" he asked. "Your house? Did you watch movies with your family and eat dinner together?"

I squinted at him. After Jake died, I'd been so sure everything about home had been bad, I hadn't wanted to even think about it, not even when I was six thousand miles away.

"Yeah," I said, remembering Jake and Ronnie, before their first kiss even, when my mom used to bring us cookies to Jake's room, because we were all making racetracks with several Christmases of accumulated Hot Wheels sets. "Yeah. We had good times."

"Huh," Sonny said, pondering, and I think he chewed on that for a while too.

I think we both thought the other through, ground the other's goods and bads and scaries and strengths all down in the mill in our minds. It was a good time, and a time I loved, but here, looking at Jai saying he made minimum wage and he still wanted to stay, I realized we suddenly had more than me and Sonny to ponder.

"Sonny," I said that night, poring over our books and our receipts, "we've got to pay Jai and Alba more money."

"Yeah, I know," Sonny muttered glumly over a beer. He was sprawled on the futon, and I was sitting at the counter. "Alba said something about saving for school. I don't know how much that'll cost, but I think it's more'n we're paying now."

I blew out a breath. We had enough in the bank to keep us afloat for a while when we were getting our feet under us, but not enough to keep afloat a family of four.

"A couple of big races," I said, not wanting to bring this up but having no choice. "We do a couple of big races. We win. I won't have to race for a while, and maybe, we make a big enough name, we'll get some more commissions for racing cars, like you had. And we can pay Jai enough so he don't have to go back, 'cause we both know he don't want to."

Sonny took a gulp of beer and set the dead soldier on the table. "You get killed, Ace, I'm goin' out and blowin' the first ten guys I find. I'll curse your name every time they come."

He glared at me, his eyes narrowed, and I had no doubt. I fucked this up now? After showing him a taste of home and what it was like to belong somewhere? The man I loved would spit on my grave, and he'd make it stick.

A big black pit opened before me, and I wondered if Jake had lived with this pit from the moment he'd cut Ronnie for standing too close.

"You do it before I'm dead, I'll kill myself in front of you," I said, meaning it.

Sonny nodded. "I'll send some feelers out. We're not goin' through this for chickenshit, Ace. We're gonna fuckin' win big."

# HOLES BENEATH OUR FEET

OUR first race was Utah.

Longest, most boring drive ever—well, in the United States, anyhow. I know Iraq and Pakistan would have been just that boring if there hadn't been the threat of explosions or imminent death, so I guess it's all relative.

Without the threat of war to keep our adrenaline up, Sonny and I took turns driving, and both of us seriously thought about getting an installable backseat so maybe Jai or Alba could ride with us if we had to go any farther than that.

"Alba might talk the whole time," Sonny said glumly, and I glanced at him like he was crazy.

"She doesn't talk any now!"

"Yeah. I like that about her."

I laughed a little. "Jai would spend the whole time thinking about doing you. I might have to kill him."

Sonny looked at me sideways. "You'd kill him for that?"

I grimaced. "I'd kill someone for trying to hurt you," I said, thinking about Galway, "or for touchin' you when you didn't want it."

"But those guys at the shower you let live."

I looked sideways at him. "Not gonna let that go, are you?"

Sonny grunted. "Do I got a say here?"

"Absolutely. Why wouldn't you?"

"Then I say no one touches you either."

"I kind of figured that," I said, feeling a smile relax at my mouth. "I swear, Sonny, I wouldn't fuck around on you like that."

"Why is that funny?"

I shook my head. "Because it's like the last few months didn't happen for you. All those things I did to build us a home, a business, a relationship—that's not what you see. You see some surfer groping me."

Sonny let out a gruff breath. "You are the only thing in my life that's ever been mine," he said. I was surprised then by the warmth of his hand on my thigh. "Would like to keep you."

"Well, let's maybe see if we can do that without spilling any blood."

"Yeah. Fine. You wanna be picky about it, we can do it your way."

I don't think he was kidding, really. But then, I didn't fuck around *about* him any more than I'd fuck around *on* him. Make no mistake. Sonny is *very* serious business.


UTAH looked like Wile E. Coyote country—at least the part we saw, which was all sand and salt flats and basically the beach of the badlands, without any water.

Racing in that desert was a thrill, in spite of the heat, and I swear when I stepped on the gas, the skin on my face went flapping and making wahwahwah sounds around my lips like the guys in the cartoons, and we murdered every time in every heat.

We drove away with ten grand, free and clear—or so I thought.

I checked us into a nice hotel at three in the morning after we won—figured we could shower and get some sleep, and I paid for two days too, so we didn't have to take off until we were good and rested.

We were tired, hauling in our one duffel between us and grateful to get away from the smell of gas and exhaust and NOS and dust, and the grit sanding our faces and arms. I dropped the duffel, pulled out a clean pair of boxers, and got into the shower. Sonny was welcome to join me or not, but I *had* to get clean.

I'd been under the spray and had washed once when he pulled back the curtain and got into the tub with me. I started soaping him too—his neck, his shoulders, his back, between his shoulder blades. I soaped his thighs and his asscrack and between his thighs and his groin, and he stood there, letting me handle and hold every piece of him and make it clean.

I stood up and smiled a little, hoping for a reaction. "Aren't you happy, baby? We won?"

And that's when he started shaking. Shaking like a Chihuahua in a hurricane, and when I stood up and held him, rubbing his arms, whispering into his ear, nuzzling his neck, his jaw, it just seemed to make it worse. Finally, all I could do was wrap my arms around him and turn the water up to scalding, waiting there, like that, under the deluge of boiling water, trying to get the feeling back into his limbs.

Finally the water ran cold, and I pulled him out and toweled him down, then helped him step into his boxers. We fell into bed like we tripped on it while running, and Sonny tried to crawl into my skin for a few moments, burrowing there under the covers, before we finally fell asleep.

The next morning I got up and left a note saying I was going out for food. When I got back, he was still asleep, but his hands were out like he was seeking me while he slept.

I shook him awake after a moment. "Soda and egg burrito?" I asked while he was still blinking at me sleepily, and I was relieved when he nodded. I let him get halfway through his egg burrito before I said, "Wanna talk about it?"

He shook his head violently and kept plowing through that egg burrito like it was something assigned by the army.

"Sonny—"

"Nothin' to talk about," he mumbled. "Not until you're done for the winter. We've got three more races to go."

I nodded and then reached out and put my hand on his bare chest until he stopped chewing enough to notice I was touching. His entire body went a little limp, and his chewing slowed down.

"I will comfort you if you are scared, Sonny Daye. That is allowed."

"Yeah, what am I gonna do if you go away and can't comfort me anymore?" he asked, his voice breaking.

I took the egg burrito and set it down, and set the soda down beside it, and kissed him, suicide soda and all. Our bodies were clean and we'd slept, and we had all the time in the world to kiss and feel, to hold each other's cocks in our hands and squeeze and gasp and come.

THERE was no talk of fear after that, but that didn't mean it wasn't there, weighing us down with every race. I could forget about it when my foot hit the gas, and the next time we took her out, the next time we raced, I did.

But that next race was in Arizona, and I did the same thing I did in Utah. I stopped at a nice hotel, one that had covers that weren't made of nylon, and got us a king-size bed and a little spa tub.

This time, I half filled the spa tub with hot water and pulled Sonny in with me, then sat down with him between my spread legs and washed the grit and grime and fear off of us, until we were both so weak we could hardly climb out.

That was a good moment. I liked that one, and the things we did in bed the next day. But the next race was in the middle of September, and I could feel the fear backing up in Sonny's chest.

That fear was like a thunderstorm but worse, more like a hurricane, just waiting to break. It hung over our heads and made the air wet, even in the desert, stuck to our lungs and settled in our chests. And it drove me to do something I didn't think I'd ever do.

If the next race hadn't been in Bakersfield, I wouldn't have done it—wouldn't ever have occurred to me—but it was, so I did.

"Mom?" I said over the phone one day. Sonny was out, working on a Buick with Jai—who was thrilled to find someone else who appreciated an oil tanker on wheels like he did, apparently—and I'd told them I was going in to drop the kids off at the pool. (Not really. I said I was gonna go take a dump 'cause breakfast wasn't sittin' well, but normally, when Alba was there and listening, we tried not to be too crude.)

"Ace, honey! So glad to hear you!" Mom's voice was, well, it was middle-aged, plump, and tired. I don't know. Maybe it wasn't possible for a voice to have all those things—maybe it was just me thinking about Mom like I'd seen her last, busting out of her pants, forgetting to dye her roots, letting me and Angie get away with absolute murder because we were the youngest and she just didn't have the wherewithal to make us mind.

"Hey, Mom. I was, uhm. See, my friend and me—"

"The one you were starting that business with?"

"Yeah. Well, Sonny and me, we were gonna be in town in a couple of weeks. I was thinking maybe we could stop by Saturday afternoon for a bit, say hi."

"That would be real nice, honey! Your dad won't be there, though. He's working an extra shift at the plant—they're gonna make him retire soon. That money will come in handy."

He still had a job as a foreman at a food processing plant. That was actually real lucky—I didn't want him to lose that.

"Yeah, Mom. That's okay. I sorta wanted you to meet Sonny. And I kinda needed to talk to you."

I closed my eyes, not sure if I wanted to tell her now so she could tell us not to come, and Sonny wouldn't have to even know I'd called, or tell her when we got there.

"What's this about?" she asked, all those years of motherhood setting something pinging in her head like an alarm.

"Mom, you remember Jake and Ronnie?"

Her voice got flat. "He was my son, Jasper. I don't forget."

"Yeah. Well, what if they'd had a chance to be happy? Would you have let Ronnie come eat at our table then?"

Mom's voice dropped. "Probably not," she said, her voice husky and torn. "And your father, definitely not."

"No," I said, thinking of my father, the bitter bend in his back, the slit of his mouth that didn't seem to move, even when he was sucking on a smoke. "But you just said he wasn't gonna be there Saturday."

Mom's voice caught. "I... it would be a shame," she said, and the little boy she'd used to bring cookies to when he was playing Hot Wheels almost withered and died. Then she spoke into that quailing silence, her voice a little firmer. "I have one son who will never come home for dinner," she said, trying to pull a cloak of dignity around her naked voice. "It would be a shame if I had two when one of you is still alive."

I closed my eyes real tight. "No one needs to know but you, Mommy," I said, feeling silly and young. "No one needs to know. But he ain't never had family, I don't think. And I'm racing, and he worries, and—"

"You're racing?" Her voice went sharp, and I tried to shore myself up, because the whole blast furnace of family had not yet nailed me to the ground.

"Remember when Ronnie tried to make Jake's dreams come true, Mom? This is safer than knocking over gas stations, okay?"

"Jasper…." She sounded hurt, so hurt. "Ronnie died of an overdose last month. I'm sorry—we… we don't say his name much in this house."

I was standing at the counter by the kitchen, and suddenly I was sitting, clutching the wireless house phone to my ear. "Oh," I said, thinking of that little dark-haired, dark-eyed kid my brother had kissed so sweetly while holding his hand under Ronnie's chin.

"Well, I don't want to end up like that. And I don't want Sonny to neither." Funny, I sounded so normal when my vision was all wrapped up in black. "So, can we come home and eat at the table?"

"Yeah," she breathed out. "Don't… Juanita will be here with Dulcie and Molly—don't, you know—"

"No one'll know but you, Mommy," I said again, and I couldn't even hate myself for the crack in my voice. "I promise."

"We'll see you then, Ace," she said quietly, and then she hung up.

I stayed sitting on my living room floor, shaking, hugging my knees to my chest. I wanted Sonny suddenly, wanted to tell him all of this, but I couldn't. I'd do what he did, and wait until after the race, and let out all my scared on him then. We could let out our scared together.

The thought comforted me. I climbed to my feet and rested the phone back in the cradle, washed my hands and my face in the kitchen sink, and went out into the August heat to work on a car so old and broke down, it shoulda been shot instead of fixed.

"So THIS is our last one?" I said to Sonny as we got ready to leave for Bakersfield a few weeks later.

"Not quite. There's one more," he said, but he said it real jumpy like.

"One more?" I scowled at him, throwing our duffel in the car and waiting for him with the three big plastic jugs full of drinking water. He wouldn't let me carry those. It was like his last holdout way to baby me after the wreck.

His gaze jumped left in a way I hadn't seen since I'd asked him about his name that first time. "Barstow. It's a big pot. Too big." He shook himself all over like a small dog. "Too big to ignore, Ace. We gotta go." He wrinkled his brow and cemented the impression of a very worried terrier. "We gotta."

I shrugged. "No, we don't," I said, not liking the way he was talking. "You got a feeling about this, there's no reason to go out to Barstow."

He swallowed then and muttered, "No reason to cheat ourselves 'cause I'm afraid of ghosts. No reason. None."

I stopped there behind the car and stared at him. "Ghosts? You got *ghosts*?"

Sonny scowled. "Everyone's got ghosts!" he snapped, and I nodded.

"Yeah, yeah, they do. But you ain't never told me about your ghost, and forgive the fuck out of me for being interested!"

The scowl backed off for a minute and was replaced by sheer misery. "You think something of me," he said, so soft I almost couldn't hear him.

I lowered my mouth to his ear and said, "I think you're my everything." I pulled back far enough to see him close his eyes.

"I don't wanna give that up," he said. He swallowed then, resolved. "I'll just keep being your everything. You don't worry about my ghosts none—"

"But Sonny—"

"No!" He shook his head. "Now get in. If we're gonna stop and see these people for lunch, we gotta get a move on."

I sighed and got into the driver's seat, then waited for him to get in the passenger side. Then I started the car.

"Yeah. About these people...."

I finished that idea and waited for the explosion. Sonny ain't never disappointed me yet.

"Your *family*!" he screamed. "We're having lunch with your *family*?"

"My mom, my sisters Darlene and Angie, since Cathy couldn't make it, and my sister-in-law, Juanita. There's gonna be five kids—Juanita's two, Molly and Dulcie, and... well, fuck, I forget Darlene's and Angie's... Mom just kept writing me like I knew, but no one sent me a birth announcement, and I sort of lost track. There might be more. There might be seven. Anyway, there's gonna be people."

"Let me out of the car," Sonny said seriously, and it was my turn to glare.

"The fuck I will."

"I mean it, Jasper—"

"And *I* mean it, Sonny Daye. You worry yourself. You worry yourself into an ulcer every time I get on that road. You think if something happens to me, there won't be anyone else to belong to. You need someone who knew me. Juanita's been living with my folks since I left—she needs someone who loved Jake, and even though they don't talk about Ronnie, well, she needed someone and my folks came through. My dad, he might never know who we are to each other, but my mom, she knows. If I ask her to take care of you, she will. She will. And you won't be alone. You won't ever have to be alone and look at God knows who and say, 'I'll do anything', because I'm taking care of you, and I won't ever let that happen, you hear?"

"I don't want strangers!" he shouted. "They're nothin' but strangers to me now, and I ain't got no business sitting at no nice people's table!"

"They're not that nice!" I snapped, trying not to panic. An intractable Sonny wasn't no news, but he had to be on board with this or I wouldn't be racing tonight, or at Barstow, or ever again. I couldn't deal with his fear. It was starting to creep into my toes as I waited to start, and taking the lead off my foot as I tried to haul ass to that finish line.

I needed him to feel safe.

"The girls are bitchy and my dad's a right bastard. But they're family, and after today, they're gonna be your family too."

"What! You're gonna waltz on in there and say, 'This is Sonny, I fuck him up the ass every night! You feel free to do the same.'?"

I was going down the highway by this time, just starting to accelerate to around ninety, which was cruising speed for us until we hit civilized places where it was too dangerous, but at his words I veered right, onto the vast acres of desert shoulder, and slammed on the brakes.

The car swerved, skewed, and spun 360 before coming to a stop, and I stared at Sonny with absolute horror and absolute certainty in my eyes.

"Who...." I took three deep breaths. "Who did that to you?"

Sonny looked away, and so much time lapsed, I could feel the tickle of sweat dripping down my forehead, the small of my back, soaking my underwear. He spoke and his voice dropped, so low I almost couldn't hear him over the sound of the motor. "It doesn't matter. It's a long way away." He closed his eyes. "Every night I'm with you, when you're inside me, my mouth, my ass, my hand, it's like it never happened. I forget about it then, because I'm yours."

I reached over to touch him so he'd know he was always mine, but he shrugged me off. "Don't touch me when I'm thinking about it," he said sharply. "I'm dirty then."

My temper flared, sparked by the dejection in his shoulders, the way he wouldn't meet my eyes. "You're not dirty," I growled. My arms were longer, and I reached around and palmed the back of his head to make him look at me. "Say it."

"Ace—"

*"Say it!"*

"I'm not dirty," he mumbled, looking down at his hands.

"Now say you love me."

That startled him. He looked up, eyes big and shiny in the darkness of the broiling car. We took out the air conditioning before we raced, drove with the windows open. It was 120 in there. "Ace, I told you—"

"*Say it!*" I shouted, knowing I didn't look sane. "You love me, and it's just us. Just you and me. I love you, you love me, it's *just us.* That other shit, that never happened, and it can't touch you, you hear me?"

Bullshit. I know it. I know it's bullshit. Something like what he was talking about, that dripped down your brain for the rest of your life. It snuck up on you like Galway's face when I pulled the trigger. I saw his head explode in my dreams. I saw the blood that exploded inside Jake's truck when it was being towed away. Was that what Sonny saw in his dreams? The time? The *times* that this... this *thing,* this abomination, had happened to him. Oh Sonny. Oh God.

"That's a lie," he whispered, because Sonny wasn't stupid, but God. I made us a home where there wasn't nothing. I made us a business out of a bare building. I made us family out of just not being an asshole. Dammit, I could make him safe from this. I could.

"Just have some faith in me," I said, wanting to weep. "Have some fucking faith, Sonny. I love you. Ain't changing."

Sonny closed his eyes. "I love you too," he said. "That first day, I said, 'I'll do anything.' I woulda done anything then just to have you. You didn't make me do anything, you just gave yourself to me. I love you. Don't ever leave me."

"Never."

"Don't ever give me away."

"Never."

"You marked me."

"Forever, I swear."

"Say it again."

"I love you. Forever. I'll keep you safe, I swear."

He opened his eyes and stared right into mine. "I'll hold you to it, Ace. Don't let me down."

"I'll die first," I said. I meant it.

"Dyin' don't keep me safe," he growled, and I nodded.

"I hear you. Barstow. Our last one."

"Ever," he said unequivocally. "We'll have enough to last us in the garage for a year, to pay Alba and Jai like they deserve. If we can't keep it going, we can't. We give up, get jobs doin' something else in a shitty apartment somewhere else. You went to all this work to get me a dream, Ace, but you're the only dream I ever wanted. Our last race. Hear me?"

"I hear you," I said again, and I was starting to hear him for real now, hear him loud and clear.

MY PARENTS lived in a steady part of town, the kind of place where people would rather pay their mortgage than mow their lawn. There were some For Sale signs around, but not as many as the neighborhood one level worse and the ones two levels better. The grass was getting long, but there were still kids outside. A boy about twelve, playing something electronic, a girl about the same age ignoring him and playing with the others, four girls and two boys, and I tried to add them all up in my head and couldn't.

The older girl I recognized, though. She had my and Jake's dark eyes and red-black hair, and a face that was wide and flat at the sides and came down into a long jaw. I had to admit it looked better on me and Jake than on a girl, but she was playing really nice with the other kids, and looks weren't everything.

I pulled the big hornet-yellow SHO into the last space of the long driveway, the kind with two concrete tracks that went from the street to the garage and had weeds growing up between the concrete since the old man had forgotten to spray for what looked like years. The weeds were stained with oil, which meant he wasn't taking care of the cars either, and I sighed. You'd think Duane the Dentist would pop in and nag them a little, since he *lived in town*, but then, he'd probably been pretending this side of town never existed.

Honestly, this was the sort of thing I could see Jake doing as he aged. Jake would be in his thirties now—wouldn't he be doing that?

I got out of the car gratefully. It was a little cooler here in Bakersfield—at least on this street, because there were trees—but that smell of sweat wasn't ever going to leave us. I'd packed for this, though, and I reached into the car and grabbed two extra T-shirts I'd put in the back.

"Dulcie?" I called to the oldest girl, the one sitting at a little plastic table and pretending to drink tea with all the other little girls. She looked up without recognition.

"Yeah, darlin'—I'm sorry. I ain't seen you in forever. I'm your uncle Ace. Is there any way you could turn on the garden hose for me? It's right by—that's it. Thanks, sweetheart."

I stripped off my T-shirt, which was practically crispy with the dried sweat, and nodded to Sonny, who came around and did the same. Both of us stood, our dog tags dangling on our white chests, since the last of the tan we'd picked up at the ocean had faded. I picked up the end of the hose, which was right by me, and sluiced off my upper body, then used my T-shirt to wipe myself off. "Ready?" I said, and Sonny nodded, so I did the same to him.

When we were a little cleaner and sorta dry, I put the hose down and we pulled on our fatigue T-shirts, which were clean and almost pressed. We didn't like wearing them much, but I figured they'd make a good impression on the family, remind everybody where we'd met.

My family would care that we'd served, and I wasn't above reminding them.

Feeling a little cleaner, we draped our shirts over the car to dry and started in, mindful that we now had the kids' complete attention.

My mom was at the porch by now, and a few things hit me as we walked up.

She wasn't fat no more.

She wasn't *skinny*, but all that comfortable pudge around her waist and shoulders and neck—that was gone, and not like she'd tried. It was like stress had worn her thin.

She also wasn't middle-aged, not really.

She was old.

I tried to do the math. She'd had Jake when she was twenty-three—she hadn't gone to college, but Dad used to say she was plain and no one wanted her until he saw her. Yeah, I know. Nice. But he used to look at her soft when he said it. I wondered if he still did.

If Jake woulda been thirty-three, that put her in her midfifties, and... well, she wasn't one of those society women or women on the TV. She was a plain woman who worked in a gas station and had six kids and... well, a lot of grandkids. I was done counting, 'cause Cathy and Duane the Dentist had some too, but they weren't here. Her hair had been blonde, but it was now gray blonde, and wispy from her ponytail. She was wearing red stretchy shorts and a man's red T-shirt—and a tentative smile.

"Heya, Ace," she said, coming down to kiss my cheek. "You boys made it. I didn't know if you would."

I shrugged. "I promised, Mom. You can usually trust that."

"Always," Sonny said quietly next to me. "You can always trust Ace's promise. Pleasetameetya, Mrs. Atchison. I'm Sonny—"

Mom nodded and smiled, and no matter what she may have been thinking, her smile was just as sweet as the one she'd given me. Sonny had extended his hand, and she took a few steps—they were almost eye level—and kissed him on the cheek.

"I know who you are, Sonny," she said quietly. "It's real nice to meet you. I understand you and Jasper served together?"

"Yes'm. Ace here was in charge of new recruits, and I was as green as they got. He kept me alive, that's for sure."

I grimaced. Yeah. I didn't want to tell my mother I'd gotten away with cold-blooded murder. That was not the way to get approval for your mate.

"I was your staff sergeant," I said. "That was my job."

Mom laughed politely and ushered us into the house. There were about five standing floor fans positioned around the kitchen to keep a nice cross draft through the cool of the back of the house to the front, and Mom sat us down by one. Sonny and I took a few minutes to luxuriate in the cool of the fans and appreciate the hell out of the sweet tea Mom served us before we managed to focus on the conversation.

"So Dulcie is in middle school, and isn't that a rough age—"

"She seemed okay," I said, thinking of the girl with Jake's cheekbones and eyes, helping the little kids.

"Yeah, but kids are giving her crap about her dad and Ronnie, and the whole town knows, and every other word out of her mouth is LTQBG or something like that—I can't make heads or tails out of it, but it's driving her mother batshit. Every time Dulcie talks about it, Juanita goes screaming in Mexican into her room about going to hell and faggots—"

Mom stopped and looked at us with big eyes, and I grimaced.

"It's a word, Mom. Not a great one, but it's a word."

"Well, I was thinking it would be nice if you two could talk to her and maybe talk her out of that—"

"Talk her out of what?"

"You know. That QTLGB thing."

God. I'd been stressing about being me for so long, I'd forgotten there was a name for it besides the one I didn't like.

"It's LGBTQ," I said. "I think. And why would I want to talk her out of it?"

"Jasper, you know how people talk—"

"I do," I said, knowing in my gut what they'd been saying about Jake and Ronnie before Juanita had come up pregnant. "I do know. And it sucks. And they'll be saying it if she's for it or against it. If she's got a group or some people at school or a teacher or a—"

"GSA," Sonny said, shocking the hell out of me. "Alba said it's called a GSA."

"You talk to Alba?"

Sonny looked uncomfortable. "She gave me a pamphlet. It was weird. I had to ask her to help me read it, but it said something about… I don't know. Not being bullied. Whatever. It said something about people not screaming every time someone mentioned they were gay. And a day of silence and some other shit I didn't get, but, you know, I'm all for kids not getting the shit kicked out of 'em. There's plenty of other reasons kids get beat up, we don't need one more goddamned reason, right?"

"You brought her something," I said flatly. "What did you bring her to make her think you were nice?"

He fidgeted with his iced tea glass, tracing the outside of the glass with a design that made me smack his hand.

He looked at me and smirked and then looked at my mom in panic, and then wiped the glass.

"A chocolate ice cream bar," he said after an embarrassed moment. "A box of them. I brought them over with the ice chest and put them in our freezer, so they were hella cold all day long."

I laughed softly. "Did you share with Jai?"

His gaze darted sideways. "Yeah. It was when you went to town the other day. You were coming back with ice cream, but, well—" He looked apologetic, but I laughed some more.

"Well, that was real nice. And it would be good if you weren't always a dick to her. Keeps her off-balance. Anyway, what she said about that thing at school, is that what Dulcie's into, Mom?" I asked, and my mom shrugged.

"Yeah, whatever. But really, Jasper, in this family, does it really need to be brought up? It's salt in Juanita's wound every time she says it…."

Which is, of course, why she was doing it.

"Does anyone ever talk about Jake to her?" I asked. "Not... not him and Ronnie. But, you know, just... just him."

Mom stopped suddenly, still like a tree. "No," she said, her voice a wet humid blanket over us in the cooling kitchen. "It... your father doesn't let us mention his name."

I scowled. "Well, great, Mom. That's awesome. Has anyone ever thought that maybe she just wants to hear her father's name?"

Mom shook her head, midway between the oven and the stove. "No," she said again. "I can't, Jasper. I... God. Everything I'm so afraid to think."

I looked at Sonny miserably, and he shrugged.

"I'm gonna go change your mom's oil," he announced. "Mrs. Ace, do you got any extra oil? Them weeds was looking awfully goddamned black—someone's gotta fix that car."

It was so exactly what I was thinking that an imitation smile twitched at my lips. "Subtle, Sonny. Real fuckin' subtle—"

"Jasper!"

I ignored her, just like I had in high school. "Look, go take the car and get some forty weight and a new filter. You saw the town when we came in?"

He nodded. "I can figure my way around."

"Good. Good. You do that, and I'll let my mom finish up dinner here. How long, Mom?"

She looked around at the kitchen. "Well, if you're not here, I can call Juanita to help—"

"Why can't she help if I'm here?" I asked, and Mom shrugged.

"You're... you're his spitting image, Jasper. You look just like him, except your eyes."

"My eyes?"

"Yeah." She sighed. "Your eyes... they're narrower. They're... hard."

Yeah, well. "Two tours, Mom. Wasn't the YMCA. Anyway, I'll go out and talk to Dulcie. You and Juanita do whatever you gotta do. If the old man is coming home, you'd better warn me, because I'm about at my limit now to deal."

I downed the rest of my iced tea and, just for my own satisfaction, put my hand in the small of Sonny's back. I didn't care if my mom saw or not—it needed to be there. His skin was slightly damp under my touch, because there was just no escaping the heat, but he relaxed against my palm. I sighed and brushed my lips against his temple.

"Don't be long," I said quietly. "We're blowing as soon as dishes are done. I want to check into a hotel before the race."

The hope on his face was pathetic, and a part of me hated myself for dragging him here. He nodded, took the keys from my hand, and went trotting off, eager to get the hell out of there.

I watched him, wondering for the umpteenth time if I was doing the right thing, and then caught my mom looking at me.

"What?" I asked, jutting my chin out like I'd taught Sonny to do when he didn't want any bullshit.

"He's sweet," she said after a moment, her gaze jumping around the kitchen like a little poison frog. "He is. You two… you're making a life together?"

I looked at her cautiously. "Yeah," I said.

"Do you think… was it Jake that made you that way?" she asked, and I had to fight not to get pissed and say something unforgivable.

"Don't you read? God made us this way. All you have to do is love us."

Mom flinched back. "I loved you kids—I loved you all—"

"Well, then, you ain't done nothin' wrong," I said, but I didn't feel that, not in my heart.

"Jake never said he… you know, he never told *me*…."

"What would you have done if he had?" I asked, dying to know.

She busied herself pressing garlic into the mashed potatoes. The smell… God, I missed her cooking. Sonny was getting better, but something about Mom's cooking, in the kitchen I ate dinner in as a kid—it was a powerful thing.

"I mean—how was I to know it wasn't just a phase?"

My hands gripped the back of the wooden chair so hard my knuckles were white. "I killed a man for him," I said, surprising her, and surprising myself badly. "He was a bad man, and he wanted to beat Sonny into the ground, but I shot him. In the head. I shot him in the head. And we got away with it. Got away with murder, because he was a bad man, and no one wanted to face that he was a bad man. Me and Sonny. We took care of the army's little fuckin' problem for them, and it was all good."

"Jasper?"

I looked up from my white knuckles. "I killed a man to keep him safe. Jake killed himself out of grief. Which part of this is just a phase?"

Her half sob made me want to comfort her, but I couldn't. I couldn't comfort myself.

"Don't answer that," I said. "I'm gonna go outside and tell Jake's daughter how to lie to her mother so she don't get kicked out of the house until she's good and ready. I got things to do."

DULCIE was telling one of Darlene's kids a joke. (Darlene's husband was Mexican—one of Juanita's distant cousins, I think. It was scary how much alike Dulcie looked to her little boy cousin. The five-year-old girl who looked just like them both must have been her younger sister, Molly, and they could have been from the same egg.)

"So, why did the elephant paint his seat yellow?" she asked, and the little boy shook his head.

"I don' know!"

"So he could blend in with the custard!"

"What's custard?"

"I don't know—I think it looks like mustard, but it's sweet."

"I ain't never seen an elephant in sweet mustard," the boy said, and Dulcie started cackling with glee.

"Exactly! That's how you know it works!"

I chuckled as I walked up. That was a good one.

Dulcie looked up at me with smart eyes. "Hey—you're our uncle Jasper, aren't you?"

Her hair was curly, like mine, and pulled back in a wild ponytail. "Yeah," I said, wondering what I was doing here.

"Who was that you came with?"

"My partner, Sonny. He went to go fix your grandma's car."

"Yeah, he ran away from us. I don't think he likes kids none."

"He's afraid of you," I said seriously. "He's afraid he's gonna screw up around you." It was how he was with Alba, had been with the girl in Iraq. I didn't see no reason for that to change.

"How's he figure?" she asked curiously.

I thought about it when I hated thinking about it. "I think everyone looking after him when he was a kid let him down," I said, and she looked sideways.

"Yeah. I know the feeling."

I stood up and wandered to the far edge of the shade, looking at her to make sure she followed me.

She did.

"Your daddy let you down," I said, and she bristled. I loved her for that.

"He did not!" she snapped, and I looked at her, just looked at her, and saw Jake as he should have been there.

"He did," I said quietly. "He could have left your mom—he still would have taken care of her. I mean... he was trying to take care of his business, and it crushed him, because—"

"Because nobody in this town would accept him!" she said staunchly, and I nodded but kept looking at her.

"I would have," I said softly. "I worshipped him. Do you think I wouldn't have still loved my big brother, even if he fucked up?"

Dulcie swallowed suddenly. "But you—you're...." She scowled at the SHO as it bwap-bwapped down the street.

Sonny parked again and got out, four quarts of forty weight and an oil filter dangling in the bag in his hand. He nodded at us and then walked with purpose down to the garage next to the house. It didn't have a padlock on it or anything, and my dad's tools should be right there and easy to spot, like they had been when I was a kid, so I let him be. He had his happy place—I wasn't going to take it from him.

"Yeah," I said softly, wishing I could join him in that happy place. Wishing I was anywhere but here, talking to my dead brother's daughter. "I am. We are. Just like Jake." I looked at her, and the almond shape of her eyes made me ache. "Don't you think I could have used your dad when I was growing up? Don't you think I would have liked him to know? Don't you think I'm mad at him too?"

"What's your point?" she asked, but her voice was cracking, and I wished I knew her better so I could hold her.

"You keep on being active," I said. "You stay in the GSA, and you keep fighting for rights, because the world needs you. But... I know your mom, she's got to be plenty bitter, and your grandma and grandpa, they're pretending it was an accident on those tracks and that none of the people in this house had nothing to do with it—"

"But why can't they just see—"

"Because they can't," I said quietly. "They can't. But they're feeding you. They're buying you clothes. They're checking your grades. They give a shit how you live your life." I looked at Sonny, thought of all the things he'd said and hadn't said. "Dulcie, you need to believe me when I tell you there are worse people than those who won't see. You're already older than they are, you already know more. You don't need to rub it in, honey. The things you know, the things you feel, they ain't gonna change. But your mom, your grandfolks, they're only going to be able to take care of you for so long, and be able to love you like their little girl before you go on and leave them. Sweetheart, don't make that time bitter. I know you're twelve, but you'll regret it."

She took a deep breath and wiped her eyes with the back of her hand. There wasn't any makeup there yet, and I was glad. "They won't even talk about him," she said miserably.

"That's a shame," I said, looking from our spot on the lawn to the shade under the trees that lined the walkway. There weren't any fences between these houses, none at all. "He was a good guy. He… he loved boy things. Poker, knives, cars."

I glanced at her and saw that she was looking at me like I hung the moon.

Well, I might as well hang the sun and the stars too.

"Did you know he gave me my nickname?" I said, and she shook her head, her gaze so avid it made my stomach hurt.

So I told her the story. I told her about us playing Hot Wheels. I told her about him letting me steer the car when I was six and he was sixteen. I told her about how he'd blushed when we'd given him crap about her mother.

"But wasn't he—"

God, even his daughter couldn't say it.

"Honey, she was a pretty girl, and she was nice to him. Being gay, that doesn't change that he liked her, that she was his friend."

She nodded and hiccupped, and I threw an arm around her shoulder. My mom called the kids in, and I kept talking until Mom called us one more time.

Before we walked into the house, she gave me a quick hug and a kiss on the cheek. She said, "Thank you, Uncle Jasper," and I nodded her in and went to fetch Sonny.

He'd finished changing the oil about ten minutes before, and had even washed up. He just didn't want to go inside my mom's house and face the women, and I didn't blame him.

He peered at me closely as I walked up to get him. "That looked like it hurt," he said clinically, and I shrugged.

"Yeah, well, I'm stronger than I look."

His gaze roamed the shade behind my shoulders as he chewed on that. "I'm not," he said after a moment. "I'm glad I didn't have to do it."

I looked into his big gray eyes and smiled a little. I wanted to kiss him again. God, I wanted to kiss him always.

"Lucky me," I said drily. I grabbed his hand for a moment and then let it go, and we turned and walked up the porch to face a full-course meal on a hot September afternoon.

DARLENE was still a superficial bitch, obsessed with her looks. She bragged about her children constantly—told me how smart her youngest boy was. I didn't have the heart to tell her I'd seen that custard thing coming a mile away and he missed it, because, hey, that's mean, and I certainly didn't tell her I hadn't seen her oldest do more than look at his computer. They were kids. They were dressed nice, they used forks and spoons, and they seemed to have a better sense of family than I had at that age, because they were nice to their grandma and offered to help set the table.

I nodded and smiled and told her no, I didn't think she'd need work done, and pretended Sonny wasn't clutching my knee under the table.

Angie was closer to my age, and her children were the two little girls and the boy who'd been sitting with Molly when Dulcie had been playing mama hen. Angie had Mom's looks—oval face, bluish eyes, reddish hair. Angie played them up a little, but in a soft way— understated makeup, a nice fitted T-shirt and shorts instead of a full-tilt makeup job and sundress like Darlene. I heard her talking about swim class, so I think the streaks in her hair were from sun, and she let it curl a little, unlike Darlene, who must have spent more time straightening her hair in a day than I spent slicking mine back in a month.

"He spends all his time on that thing," Darlene said indulgently, looking at her son—Austin? Dallas? Houston? Fuck, somewhere in Texas, that kid had a name!—as he shoveled my mother's cooking in his mouth with one hand while playing his iPod with another. "We only let him download the educational apps, and his teacher says his math scores have gone through the roof!"

Sonny was sitting at attention at the table, eating with one hand, keeping the other on my leg. He looked at the kid, looked at his plate, and then gave it up and stared at him again.

"His math scores may be up, but his manners suck," Sonny said to me, and unfortunately, the entire table had gone quiet at that time.

I grimaced, but I had to agree with him. I nodded, and Darlene said, sort of shocked like, "I beg your pardon?"

Sonny looked at her in my mom's overwarm kitchen, and his face was flushed from more than heat. He swallowed—I don't think anything in his makeup prepared him to deal with my sister—and then looked at my mom. "This is real good chow here," he said deferentially. "I keep working to cook like this, but I can't. I think it's a shame that kid don't know what he's missing. He doesn't know what he's got. That's a shame."

My mom jerked her head back, and I realized he was right. "Real good food, Mom," I said belatedly. "Thank you. Sonny does all right, though—he keeps looking up new stuff on—what was that place?"

"Pinterest," Sonny said, nodding. "It's got good hamburger recipes."

"Yeah. Your cooking's getting better, but"—I smiled at my mom winningly—"he's right. I sure did take your cooking for granted. I'm sorry."

My mom's mouth was open, because I guess no one had said this to her, and Darlene was glaring at me like it was all my fault for being the smartest/prettiest/nicest one for once, and Angie tilted her head.

"Damn, Ace, you really *did* grow up," she said, sounding pleased.

I shrugged. "Sonny keeps me straight. There's some shit—erm, stuff—you shouldn't assume everyone else has."

Sonny made an uncomfortable sound next to me, and I twisted my mouth. Well, I was keeping it vague and that was the best I could do.

And then I looked up and saw that Darlene's kid hadn't put down his damned game.

"Hey!" I snapped. "Hey—Austen-Houston-Dallas, whatever your name is!"

The kid looked up blankly. "Dayton," he said, affronted. "My name is Dayton."

I looked at Darlene incredulously. "Really?" I was off by an entire state. But, well, Texas had a Dayton too. And, besides—"You could always name him Burkettville and just solve *that* mystery completely."

Her look was as blank as her kid's, and I shook my head and turned back to him.

"Dayton, could you put the damned game away? You are sitting with family, and they give a damn about you, and you are old enough to be a human being at the table, and old enough to *learn* that not everybody on the planet has the luxury of a family. So put the game away and show your grandmother some respect."

I expected somebody to chew me out. My last sit-down at this table, I had been the youngest, and the most inclined to shoot off my mouth. Of course, Dayton had been maybe three years old then, and Darlene and her husband had been living in Arizona, and I hadn't even had a chance to see the kid. But now? Now he needed to put the damned game away, and not a soul told me I was wrong to say otherwise.

Not even the kid, who turned the game off and put it in his pocket, regarding the rest of us with huge eyes.

"I'm sorry, Grandma," he said quietly. "I didn't know I was being rude."

My mom reached across the table and patted his hand. "It's okay, sweetie. I think Jasper and Sonny just reminded us of how important it is to remember family is a blessing, that's all."

Dayton looked at me uncertainly. "I thought your name was Ace," he said, and the tension that had suddenly set down eased up.

"You can call me either," I told him easily. "Ace was my name in the army. I answer to both."

Darlene was all huffed up for the rest of the meal, but Angie talked, and that was nice. She told us about her *imperfect* children, and about how no cat was safe from her infant daughter, and how her son liked to take off his clothes in any situation.

"Okay," she said, nodding seriously. "So, right after I got back from work, I start dinner, sit down to feed Darcy, and Ian's in the backyard, right?"

Sonny and I nodded, because she'd been nice to us so far and we could deal with a kid story if it was funny.

"Anyway, so there I am, feeding Darce, and she's eating like a champion, and about the time I realize I haven't heard Ian for a minute, there's a knock on the door."

"Oh no," Sonny said, completely lost in the story.

Angie nodded at him. "Oh yes. So I open the door, and there's not one, not two, but *three* neighborhood mothers, with my firstborn. One of them is holding his tricycle."

Sonny and I were snickering, and then she added the cherry on top.

"He is *naked.*"

And that did it: we broke up completely, laughing so hard that we almost lost the last of the story.

"And the lead woman, the one with the trike, goes, 'Now, the first time we saw him go around the block, we thought we'd see a mom coming after him. Around the third time, we thought he might have escaped from somewhere.'"

By this time I was laughing almost too hard to breathe, and so was Sonny.

"There goes *your* Mother of the Year, Angie!" Darlene said spitefully, and my mother stepped in to keep the peace, because I think that came with the job.

"No, no—actually that same thing happened once with you and Jake, Darlene. I'd just sat down to feed you, and dinner was on the stove, and then I get this knock, and there's the next-door neighbor— apparently your brother was running naked through her sprinkler in the front yard."

"See?" Darlene's voice was unbearably smug. "Even then, there were signs."

"Signs of what?"

Jake's wife used to be pretty. She had black hair and almond-shaped eyes, a heart-shaped face, and a tiny tip-tilted nose. I'd never wondered why Jake had turned to her when Ronnie had told him no— she'd laughed a lot, she'd been smart, and she'd honestly loved my brother.

You couldn't tell any of that now.

She looked forty at thirty-three. She'd put on weight, and her face was round and doughy, her little point of a chin obscured by the perpetual frown that lined her mouth and the brackets by her nose.

But it was more than that, because Angie wasn't a size six anymore either. The frown that etched into her mouth and the lines at her eyes also made her brown eyes small and flat and added a divot to her forehead.

"Signs of what?" Juanita asked, and I'd heard snakes hiss with less venom.

"Nothing," Darlene said uncomfortably, and I found myself meeting eyes with Jake's daughter.

It was time someone stood up for her daddy.

"He sure did like to make an entrance," I said mildly. "That sounds just like him."

"Oh my God!" Angie said, keeping her voice as light as mine. "Remember his first car?"

I grinned. "How could you forget a Camaro? That thing got as much attention as any nekkid boy you ever seen."

"A Camaro?" Sonny asked avidly, and I nodded.

"Oh yeah. A Camaro—you shoulda seen it, Sonny. It was bright electric blue—like Cadillac blue, but he added just a hint of purple to it—"

"Did his own pinstriping?" Sonny's voice was reverent. He'd painted the Taurus, but that was all one color. He'd always looked wistfully at the cars with trick paint jobs, but knew himself well enough not to try.

"Yeah!" Angie said at my shoulder, looking at Dulcie just like I had. "I forgot about that. He used to do that to his bikes as well. Remember that, Darlene? All his friends used to come over with stolen spray bombs to have Jakey paint their bikes?"

Darlene nodded, a small smile on her face, and I loved her for that, because it meant she remembered our brother as a little kid, and not as a fuckup or a faggot or any of the other things she'd been thinking about when she'd been a bitch.

And the conversation went okay after that. We told kid stories from when we were kids, and even Juanita told stories about her own children, and for a moment, family really was a blessing.

Sonny and I offered to do the dishes, and we were just finishing up when Sonny said, "Ace, if we're gonna find a hotel before we go…."

He looked at the clock, and that's when I realized—"Oh shit! Is it five o'clock already?"

I hurried up drying the last pot and put it on the wiped-down stove top, and then ran and dried my hands.

"Ace," Mom said, her voice gentle, "you were going to have to see him sometime."

I swallowed. "Yeah, but I told myself you'd be enough. It's been a good day. Dulcie, she was real nice to her mom there at the end"—because she had been, as we'd told Jake stories—"and Sonny got to see something nice. I don't wanna—fuck."

Mom didn't even call me on my language. I bent down and kissed her cheek and called out a bye to everyone in the living room. Sonny paused to say good-bye to Mom and then was at my heels as I trotted out the front door as quick as I could, but it was too late.

I'd seen my dad's old Chevy round the corner through the kitchen window before I left, and there it was, parking in front of the house as my dad got out and stared at our car like it was sprayed with the symbols of Satan and the Antichrist in rainbow-colored paint.

Well, he didn't know, did he? I reminded myself of that.

"Sonny, could you pull us out so Dad can park in the driveway?"

Sonny nodded and hopped in, and I walked up to Jacob Atchison the first.

"Heya," I said, smiling greenly, and Dad glared at Sonny.

"Who in the hell is that?"

My father was shorter than I was. I was not six feet, but he was about two inches shorter than I was. This was something I'd known, but it felt like a bigger gap now. Maybe it was all that standing at attention at the army, but that two inches was suddenly a lot more than that. He'd aged sort of like Jake's wife, but worse. His face was lean, with wide cheekbones, like me and Jake, and those cheekbones stood out like he'd been starving, and his cheeks curved in. I wondered if all those grandkids in that house were as afraid of him as I'd been.

"That's Sonny. He's my partner—we go racing, he outfits the cars." I am a coward. I never realized how much of one until I qualified the last part. "We run a garage together."

Dad grunted. "You couldn't visit before now?" he asked, and I grimaced.

"I was setting up for Sonny and me," I said, and it was true. "Mom and I talked."

"So that kid's more important than your own family?" he asked, glaring, and suddenly I wasn't a coward anymore.

"He's my family, same as you," I said. I didn't have to live with this man anymore. My mother had sat down with me and Sonny at the table, and my mother had pressed a kiss to Sonny's cheek as we'd left. I'd seen.

Dad grunted. "You be respectful to your family," he said obliquely, and I sighed.

"Dad, you be respectful to Sonny, I'll show you all the respect you can ask for. I'd like to come back. Jake's daughter, she needs some raising. My sisters aren't entirely annoying. I'd love to see Cathy at the holidays, and even Duane and his family. You tell me I can bring my family to stay with your family, I'll respect the hell out of you."

Dad looked away. "It's more'n your brother ever gave me," he said. Then he turned and startled the hell out of me.

He hugged me.

"I'm glad you got back safe," he said, his voice gruff. "I'd be happy to see you again."

I swallowed. "See you at Thanksgiving," I said. "Sonny'll try and make something. He's pretty good."

My dad's mouth worked, and I saw that his hair wasn't the same color as mine and Jake's anymore. "Well, bring him," he said, his voice quavery. "He serve with you? I saw the tags."

I nodded.

"Tell him thanks for the service. Thank you too."

I nodded again, and Sonny waved. "We gotta go," I said, because we did if we were going to get that hotel before the race. I reached out my hand and he shook it, and then I swung into the car and pretended like I didn't want to fall apart.

# PRIDE IN OWNERSHIP

SONNY didn't say much on the way to the hotel.

We got there, checked in, and took a quick shower. We rinsed out our grimy T-shirts and shorts so we could wear them home, and hung them from the shower cubicle, and I know it was low-class, but we just liked the sheets, we weren't trying to match the hotel.

Sonny took his shower first, and when I got out of mine, he was sitting on the bed, a towel wrapped around his waist, staring into space.

"What?" I asked, because he was chewing on something.

"I…." He grimaced and then stood up. I was just wearing a towel too, and my skin was damp and pink. He walked to me and, to my surprise, feathered a touch—something delicate and crystalline but warm—from my stomach to my nipples, jingling my tags as he went.

"We got three hours before we gotta leave," he said, and although I didn't feel like laughing, I waggled my eyebrows, just to make him smile.

"We could do a lot of damage, then," I said, and he shook his head.

"No, that's not what I mean. I mean yes, I wanna do that, because, seriously, Ace, I could bend over for you on Main Street during a hurricane, but that's not what I'm talking about."

I grabbed his hand because it was starting to tickle. "What *are* you talking about?"

He looked up into my eyes, cupped my cheek with one hand, rose, and pressed a gentle kiss on my mouth.

"That was real nice, meeting your family," he said. And then he swallowed. "But it was hard on you too."

I leaned my face into his hand. "I can't argue."

"You need me," he said, and I nodded and closed my eyes, drinking in his touch on my skin.

"I do," I admitted, and the syllables hurt.

He kissed me again, this time opening my mouth. I let him, groaning, drinking his kiss like I absorbed his touch, thirsty for him.

"Let me give you something," he whispered, and he kissed me some more, and some more, and some more.

He took over then, kissing me, gentling me, pushing me to the bed. He didn't fuck me but he took charge, laying me flat on my back and kissing from my hips up to my neck. When he pulled out the lube, he greased me up and then sat down slowly on my cock, closing his eyes and letting out little happy noises as I filled him more and more.

He moved, and when I grabbed his cock and stroked him, he grabbed my wrist and helped. He came across my chest, and we didn't wash that off before the race—I'd wear his smell on my skin for luck. I came deep inside him, and he collapsed on top of me, kissing my chin, my cheeks, my neck. Finally our mouths met again, and I groaned as the quietness of our sex faded. The blood rushed in my ears at the thought of holding him, for this moment, for our lifetimes, forever, and the sound was loud and pounding and terrifying, like a helicopter landing to take us both away. I could hear the beating of the rotor blades in my head as they pounded my dreams of him with a nameless fear.

THE noises at a race are deafening. Everyone's revving their engine, slapping their big metal dicks around so we can see how fast they're going to be.

Of course, it also warms the engine up so it's all loose and sloppy and tight when it needs to be, which is sort of sexual too, so I guess it's a fuck-fest all the way around.

Sonny was sitting next to me, and we were in a big whack of cars, all waiting for our turn. Sonny was, of course, telling me not to get cocky, because he knew what all of the cars around us were capable of doing if they had a Sonny under the hood.

I was quick to point out that they didn't.

"Now see that Mercedes?" he said, clinical like, at the silver-and-chrome monster that glided instead of rode. "That thing's got some potential. It's streamlined, see? And the motor, that's something else. You modify that a little, bore out the pistons a few milliliters, give 'er racing cams an' NOS delivery—"

"She don't got no dirt on her, Sonny. See? That car don't even go on practice races. She's too clean. Driver's all for show. All about having the pretty car—probably races to get laid."

"He coulda washed it—"

"There's not even any dings or shit—nah, that car'll place and do good in the heats but won't win. Not practical. You'll see."

"That truck's got dings," he said, pointing to an electric-blue modified Chevy. "And the engine, possibly a V-12, that'd be a problem!"

"Not on a quarter," I said. "Maybe on a half. Bed's too light, all fiberglass, he tries to blow that thing out with no momentum, he'll be skewing all over the fuckin' place. We go to a half-mile track I'll worry, but I can still outdrive him—them things got no suspension."

And so on. It was important, but not 'cause of the cars. It settled us, got us thinking about things scientific like, so he wasn't scared for me, and I wasn't scared for him. It was a real good pattern, and I thought I was gonna miss him as I looked around for someplace to drop him off before I lined up at the starting line.

"There ain't no good place," I muttered. "Think you can hold on for the ride?"

"Yeah," he said. "I'd rather be here anyway."

I risked a look at him and winked. "But how you gonna hook up with the money man?" I asked, and Sonny shrugged.

"Maybe you pay if you lose?"

At that moment there was a banging at my window from someone who had braved the jostling herd of metal cattle, and I stepped on the brake and rolled the window down. "You need our stake?" I asked, and the guy nodded.

He was in his late thirties, his hair cut short, his face stubbled. He smelled a little greasy but not too bad—probably like me and Sonny, working with cars all the time—and he wore a grease-stained red T-shirt and jeans. There was a girl behind him, underage, with dark hair and a thousand-yard stare. Her blue eyes were as dead as a fish.

"Two grand stake," he said, and I held my hand out 'cause Sonny had the money, but nothing slapped into my palm.

I turned and looked at Sonny, and my heart stalled out. He was backed into the corner of the seat and the door, and I've never seen a live human with a face that white. He was shaking like he was dying of cold, and I could hear the faint chattering of his teeth.

Gently, I took the money from his hand and looked at the guy with half his body in the car.

He was smiling like he'd just spotted an old girlfriend in a crowd—the easy old girlfriend with the hot friends who liked slumber parties.

"Martin?" he said. "Martin Richards?"

"No," Sonny said, although I don't think it was to the guy's question.

"No," I said more strongly. "That's not his name, and you're scaring him."

"Not his name?" the guy said, turning to me. He had squinty eyes and a mouth like my old man's—two lean lines instead of lips. His nose had been broke at least twice, and there was a scar on his forehead underneath the grime.

"His name is Sonny," I said, my voice hard. "Ain't no cause to go calling him any other name, 'cause that's not who he is."

I knew. I knew. This was the big bad, or part of the big bad, that Sonny would not talk about.

"Bullshit." The guy turned his head and spat, and I watched tobacco sizzle on my hood. "You think I'd know my own goddamned property!"

His hands were draped over my window ledge. I grabbed his forefinger and bent it back sharply, dislocating it in one pop. The guy screamed and fell to his knees right in the middle of all those jockeying cars. Then I took the two-grand stake and shoved it in his other hand, the one still clutching my door.

"His name is Sonny," I growled into his face. "And he ain't my property, but he's mine."

"I'll fuckin' get you for this!" he screamed. "That's my property you got! His mother took two bricks of meth for him, and you fuckin' owe me!"

I might have killed him then, but the car in front of me moved and Sonny made a sound I couldn't even classify, and I just followed the crowd like the rest of the steel cattle.

"Ace," he muttered as we took our place behind the cars about to go. "I gotta throw up."

I reached over, grabbed his clammy hand, and squeezed it. The girl in front of the cars dropped her flag, the cars disappeared. Everybody watched them go, and we took the place of the racing-green Acura in front of us.

"Can you hold it one minute?" I asked. "We gotta win this here race right the fuck now."

He swallowed hard, still shaking, and I reached behind me and handed him his helmet. Mine was on, and my hair was sopping with sweat underneath it—but not, I don't think, because the helmet was hot.

"You'd better make it ten seconds," he said, his voice on edge.

The girl raised her hands, and I said, "I can do it in three."

It was like we snipped those three seconds out of time. One second my foot was on the gas. The next second I'd skidded to a halt at a lonely stretch of road beyond the race, and Sonny was on his knees in front of the car, retching.

I tore off the helmet, shut down the car, grabbed a bottle of water, and fell on my knees beside him. The ragged stickers under our knees jagged their way through our jeans, but I didn't give a rat's ass.

"I'm sorry," he muttered, and I ripped the bottom of my T-shirt off to wipe his mouth.

"You got nothin' to be sorry about," I said, and he shook his head, wiping his eyes on his shoulders.

"I'm sorry. I'm sorry, Ace. I should never have followed you to San Diego. You promised something, and I wanted it so bad, and I shouldna gone. I shoulda stayed in the army 'til I didn't come back, I shouldna—"

"You don't belong to him," I said, my voice coming apart like the rest of me. "You don't belong to him. *You never belonged to him!*"

Sonny nodded and threw up again. I washed him off, but it was messy, and he muttered the whole time. "I did. I did. I did. I washed his clothes, I did his dishes, I sucked him off… I was his. I was his. I slept on his floor. I was his…."

"You weren't his."

"I was!"

"You never belonged to him!" I said, my voice tilting crazy. I'd already ripped my shirt, so now I ripped his, right above the mark I'd carved into his arm myself. "You *begged* me to mark you, and I marked you, and his mark, it's all gone. It's all gone. You took it off yourself. You made it so you never belonged to him. Do you hear me?"

"I did…." But his voice was growing weak now, ragged, like my belief was blowing away the things he remembered.

"You never belonged to him!" My voice rose, cracked, and now I was the one who was going to throw up, because what he was saying, what he was describing, the things that guy had said—it made me want to scream, to howl, to shriek like tortured steel, *"You never fucking belonged to him!"*

"I did!" Sonny sobbed. "I did, I did, he owned me, he owned me, he fucked me and marked me and used me, he owned me, body and soul—" He was blubbering now, spit and snot sputtering out with his words, and I grabbed him and pressed him to my chest and held him, barely giving him room to breathe.

"I've got you," I said, willing it to be true. "I've got you. I've got you. I've got you. He won't touch you. Won't touch you ever fucking again." *I've got you. I've got you. I've got you.*

"You got me, Ace," Sonny mumbled when the heat and the stickers and the cramping got too much. "You got me."

"I've got you," I said, my voice choked, clogged, like weeds in a lawn mower, broken, sharp, and aching.

"You got me."

"Ain't never letting go."

"You got me."

"Ain't *never* letting go."

"Swear, Ace. Swear."

"Never. Ain't never letting go. Swear. Won't ever let you go."

"Please, Ace. Don't ever let me go."

I could only hold him, hold him and wish I could scream. Wish I could scream, and wish I could kill. I'd kill the man right here, in cold blood, if he stood before me, but that's not what Sonny needed, not now.

"I will fuckin' *never* let you go."

It must have worked. I kissed his temple, his sweaty head, his forehead, and eventually we got up. I pulled him to the car, took off his shirt, and put him in the passenger seat before settling his racing harness because his hands were listless, and he couldn't seem to focus. I took off my own shirt and rolled both of them into a ball, figuring we could wash 'em out and use 'em as rags, and we rode back to the gathering in the usual big loop. The shadows were lengthening and the sky getting a deeper blue—late. It was getting late. We got back and the money man was easy to spot—he had a gathering of people around him, and he was pointing at our car with the finger that wasn't broke.

With a sinking stomach, I remembered the magnetic signs Sonny and I had bought last week advertising our garage, our names, our phone number, everything. I looked at Sonny through the window. "We can live without this pot if we need to," I said, and he nodded.

"We won that race fair and square," I shouted, leaning against the car. "You don't give us the pot, everyone's gonna know you're full of shit. No one's coming to your race ever again."

Our guy had his hand wrapped in a wet T-shirt, and he was talking to a much bigger guy, this one with long blond hair, a beard, and a back like a tabletop—all muscle, no fat, could probably drop me with one blow from his hammer fist. Was there a rule? Did all the guys who ran these races have to be huge?

The big guy came up to my window. "He says you broke his finger."

"That or dislocated it," I said, nodding.

The guy raised his grizzled blond eyebrows. His face looked like two tan slabs of ham, his cheeks were so long and lean. "Care to tell me why?"

"He was making claims on my mechanic," I said. "Claimed he 'owns' him. That man served two years in Iraq. Saved my life at least twice. Nobody owns Sonny but Sonny."

The guy nodded and thrust a wad of cash at me. "I hear you. Fair enough. You took the pot—that's fair. But you and your man—you're trouble. No more racing here. Ever."

"Who is that guy?" I asked. "Where's he out of?"

"Barstow." Blond guy shrugged. "He stakes the pot sometimes when he can. There's a little apartment in Barstow—he's lived there for half his life, I guess. Sells meth but isn't stupid enough to make it. He's their big dealer."

"What do they call him?"

"His real name is Albert. We call him Animal."

I could see why. I held up the wad of cash—it was about fifteen grand, all told—before shoving it in my pocket. "Thanks for the winnings, and we'll get out of your hair. Don't worry. Ain't no reason for us to go to Barstow, ever," I said. I was wondering if maybe I shouldn't call in my big marker from Jai's family on this one—at least to rough the guy up and convince him that looking for us would be a really bad idea. I started searching for him in the crowd, and I could tell blond guy was doing the same, and about the time my stomach started to chill, I whipped my head over as he gave a shout.

"You! You put him back!"

And then Sonny screamed.

He screamed my name, desperate like, and my knife was in my hand before my brain even knew it was an option.

"Put him down!" I snarled. The car had been unlocked, and the Animal… he'd opened the door, reached in there, and grabbed him? Just like that? How could he do that? "Sonny, goddammit, you're a soldier of the US Army, fight the fuck back!"

Sonny looked at me with stunned eyes, and for a horrible moment, I thought he wouldn't. I thought he wouldn't be able to, that he was trapped forever in that place where he was helpless and this guy owned him, body and soul.

The guy had a knife too. I'd dislocated the finger of his right hand, which must have been his good hand, because his left hand wasn't too steady on the knife as he held it to Sonny's throat.

"He was the best one I had," Animal said wistfully.

Sonny looked at the knife quizzically as though figuring out what to do, and out of nowhere, his scowl snapped his brows shut and he screamed, "I wasn't yours!"

His foot came down on Animal's instep at the same time, and the guy grunted and backed up for a moment before grabbing Sonny's arm around him and shoving him against the car.

He looked up at me and grinned, brown spit trickling down his chin. "I should thank you," he said, wonderingly. "It looks like you gave him some spirit. He was 'bout used up when he ran away, but he'll be more fun now."

"He'll kill you in your sleep," I said, baring my teeth. "He'll laugh while he's doing it. I'll love him for it. Don't you doubt it."

"Oh, now, I broke him once," said Albert the Animal. "I can break him again."

I looked him dead in the eye. "I don't think you'll live that long."

I meant it. He was laying hands on my Sonny. Sonny was snarling, thrashing under him. Animal grunted and howled in pain, almost crumpling, and I'm pretty sure Sonny dislocated his kneecap, because he could barely stand.

Sonny took his chance and turned around to face his opponent, and I took two steps and used my right arm to vault over the car.

And Albert saw me up in the air, and saw Sonny helpless and ready to fight. His knife hand was wobbly and he had no weight behind it—which is the only reason Sonny survived when Animal thrust it in his gut.

Sonny sank to the ground and Animal danced backward, wobbling on his one leg and hooting in excitement.

"Whoo! You see that? That's what you get when you stand up to me, boy, that's what you get! You think you can drive that thing fast? You drive that thing fast enough to save his life!"

My vision was red when I threw my knife. That's the only reason I hit his shoulder and not his chest.

He howled and fell on his ass as I got to Sonny. The knife was halfway in his stomach, far enough to hit the bad stuff, not far enough to hit the shit that would kill him right off.

"No, don't touch it," I snapped as he went to pull it out. "Leave it in until we're almost there."

"Where we goin', Ace?" he asked, looking up at me, as trusting as a child.

"We're gonna get to the doctor's," I said. We'd seen wounds, both of us, in Iraq, and I could tell it would be touch and go, and it all depended on how quick I got him to help.

I looked up and saw that the crowd had dispersed at the first sign of blood. Animal had pulled himself up and was off in the distance, heading for the parked cars and screaming for the girl, and there wasn't nothing I could do now, because Sonny needed me more. The blond guy was standing, though, stunned, on the other side of the car.

I scooped Sonny up, lifted him like a doll, and carried him to the car. I belted him, careful of the knife sticking out, and tried not to throw up. I paused and kissed his temple. "We're gonna get help," I said, and behind the words I felt a breaker crash—the terrible fear, the knowledge that every plan, every wish I had for the two of us depended on his sturdy little body fighting clear for the next few hours.

I stood up and ran around the car only to be stopped by the guy in charge of the race.

"I'll keep your name out of it," I snarled. "Just get out of my way."

The guy swallowed. "You do that for us," he said seriously, "we'll keep quiet for you."

I was going to grab him by the throat, tell him we hadn't done anything. And then I took his meaning, and my world—which had been hot, glaring, unfocused, and chaotic—sharpened to a crystal point.

"I hear you," I said. I didn't say good-bye.

"Ace," Sonny muttered. "Ace, it hurts. Man, I thought it wouldn't hardly hurt, but it hurts."

I closed my eyes for a second against the twilight from the road, opened them, and tried to fathom what this meant.

"It's good," I said, my throat raspy. "It's good. It stops hurting when shit gets bad. You know that. We saw guys die. You saw me pass out. Didn't hurt."

"Thank God," Sonny murmured. "Fuckin' hurts. Hur-fuckin'-ray."

A laugh barked out of my chest. "Yeah. Sonny, while you're still awake, could you look at your tags for me? What's your blood type?"

"Why you need to know that?"

"I'm gonna call an ambulance," I said. "Sonny, when they ask you who did this, I need you to do me a favor."

"I'm gonna live that long?" he asked.

I pounded on the steering wheel and screamed until my throat gave out. When I spoke again, my voice was ragged, but he still heard it.

"Yes! Yes! Fuckin' *yes*, you're gonna fuckin' live! Now give me your fuckin' blood type, Sonny Daye, we're gonna get you some fuckin' help!"

"A-pos," he muttered. "What's your goddamned favor?"

"Remember what Galway looked like?"

"Alive or dead?" Sonny asked. There was enough edge in his voice to give me hope, which was good, because I sounded like I had it all together, but it was a fucking lie.

"Alive."

"Yeah, can't forget."

"Good. Pretend he's the guy who stabbed you in the stomach," I said, and God bless him, he didn't question, he didn't ask.

All this time, I'd wondered if he would ever believe in me, but now I knew.

"All right, Ace. Sure. Don't give a fuck who did it, just want him dead."

"That's the idea," I muttered, but I'm not sure he heard me. I pulled out my phone and started pressing keys. It was real easy. Nine. One. One.

WHEN I'm dead, I'll know I'm in hell if I'm back on that road, with the twilight stealing over us like the chill of death.

Sonny was tough, real tough. He hardly moaned, hardly screamed, but he hurt, he hurt so bad, my body sweat with his pain. I kept my cool as I called the operator, told her my man had been stabbed by a guy on the side of the road, and we were heading south on a frontage road to Highway 5, and was real fuckin' grateful when she said she'd have an ambulance heading toward us, stocked with A-pos.

It was a chance. A real chance, because we were an hour out from medical care, forty-five minutes if I floored it and twenty-five if there was an ambulance coming the other way.

I hung up because I didn't want to crash, but that wasn't the only reason.

I couldn't talk to Sonny if I was talking on the phone to some woman trying to tell me to keep calm.

I was bein' calm. I was bein' as fucking calm as I was gonna get.

I drove like a pro, keeping my eyes on the road while my brain played out the worst moments of Sonny's life for me, whether I had the details or not.

God.

I'd wanted to do this in a quiet room, hold Sonny, make each other better, but that precious dignity I'd been trying to give him had just walked up and knifed him in the gut, and we did not have that, now did we?

"I'm sorry, Ace," Sonny said, and I screamed again.

"This ain't your fuckin' fault!" I panted when the scream was out of my chest. "It ain't your fuckin' fault, and I won't hear it."

"I just wanted to be... you know, he'd started passing me around, but my birthday was coming up, and I ran. I figured the army, right? 'Cause the commercials." His sigh hurt. "I wanted to be strong like them guys." A husky, bubbling sound that might have been a laugh. "'Course I had to hide on the streets until I found a crooked recruiter, and that took me ten tries, but no one else would pass me!"

"Why the tenth?" I asked, trying to keep him awake. The thought that... that... I couldn't think it. Not with him bleeding next to me. It couldn't even be a possibility.

"The others were good guys. Our army gots good guys in it," he mumbled. "Even the guy who was crooked—he fixed me up with my ID and my numbers. Got me a ticket to Fort Benning. Good guy. Just needed to be touched, but not a bad man. What'd you call that? Irony? I wanted to be a good guy so I had to find a sort of bad guy who'd let me blow him so I could get my fake ID to be a good guy?"

"Yeah. That's irony, Sonny. What made you snap? Just your birthday?"

"He... he was a fucker," Sonny muttered. "He was a bad man. But it was just him for a while. He started passing me around, though. Made 'em wear rubbers, which sorta makes it worse, 'cause he said he didn't want no fuckin'-around AIDS, but he... I thought I was his. Wasn't great, but even a dog belongs to somebody."

"You're a person," I told him. "You remember that. You're my person. You fought him. You fought back against him. You're stronger'n him."

"I shoulda pulled my knife," he said, his voice wandering. "Was gonna. Then I remembered I didn't have one. You had one. I didn't. I didn't have one."

"That's 'cause it's my job," I said firmly. "My job to take care of you. I failed, Sonny. I'm so sorry I failed. But it ain't never happening again. You can believe it. It ain't never happening again."

He lost consciousness about ten minutes after that. I was screaming his name when I saw the lights in the distance. It was the ambulance, and they had a shit ton of A-pos.

At the last second, as the ambulance skidded to a halt by us on the shoulder of the road, I remembered to use Sonny's T-shirt to wipe off the knife. No fingerprints. Nothing to connect Albert the Animal, no last name, to us.

Some people might say that makes me cold-blooded, and maybe it does. But I couldn't think of Sonny dead, I had to think of him alive, so that left this course of action. That was all.

And this course of action would only work if no one thought an army corporal named Sonny Daye and a staff sergeant named Jasper Atchison had any reason to know a guy called Albert the Animal.

It was like God drew the plans in my brain, that's how clear it all was.

But first, it depended on that one thing, that thing I couldn't think about, the thing I wouldn't face—it all depended on that one thing not happening.

I followed the ambulance back to the hospital in Bakersfield, cursing the fact that it could go as fast as it wanted, and it topped out at ninety.

THE hospital was a blur. There were nurses who gave me scrubs over my jeans because I was bare-chested and that offended them, and then there were police, lots of police, who asked me over and over again what happened.

It was real simple.

There was a guy on the side of the road in the desert with a flat tire. We stopped to help him; he pulled out a knife and tried to take our money. Sonny tried to be a hero, the guy stabbed him, I smacked the guy with a crowbar, and I got Sonny and ran.

So what did this mystery villain look like, Mr. Atchison?

He was tall, a little taller'n me, and he had ginger hair, and big green freckles, and squinty green eyes, and a scar up by his right eye.

When the sketch artist held up his first try, it looked like a mirror image of Galway, with the scar on the wrong side.

"It's perfect," I said, nodding, shivering, because I still saw his face in my nightmares. "I'll dream about that guy for the rest of my life."

I didn't say it wasn't the worst dream I'd ever have.

They asked me who Sonny was to me, and I said, "My partner," and left it at that. I have no idea what they thought of the two of us, and I cared less.

I just wanted to pace the room, waiting to hear about him.

Two hours into surgery, I had the good sense to call Burton.

"Dammit, Ace, I said this phone was for emergencies—"

"Sonny's been stabbed."

"That qualifies. Who did it?"

"I ain't tellin'. How do you get away with murder?"

There was a silence on the other end. Then: "Ace, this is a bad idea."

I closed my eyes and knew I wasn't as strong as Sonny on this. Someone had to know. "You know how Sonny was broken?"

Another silence. "Yeah."

"It was the same guy who done it. And he knows where our garage is now. He knows where we live."

Burton grunted. "How's Sonny?"

My voice broke. "He's gonna be okay because I said he was and I ain't never lied to him yet. You understand that, Burton? I ain't never lied to him. He's gonna be okay, we're gonna be okay, it's all gonna be okay, because I ain't never lied to him. *Make it so I don't never lie to him!*"

I wasn't sane, and he knew it. But he must have also known a whole lot of other things too, because the shit he told me was real fuckin' useful when all was said and done.

"I can be in Bakersfield in three hours," he said when he'd finished. "Wait until I get there."

"I wanna leave before," I said, "if he's in recovery by then. I don't want you—"

"Yeah, you do. If I'm implicated, I can pull some strings. Trust me on this. I'm not gonna stop you, and I'm not doing it for you, but Sonny can't be without you, Ace. Getting you to him will be my job if it comes up, you hear?"

"Yeah."

"Anything else I should know?"

"Yeah. If you see a picture that looks real fuckin' familiar, try not to say the first name that comes to mind."


I HAD five minutes with him when he was in recovery. Five minutes, and I spent them weeping like a pussy. Weird, the shit you regret.

He wasn't conscious, really. Kept saying my name, and I held his hand and cried, realizing I'd been praying this entire time and didn't know it. I must have been praying, I must have, because as I sat there, watching his chest rise and fall with every breath, all I could think of was, *Thank you, thank you, thank you.*

I've never felt so much gratitude, such a swell of anything, in ever my entire life.

His face was white under his tan, and I saw him for a moment like the rest of the world might see him.

They wouldn't see the toughness or the man who'd wept over a child in the rubble of war.

They wouldn't see the passion for cars that I did, or how working on them, making them orderly and tidy and run like a watch, must have done something for a man whose world that was chaos.

They'd see a small young man, someone vulnerable, someone who needed protecting. I'd tried. I'd tried, and I'd failed, and now if God saw fit to make sure he lived, I owed for that. Sonny would live to fix another car, and I'd make sure he'd be safe. It was my job. It was why God put me into this world, sure as he'd put Sonny here to work on cars.

It hit me then. I didn't know how he got to know cars—I'd ask him later, maybe—but he did. Someone had shown him. Someone had handed him a wrench and told him what made things work. Whether it was a good guy or a bad guy, that person had saved his life.

I'd ask him, I thought while my tears flooded whether I wanted them or not.

No one else would see the brokenness inside that no one could fix but maybe I could bridge. I could span the broken thing in him, and together, we could be whole.

I couldn't be whole without him.

"Sonny?" I whispered, because the nurse was pointing at her wrist, where a watch would be if she wasn't wearing it around her neck. "Sonny, I'm gonna go for a little. Gonna go get you some new clothes for when you're up and around." It was a lie, a big one, but I didn't have a better. "I'll be back, okay?"

"Ace?" he moaned, and I clutched his hand.

"I'm here."

"Ace?"

"I'm here."

"You promised you'd keep me."

"Forever. I'll keep you forever."

"Promise."

"They'll have to drag me away," I said, and my brain looped around and around the plan, because it had to be perfect, otherwise they'd do just that.

"Promise," he mumbled, and I was torn.

"I promise they'll have to drag me away to get me to leave your side."

He wasn't stupid. He knew something was up, but he could barely open his eyes, much less make sense of it. "Promise."

"I will never want to leave you. I promise I will *always* want to keep you," I told him. His mother had sold him for two bricks of meth. His next protector had passed him around. He'd signed up for the army to keep him but had opted to go with me instead. I couldn't let him down. I couldn't. "I promise, Sonny. I will try to be what you deserve."

Sonny nodded, and that was going to have to be enough. He kept mumbling, worried like, but then, that was Sonny, and I didn't blame him. I reassured him as much as I could, and he squeezed my hand and I cried on it.

When I could stop crying, that was the time to leave.

I kissed him on the cheek before I left, and he opened his eyes enough to settle down. "You're here," he murmured.

"I love you," I said. I wanted to tell him I'd be there while he slept, but I couldn't. "I'll keep you safe," I said. Because that, of all things, wasn't a lie.

I'd do anything to keep him safe.

I bumped into Burton on my way out of the hospital, and he looked me over. I was wearing scrubs, but my hair was wild, torn out of the gel by my running fingers, and I was crusty with dried sweat. "You look like hell—"

"I need to go," I cut him off. "I need to go, and I need to be back. I figure, it *should* take me five hours, but I can make it in four."

Burton grunted. "Yeah. I hear you."

"You need to watch him," I said, and then I held up my hand. "If I don't come back, here's my folks' number. It won't be ideal, but he can stay with them until he's ready not to." I figured if I died, my parents would feel obligated. They had with Juanita, and, well, it was my only option besides giving him to Jai, and this I would not do. But…. "And if I don't come back, you need to tell Jai he's got the garage, and tell him I'm calling in my favor, and his boss needs to watch out for Sonny too."

"God, Ace—you got people, you got—"

"All he's got is me, and I failed him." My voice was going to break, and I couldn't afford it to. "It was almost too many times. I'm not gonna fail him again."

There were people coming and going—nurses in scrubs, doctors in jeans and white jackets, visitors with balloons or grim looks. I was maybe the only person in the entire hospital who was planning to go out and take a man's life, and I realized I looked the part. I took a deep breath, pulled my spine up, and saw a restroom. I set off toward it, and Burton followed me without a word.

Inside, I ran cold water on my face, on my wrists, and through my hair. I pulled a little comb out of my pocket and slicked my hair back, not in a ducktail, but plain and simple, less likely to be remembered. I would have shaved my sideburns if I had a razor, but I didn't. That was okay. No one was going to see my face anyway if I was smart.

"Here," Burton said, trying to shove a wad of cash in the pocket of my jeans. I shoved it back and showed him my winnings, and he just nodded. "Good, that's untraceable too. Stop at the second Walmart you see and go shopping. Get all the shit we discussed. And for Christ's sake, get your knife back from the guy, because that's the *last* thing you want there during an investigation."

I nodded, thanking God I had a trained killer on my side. "Hear you," I muttered. Jake had given me that knife. I wanted it back.

Burton nodded back. "'Kay, Ace. You're smart—I know you don't think you are, but you're smart. But no one's smart all the time when they're doing something like this. You need to be." He handed me keys. "I rented a car, basic Dodge POS—don't worry about the inside, I got a detail man. Here's the number of a guy nearby who'll get you an ID if you need it. I took some of what you said and got an address with quick directions—I sent them to your phone. There's also directions to a shopping complex nearby, with the things you'll need. Delete the directions once you get them. Don't worry about Sonny. I'll have him meet you if you need to leave. Just... just be careful, man. Sonny's a friend, and he's a good guy, but without you—"

I nodded. I understood. Sonny would be dangerous on his own. Dangerous and unbalanced. Burton might not have to put him down, but he might have to put him in a cage, and that would be worse.

"Stay with him," I said. "The doc said he'll be out for six, eight hours. I should be back before then."

Burton nodded. "I hear you."

I shook his hand and went in for the chest bump, fighting off the feeling of being choked up. "You're a good friend," I said. "I'll see you in a few."

I WENT to the *third* Walmart I saw down the freeway, because the second was still in Bakersfield and too close to my parents' house. I walked in, bought a bowie knife like the one I threw at the Animal, a package of white T-shirts, new cargo shorts, new underwear, a black nylon track suit, cheap black tennis shoes, cheap vinyl gloves, a black beanie—the loose kind that stupid kids wore to look cool, so they were available all year—some little packets of laundry detergent, and a bucket of bleach.

In spite of what Burton said, I didn't want him implicated. It took me an hour and a half to drive from the Walmart to the shopping complex. Burton was right—they had a Laundromat. I changed into the tracksuit in the car and walked in with my armload of dirty clothes, including the bloodstained T-shirt I'd worn into the hospital, the jeans I'd just taken off, and the two T-shirts that had been rolled up in the back of the car after Sonny had gotten sick, along with the detergent and the bleach. I started the clothes, twitching in an effort not to look around and see if anyone noticed the fool sweating it out in the tracksuit and the brand-new black tennis shoes, but I needn't have bothered. Everyone likes to think they're someone from *CSI*, but the fact is, most people got their own shit to tend.

When I walked in, I checked out the parking lot; it was an old one with cracks in the concrete and grass growing up against the curbs. There wasn't a single camera there, and as long as I stayed a long ways from the gas station on the corner, there wasn't need to worry.

As it was, I walked back to the car, which was parked as far from the complex as possible, hopped in, and followed the directions on my phone before deleting the text string. The place itself wasn't hard to spot.

Old apartment buildings. Every shitty town has a few, the kind where people live because the day-to-day is cheaper and the empty rooms are rented by the hour.

This one looked like the hookers and the meth dealers and the single mothers down on their luck knew each other. All but one room had the drapes shut tight, in spite of the beauty and (relative) coolness of a September morning. The one room that didn't had the door wide open onto the concrete porch of the second story, and a television on loud. I saw a girl with dark hair through the window, and she looked familiar enough for me to place her as the girl from the race. This was Sonny's replacement, I thought, feeling ill. I would have to do this when she wasn't looking, but that didn't mean she wouldn't be the first person to find the awfulness left behind.

I worried about that for a moment as I ambled the car past the apartments and then left it behind. There were worse things than seeing a dead body—just ask Sonny.

I didn't park in the parking lot.

Instead, I just cruised on past it and found a place around the corner. It was an abandoned hamburger joint, and it backed up against the complex. I could not have planned it better if I'd been making a movie. I let the car idle for a minute, grabbed the hat out of the bag, and cut a couple of eyeholes in it with the new knife. I put it on my head, low enough to cover my hair and my sideburns, and put the gloves and new knife with the tag still stuck on the back in my pockets. Right now, I was a white guy in a black tracksuit.

I turned off the engine, slid out of the car, and clambered to the top of the hurricane fence, scoping out the back. With a little figuring, I knew which room was Albert's—and it didn't hurt his windows were open. I could hear the television and hear him screaming at the girl for some more goddamned ice, and it figured. If they had the front door open for air, they'd all be opened up for flow. Everyone else was too scared, I thought. That's why the windows and doors were closed. He had them all too scared even to look outside.

The side of the apartment complex was smooth, but there was only about a four-foot gap between the fence and the wall. I stayed crouching as I pulled my hat down, looking through the eyeholes. I put on the gloves one at a time and drew out my knife. It was stiff and alien, unlike the warm, familiar wood of my brother's bowie knife, and I wiped it on the tracksuit before I got a good hold through the cheap driving gloves. The hurricane fence was wobbly under my feet, and I figured I had about three good long steps of momentum before I went tumbling down it, so I steadied myself good.

One, two, three….

I ran, making those steps count, and on the last step, I propelled myself up and sideways, slicing through the screen with my left hand, and grabbing onto the ledge with my right.

In the army, I'd been able to do ten one-armed pull-ups per side, mostly because I am long enough that I can balance.

Right then, I only needed to do one.

I did, using the other arm to continue to slice through the screen, and when I got to the top, I took the time to put the knife in my pocket and then hoist myself into the bedroom.

It stank like old weed and old sex and a bathroom that ain't been cleaned in forever. There were stained black sheets on the bed, a dirty red velour cover, and a battered dresser spilling over with old T-shirts and frayed jeans. Takeout containers littered the top of the dresser, getting rank. A hamper in the corner overflowed with dirty laundry, tumbling over with rags stained red and yellow.

I realized that was where some of the stink was coming from. Our guy was already infected from that knife through his shirt. Well, I guess it pays to clean your shit, now doesn't it?

"Dammit, bitch! Get in here with my fuckin' ice!"

"The ice, it is all used up!" the girl said, and I heard a definite inflection of Russian in her voice. Great. This one he probably ordered on eBay. I fuckin' hate humanity sometimes.

"Well go out and fuckin' get some more!" I couldn't hear her footsteps because the TV was on too loud, but I did hear him say, "The stupid bitch forgot the fuckin' money!" to himself, so I assumed she was gone, and I was in a quandary.

Do him now, before she got back, or hide under the bed until she came back and left again?

I realized the bed was a pedestal, the closet wasn't big enough for me, and the bathroom was visible from the living room, and that made up my mind.

I ran into the living room, which had a recliner, a dog bed, a coffee table covered in pot and more takeout, bloody rags, my brother's knife, and a television with the volume on super loud.

Sonny's "owner" looked back at me from the recliner, surprised as hell. "What in the—"

I leapt over the coffee table and straddled the guy with his stink, holding the bowie knife to his throat.

"That was my brother's knife, you pig," I said softly. "I came to get it back."

His eyes rolled wildly, and I grabbed his hair to tilt back his scruff-covered throat.

"You c'n have it," he said, polite as a first grader. "I don't need it. I won't tell anyone you gave it to me. No harm, no foul. I damaged your property, you—"

My eyes caught my reflection, black masked and scary, and I realized anyone looking in could see a guy with a mask through the window. I kept the knife at the guy's throat, but I moved off the recliner and closed the drapes.

"What're you doin'?" he asked, growing bolder.

"He's not property," I said, lowering my head so we were both facing the television and I was holding his head with one hand and talking into his ear. "And neither is that girl. And there is no jail good enough for the likes of you."

I had the knife in my right hand. That's my good hand. The only warning he got was the clenching of my left hand in his hair before I pulled that blade hard and fast through his trachea, through his jugular.

He didn't scream, but since I didn't saw his head partway off, it took him a minute to die, his breath gurgling through the blood that first spurted out his throat and was now pooling on the front of this shirt. It was everywhere—the table, the television, the far wall—and his body was twitching enough to spread it some more too.

The body stopped twitching, and I let go and stood up, trying to still my breathing and remember the shit I needed to do.

And that's when I heard the gasp over the television.

I looked up and there was the girl, her eyes wide, staring at me, and I would have cursed myself for stupid a thousand different ways, but I'd known, I'd known this could happen.

I held my fingers up to my lips, moved so I was facing the Albert the Animal with the terrible bloody smile that bisected his neck, and drove the knife into the wound on his shoulder, obscuring the blade mark left by my brother's knife when I'd thrown it.

The girl's eyes were still wide but no longer rolling in panic. She looked at the man on the recliner, the one who had made her sleep on the dog pallet when she hadn't been having sex or cleaning the house, and snarled.

I didn't know what she had planned, but I was so surprised when she grabbed the knife in the guy's shoulder with two hands and yanked it out that all I did was stand back.

And watched as she stabbed him again and again and again. She probably only weighed about 115, 120, so the blows didn't go all the way in. She couldn't have done this, not for real, not with her body strength, which is probably why she hadn't.

I let her. I let her desecrate a corpse, because she'd earned it.

After a few moments, her screaming went up a few notches, and I touched her shoulder and held my finger to my lips again.

She shook her head. "When he raped me," she said, her sneer evident, her accent thick, "I screamed. I screamed every time. And no one came. No one will come now."

"Good," I said. "But that don't mean I'm going out the front door."

She looked at me suddenly, her eyes wide. "What will I do now? Where will I go?"

I blinked. "Well, do you have any money?"

Her smile was as gleeful as a Christmas morning. She ran to the back room and came back with a big gym bag. She opened it to show me piles of money, greasy bills, desperate bills, probably coated with drug residue and the film of desperate people, neatly counted into stacks, and bound, all twenties. An entire gym bag.

My mind boggled. I couldn't do the math.

"Half is yours," she said, and I was going to say no. I was going to say it was all hers, because she'd earned it the hard way.

But so had Sonny. They'd both earned it the extrahard way.

"Deal," I said. "Do you have ID? Anything legit?"

She shook her head, and I thought about Burton's guy.

"You're Russian?" I asked, and she nodded.

"Da."

"I know a town where almost the whole population is Russian. You game?"

Again, that gleeful smile. She had a long, oval Russian face, dark hair, and blue-gray eyes. She was really very pretty, and maybe, *maybe* fifteen.

I did not ask her how long she'd been there.

I didn't want to know the answer.

"Let's get the fuck outta here," I said. I looked down—she had flip-flops on, and I gave one last order.

"You need tennis shoes."

She grimaced, and I sighed. "Well, we'll manage. In the meantime, change your clothes." There was blood all over her little yellow summer skirt and the big white T-shirt she'd been wearing. "You got a garbage bag?"


I GRABBED my brother's knife while she went to fetch the garbage bag, and then I used the nylon jacket to wipe the blood off it, and off the vinyl gloves, which I kept on. I took off the track pants and the hat and left on the shoes, then put the clothes in the garbage bag so we could sling it over our shoulders. She was wearing jeans and another white T-shirt when she came back, and I'd heard her in the bathroom as she washed the blood off her body. Good for her. I wasn't risking leaving anything more in this place than I had to.

I helped her to the ground first and then dropped the bag to her, half expecting her to run away with it when I did. When she didn't, I realized that she was a lot like Sonny at this point. She needed orders.

She needed a leader. You live with that long enough, it takes a while before you can live without it.

That was okay. She needed a leader, and I was glad to have a lackey, if only for another couple of hours.

I lowered myself to the ground behind the apartment building, and then we both walked, cool as you please, around the hurricane fence, around the block, and to the brown Dodge behind the burger joint.

I used the clothes in the bag to wipe off my shoes and gloves before throwing them in the bag too. I pulled my own tennis shoes out of the backseat, put them on, and started the car.

We were going to need gas before we got back to the hospital in Bakersfield.

And that was when I realized that twenty-six hours ago, Sonny and I had been starting out from our little garage, and Sonny had been worried about meeting my mom, and I had been worried about meeting his past.

Well, you go without sleep a lot in a war zone. I could make it to Bakersfield just fine.


FIRST we stopped at the Laundromat. I took the trash bag and the bleach in and threw it *all*—tennis shoes, bag, gloves, everything—in the big power washer, and I added pretty much the entire bottle of bleach and set the water on hot. I pumped that thing full of quarters, unobtrusively wiping every quarter for my print before putting it in the machine.

I took the other clothes out of the washer and put them in the dryer, and then took the girl next door to the grocery store.

It was one of those superstore places, and yes, they had those rubber Crocs shoes, and some more clothes, and even some underwear in her size, and we bought that with cash from the gym bag that was locked in the trunk. We also bought two more gym bags.

We took our stuff to the car, and she changed. I halved the money, neat and pretty, and put half in the pink gym bag we'd bought for her, and half in the gray one, which was the only other color they'd had. Then we went back to the Laundromat, threw the dirty gym bag with the clothes into the bleach-stinking hot water, got my still-damp clothes from the drier, and left.

Just left.

If someone could track those clothes to the murder to us to the rented car, well, let them, but as I got into the car, it occurred to me. I didn't think anyone was going to miss Albert the Animal enough to go to all that trouble.

# GOOD GUYS, BAD GUYS

I LOOKED up crime statistics at one point. Seems the clearance rate for homicides is 96 percent in San Diego and in the 80s for a lot of that part of Southern California.

You'd think that would mean bad things for me. I killed a man in cold blood. I grabbed him by the greasy black hair, yanked his head back, and cut his throat—can't get much more clear-cut than that.

I had an accomplice who had lived in the apartment—and I didn't kill her to keep her quiet.

My life should have been over.

All the way back to Bakersfield, I kept expecting to hear sirens, but I didn't. I must have checked my rearview mirror six times in the first ten minutes, and an unexpected cold sweat drenched me and clenched my stomach.

The girl saw, looked at me, grunted, and turned away; I thought it was in disgust.

"Do you know what happened to the… the *pet* he had before me?" she asked.

I shook my head and tried to control my breathing.

"The bones are rotting in that place you parked. He kicked the boy to death while I watched so I knew not to run away. Then he had me board up the windows. Then he raped me while he was covered in blood."

I hadn't eaten since my mom's table. The POS had shitty suspension, and it bumped like a motherfucker as I pulled to the side of the road, threw her in park, opened the door, and dry heaved into the dead weeds.

There was no water in the car. There was water in the SHO, I thought wretchedly. Then I remembered that the Ford was parked at the hospital, and Sonny was there. Sonny, who expected me to be there when he woke up.

I reached to the backseat, to the pile of damp laundry, and found one of the torn shirts from yesterday. I used it to wipe my face and my teeth, and it felt so good, I used it to towel myself down underneath my white T-shirt.

Sonny was waiting for me.

I sat up, threw the shirt in the back again, and started the car.


WE STOP at a gas station about ten minutes later, and I make two calls.

The first was to Burton. I asked him if a friend of mine could use his ID guy. He asked me what kind of friend.

"That guy had… he had a girl there this time. She was happy to help, but she's underage and has no family. I need to get her somewhere safe."

Burton grunted. "A foster care facility I am not. I'll get you the ID, I can make the call now. You find somewhere for her to stay."

"Yeah. Sonny?"

"Still out of it. Keeps asking for you, but he wouldn't know if you were here."

I made a sound then, not sure what it meant. "He gonna be okay?"

"They say infection is the worst risk. He can avoid infection for the next forty-eight hours, he's going to be okay."

I nod. God. Forty-eight more hours? I sway a little on my feet. I needed to be there, or I would never make it.

"We'll be there in forty-five minutes," I said, because that was about how much more I had in me.

"I need a name for the girl," Burton said, and of all things, that seemed the funniest thing I'd heard in my life.

I burst into hysterical laughter while Burton waited patiently on the other end of the line. I was still laughing when the girl came out. She'd gone into the mini-mart for some food. She had a couple of sandwiches and a soda for me, on ice, and some waters, and I blessed her.

"That was real thoughtful," I said, gulping the soda like it was the nectar of life. "What's your name?"

"Katrinka," she said, and when she said it, it sounded like a fine name. "*He* called me Helga."

"Her name's Katrinka," I said into the phone, and then I hung up. "*He* was a pig," I said to her, my voice flat. "Did he mark you?"

Her eyes grew dark and troubled, and she went to unbutton her jeans. I shook my head. I knew what she was going to show me. "You can tattoo over it later," I said. "No one owns you."

She swallowed and looked at me with black-fringed blue eyes. "But what do I do now?"

"I got a friend," I said, thinking of Jai. "He's Russian too."

The hurt on her face cut through my gut. "Russian men, they don't think much of whores—"

"No!" I snapped, uncomfortable. "Not like that. He's like me. He's gay. But he likes taking care of girls. He has a sister. Treats her like a queen."

It was the girl's turn to look uncomfortable. "Gay? You like men?"

I sighed. "I like one man," I said with dignity. "And right now, he's in the hospital, and I need to be there to see if he lives or dies."

"You did this for *him*?" she asked. "And not for the money?"

I shook my head. "Not for the money."

It was her turn to laugh hysterically. I sucked my soda down and let her. Eventually she stopped and we got in the car. I made myself eat, because food is fuel, and it was quiet—no radio, nothing—for the next twenty minutes.

"Would he not touch me?" the girl asked out of the blue. "Since he is gay?"

"I about guarantee it," I said, thinking of Jai and Alba.

"If I do not like him, what will you do?"

I sighed. "Something," I said. "We got a spare room right now, but it's for someone else. We'll think of something."

"You...." She shook her head. "That is stupid. It is stupid I should ask."

"You want a promise," I said, thinking of Sonny. "You want a promise you'll be safe. I can promise you Jai won't hurt you. I can promise I'll do my best. I can't promise that the cops won't arrest me, and I can't promise that the world won't fall to shit. I can't promise that Sonny and I won't lose the garage and lose our home. I can't promise that Sonny will want me forever, and we'll never break up, or that someone won't notice Jai's got an underage girl living with him and send you to a foster family. I can't promise that Alba won't get jealous, 'cause she likes working for us, and I can't promise she won't try to rip your hair out, 'cause she's tough. I can't promise we'll have enough money. I can't promise some other asshole won't think you're pretty and try to violate you, because some fuckers are good at that. I can't promise...." My voice was breaking, and I had ten minutes to go. I took the exit off the freeway and itched at the stoplight until it turned green, and she just sat there, waiting for me to finish my sentence.

"I can promise I won't hurt you," I said gruffly. "I can't promise Sonny won't be a dick, but I can promise he won't lay a hand on you. I can promise the same thing for Jai. It's all I've got, Katrinka. It's all...."

Five more minutes. Left. Left. Right. Left. Itch at the lights like my balls are on fire. See the hospital. Remember where to park. Pull in right next to the yellow Ford, which still had Sonny's blood in the front seat.

Her hand on my thigh was cool and seemed to spread some calm. "I don't even know your name," she said gently, and I was grateful.

"People call me Ace," I said. "I'm gonna leave you in the car and have Burton take you back to our hotel, okay?"

"No," she said, shaking her head. "Take me with you. I...." Her hand tightened, and I realized it was shaking.

Sonny had needed to hide on the street for weeks and go down on the one crooked army recruiter he could find. She'd needed to help me get away with murder. Different prices, but neither of them easy.

"Yeah," I said, gathering myself. I wanted a shower. I wanted a hot dinner and a clean bed. I wanted Sonny there next to me, telling me it was all okay. "Let's go in."

Sonny was still pale, transparent, and small on the hospital bed. I didn't care. I managed a handshake and a chest bump with Burton, and then I fell into the seat next to the bed and laid my head down. I grabbed Sonny's hand and held it to my face.

"Ace?" he mumbled.

"I'm here."

"I was worried," he said, and I shook my head. My face was wet and my shoulders were shaking, but I was here, and he was here, and right now, that was about the only thing I could think about. We were there.

The girl took a chair in the corner of the room, and Burton took my hotel key to go get some shut-eye.

I lay there, my upper half stretched across the hospital bed, and shook, just shook.

Sonny roused himself for a minute. "Ace!" he said, like he was scared, and I clutched his hand tighter.

"You're safe," I said, hoping. "You're safe."

I TOLD the girl I couldn't promise anything, but that didn't mean I couldn't try to make things right anyway.

I laid my head next to Sonny and slept for six hours, and when I woke, it felt like someone had taken an axe to my back and broke it.

I stretched, trying to get the kinks out, and saw Sonny's eyes on me, big and gray and serious.

"You're okay," I said, so happy I couldn't hardly even say the words.

"I've been better!" he protested and then looked at me. "So have you."

I grimaced. "Well, yeah." My stomach growled. Those sandwiches had been a while ago.

I looked around the room, saw the girl curled up in a ball. Thought she should eat too.

"Who in the fuck is that?" he asked, and I grimaced.

"That is the second-biggest thing I don't want to talk about," I muttered, and at that moment, the police came in.

There were two detectives assigned to the case—middle-aged white guys, graying hair, one darker, one taller, and beyond that, I'm a little fuzzy. They asked us for the details of our story again, and the fact that I remembered them, and recited them, was a marvel of the human brain right there, because until the moment they asked, I hadn't thought about that.

One of them pulled out the police artist sketch, and when Sonny's eyes widened and he made a sound, the guy said, "Is this the man who attacked you, Mr. Daye?"

Sonny's gaze darted to mine, and he nodded frantically, like a scared rabbit. "Yeah," he whispered, and I knew the detectives were seeing someone traumatized by being stabbed, and I was seeing someone traumatized by a realization he didn't want to make.

"Do you got a line on him, mister?" I asked, and the detective shook his head.

"No, but he's wanted in conjunction with another crime committed in Barstow yesterday. We got an anonymous tip that placed him at an apartment building where a man named Albert Klein was murdered. Do you know anything about Mr. Klein?"

When Jake sliced up Ronnie, he'd come home with blood on his shirt. My mom had asked me if I knew where Jake got that, like I was her little man and I'd betray my brother.

Burton had just lied about the blood on my shirt.

"No, sir," I said, blank faced. "I've never heard that name before." And that was the truth.

The detectives shrugged. "Well, we'll be in touch if we hear anything. We're glad you're feeling better, Mr. Daye. It's good to see you awake."

Sonny nodded and smiled weakly, and we locked eyes as the sound of the detectives' shoes echoed down the hallway.

"Look outside and see if they're gone," he said quietly, and I did, mostly for my own peace of mind.

I turned my head then and shut the door behind me, and he said, "What did you do?"

I said, "I kept you safe."

He swallowed, and his face went whiter, and he fell back against the pillows.

"Thank you," he said. He glanced at the girl, who had slept through the detectives' visit and everything. "What are we going to do with her?" he asked.

I sank into the chair again. Sonny's stomach was taped and he had machines monitoring his breathing and his heart rate, and I wanted nothing more than to sit in that bed and hold him.

"We're gonna make sure she never has to join the army," I said, and I didn't mean to be funny, but Sonny laughed. He laughed hard, and I sat up and stretched a little and kissed him on the forehead.

He closed his eyes and the laughter subsided. "You'll keep us safe," he murmured, and this time, when he slept, it was easy, like he didn't have nothing to worry about in the world.

SHE didn't go with Jai in the end, although Jai would have kept her. But he said girls who'd been in the sex trade have a hard time getting out in the Russian communities, and he didn't want his people to find out he had a girl.

Out of desperation I turned to the one person who at least knew what to do with a girl around the house.

After we slept in the hospital, Burton showed up in the morning with the girl's papers. I had the quick discussion with Jai, who was regretful but honest. He was also worried sick about Sonny, so I downplayed that part, and I told him we'd be able to pay his salary for at least a year, and he hung up reassured on a lot of counts.

I told Burton, and he shrugged and said, "Just as well. That's a little close, proximity-wise. You need someone you don't live by, you feel me?"

And I looked around the hospital room and thought that this place was about as far away from home as I ever wanted to be.

And then I remembered that it was, and that my mother lived five miles away.

I kissed Sonny good-bye on the lips, although his breath was rank, and told him I'd be back in a couple of hours. He mumbled something about how I'd better be, and then me and Katrinka went on a little ride.

"They are nice people?" she asked as we got into the car.

"Yeah," I said. "They don't talk a lot, and they got their faults. But they'll raise you right."

"You are sure?"

"No. But it's harder for them to turn you down when you're at their table," I told her, thinking of Sonny. Once he'd eaten at their table, they weren't going to turn him away.

We stopped on the way and set up a checking account in the girl's new name. Burton had made her Katriona Olenskya, which I thought was pretty. "That way, people can call you Kat," I said, and she raised her eyebrows and smiled.

"I like that. Do you think these people will let me have a cat?"

I shrugged. "I think my mom's got a few now."

She really did have a nice smile, even though she had a big space between her teeth and a rather short jaw. I hoped she didn't stab my folks in their sleep, but I'd already seen she didn't have the body strength to do it right. Besides, I'm pretty sure she was like me: she needed the right motivation.

My mother was… surprised.

"Ace, you want me to—to what?"

I grimaced. "She needs a home," I said, wishing we'd gotten food when we'd stopped at the bank. "She needs a home, and you've got one. Juanita needs a daughter who does what she asks, and I've brought her one. She has her own money—she can buy her own clothes, and even help with the groceries—"

"We can do for her, same as we did for you. I just want to know why me? You show up two days ago with Sonny, and today you show up with a girl?"

Oh God. It was Monday morning.

"Mom," I said, feeling fractious and hungry and as intractable as a five-year-old. "If you love me—if you *really* love me—you will *never* ask me about the last two days." I needed to stop by the hotel. We had it until this morning, but I needed to get a couple more days. I had a sudden cold-shake moment about all that money in the back of the car, and then remembered I'd seen it when we set up the girl's bank account, and settled myself down.

"Ace—"

"Ever," I said, looking her dead in the eye. "Please, Mom. She needs what Sonny never got. She needs sanctuary, and she needs someone who has her best interests at heart looking out for her. She needs someone to tell her nicely when she's wearing too much makeup, and she needs someone who will cook for her and ask her to clear the table and do the dishes. She needs someone who will make sure she goes to school and gets good marks. She… she just needs a mom. She needs a mom, and I don't know how old she is, but she might need you for a few years."

Mom gasped and then looked at the girl, who was sitting on the porch. Sure enough, an orange-and-white cat—a young one—wandered up to her, and she started petting it like that was the most natural thing in the world.

"I can't tell you about years," Mom said after a moment. "But we can take her for a week or two and see what happens."

I hugged her, short and strong, and kissed her cheek. "Thanks, Mom. I love you. Be gentle with her—no yelling, and don't let Dad scare her. She's not going to be real fond of men for a while."

I left my mom before she could ask me any questions. I walked up to Kat and crouched down, petting the kitty so she would know I wasn't going to get scary anytime soon.

"You've got my number," I said, because I'd written it down and given it to her. "Ask my mom and she'll take you to get you a cell phone," I said.

"I will be okay?" she asked, and that trust, it killed me.

I kissed her forehead. "Remember all those promises I can't make?"

She nodded.

"I can promise you that these people will never mean to hurt you. They may hurt your feelings, and they wouldn't understand where you've been for the last year, but they would never mean to hurt you, do you understand?"

She nodded again. "That is something," she said with meaning, and I nodded too.

"Yeah. Yeah, it is. Call me if you get in a jam, but I think you're going to be okay."

My mom was coming up the stoop, talking the whole time. "Well, are those the only clothes you have? You're small, you can fit into Dulcie's stuff until we can take you to Walmart, how's that?"

Mom herded her into the house, talking about lunch, and the girl looked over her shoulder and waved. I waved back. I'd keep in touch, I thought. It would be good to know that someone would survive, someone would be okay.

From Mom's I went to our hotel, where I dropped my clothes as I went and showered. For almost an hour. I could not stop soaping myself, and again, and again, and my hair, and every crease in my body, and I tried not to think of the water running red.

When I was done with that, I toweled off and put the clothes Sonny and I had left in the duffel back on, registered for another three days, and drove to the hospital. I finally got some food on the way.

When I got there, Sonny was watching the news. Sure enough, there was a picture of Master Sergeant Galway there, in bold lines and black and white, with the news that he'd stabbed a man to death in his apartment.

Sonny looked at me as I walked in. "Thirteen times?" is what he said, and I grimaced.

"I only did the first one."

He grunted. "Well, that's the one that counted."

"God, I hope so." Thinking about all that had cost me.

I sat down next to him and laid my head down again. He stroked his fingers through my hair.

"Is this all over?" he asked, his voice faint.

"Do you love me?"

"God, yes."

"Will you stay with me forever?"

His voice broke. "They'd have to drag me away."

I watched the news story unspool, the big vat of lies I'd cooked up and that were being boiled into the truth by the media.

"Then let's say it's over," I said, my voice scratchy. "Let's say it's over. You'll get better, and we'll go back and try to make our living, and I may have to race again, 'cause we know now there's worse things than racing, but let's pretend this is it. That we'll be together, and we'll be that way until the police or God drags one of us away."

"I can do that," he murmured, and I turned my head to look at him. He was lying back against the pillows, and he didn't look infected. He looked tired and white, but not like he was sickening. He would heal. He raised his head a little and looked at me dead on, his gray eyes wide. "With you here, Ace, I can do anything."

I stayed facing him, and he turned off the television, and it was just us in the hospital room, and the blessed, blessed quiet, with the touch of his hand in my hair.

# WASHING SINS

HE WAS out of the hospital in a week. They told me he had the sort of constitution that kept the human race alive when other races died off, and I thought that was fitting.

On the last day, I checked out of the hotel and then checked him out of the hospital, and took him to the beach in San Diego before we went home. I got us a hotel room and lay next to him, full out, while he rested. I just looked at him with the light from a real sun on his face and played with his dog tags and stroked his chest, my throat tight with the things I could not control.

I had this, I thought. I had the here. I had the now. We had the us.

He woke up after an hour and turned to me without talking. His lips were a little rough and a little chapped, but I fell into him, into his mouth, into his kiss, like I was falling into a feather bed. This was home.

We moved slowly, careful of each other. I was afraid of hurting him, and I think he was afraid of the same thing. We stripped off our clothes and just lay there, stroking random places on our bodies.

I found the flesh of his bottom and kneaded, and he hid his face against my shoulder. "Am I still who you want?" he asked, because I guess you can't ever hear that too much if you're Sonny.

"Forever," I said. Then I grasped his chin and made him look at me. "Am I?"

He nodded.

"You sure, Sonny? You know the things I done."

"I know who you are," he said quietly. "Forever, Ace. I'll do anything."

And then there wasn't no more talking. I kissed him, starving, and drank him in, parched for the spit in his mouth, the sweat on his skin. He kissed me back the same way, and I sat up, my legs over the edge of the bed, and hauled him around so he straddled me. He wrapped his arms and legs around my body and enveloped me, made me safe in the cave of his tough little body, and I palmed the skin of his back and his shoulders and his ass like I could pull him in through my fingertips, and every vertebrae on his back was a prayer bead under my hands.

Our groins could meet only because we'd both lost weight, and there was not much else for them to do, but our erections came up between us. I reached between us and grasped our cocks, squeezing as Sonny scooted back and forth, the tender skin of our shafts and crowns rubbing together, rubbing my roughened, tightened fingers. I wanted harder, *craved* faster, but wouldn't risk hurting Sonny, not this night, when he'd just finished looking weak and sick and sad.

I lay back with him on top of me and then rolled us over on our sides. He groaned and started arching faster, and I let him, let him set the pace, let him grunt and rut in my big hand, let him moan my name and claw my chest in an effort to move faster, harder, deeper, but it wasn't enough. We needed more, more sensation, more violence, something sharp and definitive.

My cargo shorts were on the foot of the bed, and I reached into them, got the lubricant I'd brought, 'cause it was always handy when men were naked, and squirted some into my hand. I brought my knees up, reached around my back, and shoved two lubed fingers into my ass without thinking. I needed. Sonny needed. Somehow we needed this.

"Sonny," I growled, and he looked at me with big eyes. "Don't just sit there, dammit, *fuck me!*"

He did, quick, and I was grateful. There was a cock-wilting explosion of pain, and he sat there for a moment before I started to wiggle, scooting down and up and down and up. There he was, lodged in my asshole, stiff and unyielding. I opened my eyes from the red veil over them and he stared at me with concern.

"Ace?"

"Move," I whispered.

"Are you—"

*"Move! Please, God, Sonny, move!"*

And he did. Back, slowly, forward, hard, back, slowly, forward, hard, and my erection returned, grew fuller, stiffer, with every thrust. I watched him, his face scrunched up in concentration, his eyes closed, as every movement grew more and more controlled, every moment grew more and more needy.

"Sonny!"

He opened his eyes.

"Kiss me," I said, and he had to practically bend me in half while he stayed inside me, but he did. He tasted perfect, hot, hard, salty, and I wanted suddenly to suck his cock until he spilled and I had that taste in my throat, running down my mouth too.

But not this time. He groaned suddenly, his hips pumping like they were powered by NOS, and I spread my legs, spread my ass, begged him inside me with all of his strength.

He hit my prostate with a random thrust, and I cried out loudly, and I came, spurting across my stomach without touching myself, and he grunted and moaned and came inside me. I felt it hit, hot and sharp, and loved it, wanted him inside me forever.

He fell on top of my chest, his cock popping out on a gush of come, and I shuddered. Then I wrapped my arms around his shoulders and hung on, and he laid his head on my shoulder, our bodies meshed together, his resting on mine, and he cried helplessly and without reservation, and I let him.

There didn't seem to be any words.

They came eventually.

He slid off my body and we lay side by side as the sun hit the late afternoon angle through the drapes.

His voice surprised me from an almost sleep, and it was so soft, it took me a few moments to catch on to what he was saying. "I said she tried."

"Who tried?" I mumbled.

"My mom. She tried. It was easier when my grandparents were alive. She was young—real young. She was my age when they died, and I was like seven. She was younger'n Alba, even, when I was born."

"Your grandparents were okay?"

"Yeah. Grandpa used to love cars. I'd sit next to his feet for hours when he was under a car, just to hand him a wrench."

I was right, I thought. Someone had loved him. Someone had given him cars.

"What happened to them?" I was afraid he'd stop then.

"Car accident. Mom was lost. I remember lawyers and a will in probate. She had an uncle who wasn't real nice. Suddenly we were out on our own, and she had no way to make a living. Anyway, she tried. Small-time jobs, state day care. And then she got a boyfriend. And then another." He kissed my chest, but ruminatively, like it helped him think. "I don't know when the drugs started," he said apologetically. "But she wasn't the one who sold me for meth. It was the last boyfriend. He fucked me a few times, said I wasn't worth keeping around and too useless to fuck. Sold me the next day."

"How old—"

"Fifteen," he said, shrugging. "I kept ahead of Animal, did shit for him before he asked, greased myself in the morning so he never needed to worry. Got good at shit so he didn't have to scream at me. I knew cars, and he liked being around them, so I could help that way. It's the reason he kept me so long. The girl before me ran away, I guess, but me, I mighta stayed with him forever."

"But he shared you," I said, logic taking the place of emotion, and he answered the same way.

"Yeah. I knew what it was like to belong. If I wasn't going to belong just to him, there wasn't no reason to stay."

"You belong to me," I said. They could put me in the chair, and I'd always believe that killing that man was the best thing I ever did.

He talked more, his voice fading out with the dying light, and I drank in every word. How he'd worked on Animal's cars and that had been his relief, how they'd eaten takeout almost every night because Animal suspected he'd poison his food.

"I would've," I said at this point, and Sonny patted me with reassurance.

"You would've slit his throat before he touched you," he said warmly, and I conceded that this was probably correct.

The list of horrors was...

Horrific. It was awful, and painful, and I can't say I didn't cry, but so did Sonny, and when it was over, we simply closed our eyes on it and slept, because that was all the peace we had.


WE STAYED for three days. The last day, I woke up in the night, and the sea was a terrible, unfamiliar rush in my ears. I stood up for a moment and walked over to the window to see the full moon on the breakers. I realized I wanted to bathe in it, let the salt water scrub me clean of the things I'd seen, the things I'd done, the things I knew.

There was a rustle behind me, and Sonny stood suddenly there, wiggling his way under my arm, and I looped it over his shoulders and pulled him tight against my body.

"What now?" he asked, and I held him tight and closed my eyes.

"I can't make good promises," I said quietly. "I can promise to love you for the rest of my life, but I can't promise how long that will be. I can promise we'll be together for as long as possible, but I don't know how long that will be either. I can promise all sorts of things, but I can't promise I'll keep those promises. I can only promise I want you safe and sound."

He sighed and settled back into me. "I want you safe and sound too," he said quietly. "Let's live like that, then. Let's live like we can keep those promises. Let's live like the past is dead and all we got is the future."

I closed my eyes then, the moonlight bright against my eyelids, and squeezed his shoulders. "That's how you live anyway, isn't it?"

"Sir-yes-sir."

I laughed softly.

"We got money for a while," I said. "Maybe I won't have to race after all."

He hmmd. Maybe someday I'd explain where the money came from, how I'd stolen it from a dead man and given half to a fifteen-year-old girl. Right now, I'd just as soon he didn't ask.

"You want to go swimming?" I asked, and he startled.

"At night? It'll be cold."

"Yeah. Just once. One wave in."

"Yeah, okay."

He was right—it was cold. He'd be weak enough to stumble when we were done, and tired enough from that one thing to sleep the whole way back in the morning, but he was there with me. We swam out beyond the breakers and bobbed like otters, and waited for the big one, the one that was going to carry us home.

It came, and we rode it, exultant, tumbling in on the sand, purified by the water and the laughter and our love.

It was the only grace we needed, and all that we would ask.

WE LEFT the next morning, not long after the sun rose. Sonny was still tired, and as nice as the hotel was, it wasn't home. We left our sins behind us, drifting out to sea, and let the sunshine warm us as I drove that secret piece of Sonny's soul to our little plot of land and our humble dreams.

AMY LANE is a mother of four and a compulsive knitter who writes because she can't silence the voices in her head. She adores cats, Chi-who-whats, knitting socks, and hawt menz, and she dislikes moths, cat boxes, and knuckle-headed macspazzmatrons. She is rarely found cooking, cleaning, or doing domestic chores, but she has been known to knit up an emergency hat/blanket/pair of socks for any occasion whatsoever, or sometimes for no reason at all. She writes in the shower, while at the gym, while taxiing children to soccer/dance/gymnastics/band oh my! and has learned from necessity to type like the wind. She lives in a spider-infested, crumbling house in a shoddy suburb and counts on her beloved Mate to keep her tethered to reality—which he does, while keeping her cell phone charged as a bonus. She's been married for twenty-plus years and still believes in Twu Wuv, with a capital Twu and a capital Wuv, and she doesn't see any reason at all for that to change.

Website: www.greenshill.com
Blog: www.writerslane.blogspot.com
E-mail: amylane@greenshill.com
Facebook: www.facebook.com/amy.lane.167
Twitter: @amymaclane

Also from AMY LANE

BOLT-
HOLE

Amy Lane

Contemporary Romance from AMY LANE

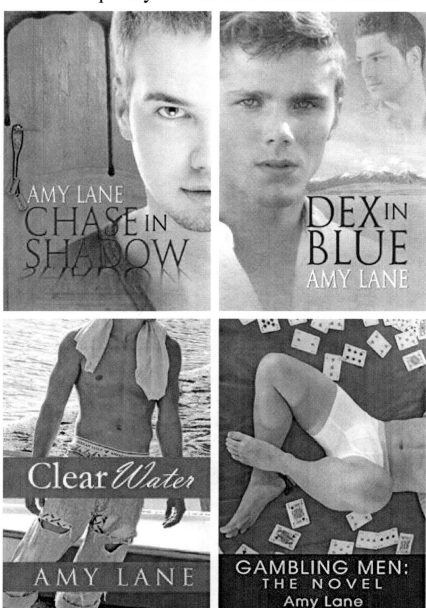

# Promise Rock Series from AMY LANE

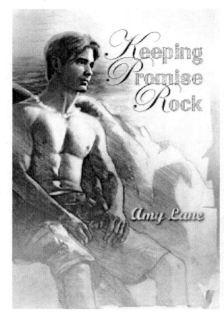

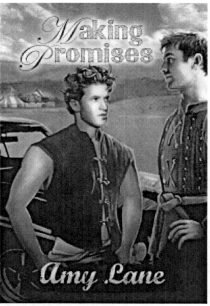

http://www.dreamspinnerpress.com

# The Knitting Series from AMY LANE

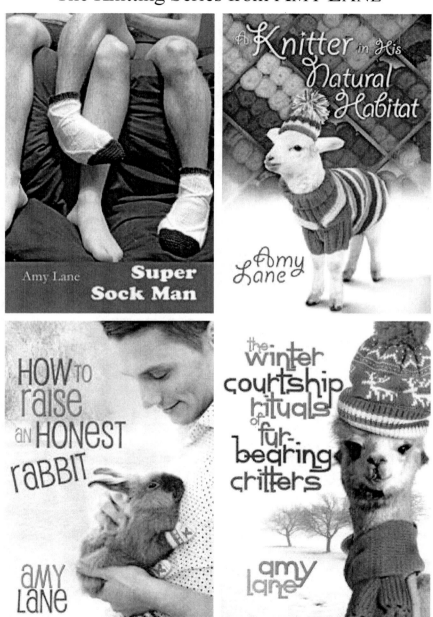

# Fantasy Romance from AMY LANE

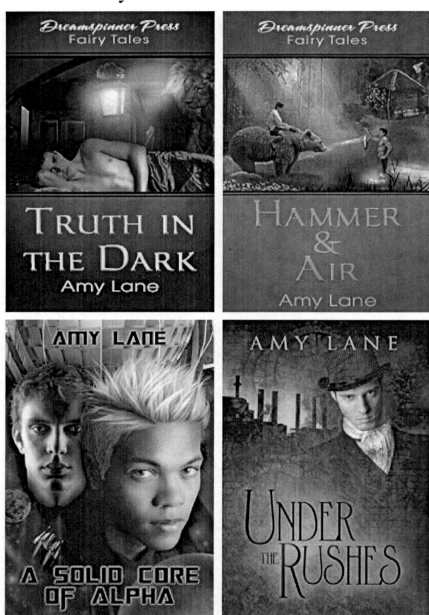

# The Talker Series from AMY LANE

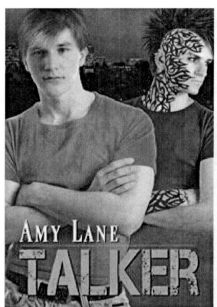

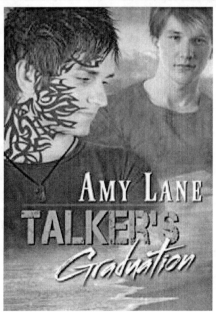

http://www.dreamspinnerpress.com

CPSIA information can be obtained at www.ICGtesting.com
Printed in the USA
LVOW10s0352041113

359774LV00004B/133/P